DANGEROUS LADY

The Marwood Family Saga
Book One

Amy Licence

SAPERE
BOOKS

DANGEROUS
LADY

Published by Sapere Books.

24 Trafalgar Road, Ilkley, LS29 8HH

saperebooks.com

ISBN: 978-1-80055-651-5

To Rufus and Robin

Is it possible
That so high debate,
So sharp, so sore, and of such rate,
Should end so soon and was begun so late?
Is it possible?

Is it possible
So cruel intent,
So hasty heat and so soon spent,
From love to hate, and thence for to relent?
Is it possible?

Is it possible
That any may find
Within one heart so diverse mind,
To change or turn as weather and wind?
Is it possible?

— Thomas Wyatt

ONE

1527

Thomasin Marwood closed her eyes and inhaled. Smoke. That musty scent of wet woodsmoke, drifting eastwards from the clearing in the woods. It was still early, barely past the hour of Prime, but the charcoal burners had been at work since dawn, crouching low to the earth, coaxing up their small flame into a blaze. And underneath the smoke, there hung the slight tang of autumnal decay, like a quieter voice in the choir. She took a deep breath, filling her lungs with the flavours of home.

Thomasin stepped across the threshold of her family home into the daylight. Eastwell Hall rose up behind her with its red bricks and twisted chimneys, a strange, bright jewel nestled in the quiet Suffolk valley. A house had stood there for two centuries, but the current one had been built by her grandfather, whose stern portrait hung over the fireplace in the great hall. She had seen it every day for as long as she could remember. Thomasin could have walked blindfolded, with just her fingertips as her guide, around this corner, through the doors, up the stairs, without so much as a tumble. While she was away, her favourite haunts would fall silent: the long gallery hung with pictures, the shady nut walk, the walled rose garden with its delicate scents. But today, at the age of seventeen, she was covered head to toe in white and yellow silk, with a rope of her mother's pearls about her neck. Thomasin idly rolled one pearl between finger and thumb, cold and smooth to the touch. It was an unfamiliar, borrowed glamour.

The clatter of feet in the hallway behind her announced the arrival of her parents. Sir Richard Marwood was a tall, imposing man in his mid-forties, whose face wore a mixture of ease and quiet resignation. He had already begun a promising career at court when the king came to the throne as a young man. Sometimes, late at night, when Father had drained his wine, he still spoke of how he'd hunted for hours a day with Henry in the old days, jousted in the lists, or danced in pageants by candlelight, dressed in Turkish costume. For a while he had the king's ear, at the most fashionable, exciting court in Europe. In the world, some had said. He had married Elizabeth, a lady-in-waiting to Queen Catherine, her fingers accustomed to lacing and unlacing the complicated farthingale skirts the Spaniard favoured, and her ears with their pearl rings, accustomed to the queen's long hours at prayer.

Thomasin could not remember those early years, when she had been a baby at court. Her first memories were of Eastwell, when she was three or four, but her elder sister claimed to recall the courtyard at Richmond Palace and the park at Greenwich. There was a full two years between them, important years at that early age, so Thomasin never doubted Cecilia's stories of ladies in wide gowns, dancing and hawking, and of riding in carriages to picnics in the forest, but it was a mixture of dreams, and a sense of longing, that she could not share. Their mother had never really forgiven their father for deciding to leave politics in favour of a quiet life. She seemed to live purely for the fragments of news and gossip that arrived at Eastwell in her brother's neat secretary hand. Thomasin, though, knew nothing but the Suffolk countryside and loved its peace and greenness.

Richard approached his daughter, pulling on his gloves. "Ah, there you are…" He broke off, calling back into the hallway.

"Here, she's outside already, she's waiting." Then he added, more softly to Thomasin, "Your sister is growing impatient."

In the doorway, Cecilia Marwood paused to rearrange the folds of her gold silk dress. The glass sequins and gold thread sparkled in the autumn sunlight. Thomasin watched her sister out of the corner of her eye. They had never been close. She had known sisters, local friends, who confided in each other, who laughed and talked together, but Thomasin had always felt a distance, a coldness in Cecilia's presence, a rivalry for her father's affection. But all that was over now. Cecilia was a grown woman, heading off to be married.

"Come on then, Mother," Cecilia called back. "We don't want to arrive after nightfall, you said so yourself. Oh, but where is the carriage? Why isn't it ready?"

"I've just sent around for it," their father reassured her. "There is no need for this worry. You will give yourself a fever."

Cecilia turned away, her mouth pursed in annoyance.

There was no denying her sister's beauty, Thomasin thought, as she watched Cecilia sweep past. She had inherited the fair colouring of their mother's family, the Russells, who were known county-wide for their looks. But it was a cold, bloodless kind of beauty to Thomasin's eyes, with its pale skin, icy-blue eyes and sharp profile. The cast of Cecilia's lips made it seem that she was always sitting in judgement, wearing her face as a kind of mask. Emotion only showed when she could no longer contain herself, and her bottom lip began to quiver. That little movement, that break in spirit, had proven to be Thomasin's victory in a hundred small childhood battles.

Thomasin had taken after her father in looks; she had his dark, chestnut-brown hair, almost reddish where the light caught it, his deep, warm eyes that sparkled and the swarthy skin with ruddy cheeks and lips that her mother disdained as common. Thomasin was curvy and voluptuous where her sister was tall and willowy; Thomasin was as ready to laugh as Cecilia was to judge, and as keen to savour life, as the bride-to-be was to cling to its rules.

And then came their mother, Lady Elizabeth Marwood, resplendent in green, like a ship in full sail, her heavy locks piled upon her head. She moved slowly. Majestically as ever, but slowly. The old malady in her breast had been giving her sleepless nights, but she hid it well. She was not an old woman, but a proud one, once renowned for her beauty, and would never have anybody know of her suffering. This was another reason for the family attending London. As soon as the wedding celebrations were over, Elizabeth would be seen by one of the best physicians in Cheapside. And cured, hopefully, with some small changes to her diet. The Suffolk physicians had done their best, riding over from Bury St Edmunds with herbs, or recommending shrines where she might pray to certain saints, but for all the caudles and offerings, in twelve months there had been little improvement in her condition.

Behind them, the smaller Marwood children came tumbling out to bid their farewells. There was a gap of five years between Thomasin and Lettice, who at twelve, was on the threshold of growing into a woman, but with the plumpness of childhood still about her face and the same dark eyes as Thomasin. Fierce and witty, she was Thomasin's favourite of the pack, although she loved them all for their differences. At nine, the Marwood's only son Digby was a solid little man, who loved his horses and dogs and making wooden ships to sail on the pond. The fair-haired Alice was five, cuddling her little poppet doll and Susanna was just a babe in her nurse's arms.

Elizabeth kissed them each in turn, and Thomasin followed.

"All will be well these two weeks," their mother promised. "Be good, do your lessons, follow your nurse's instruction, eat modestly and sleep well. I look to you, Lettice, to keep the little ones in mind of this."

"Of course, Mother."

The carriage rumbled around from the stables, pulled by four grey horses, which drew to a halt before them. The Marwood family arms were painted on the side, the intersected star and moon combination that was centuries old. Elizabeth put one hand forward as if to inspect it, but made the most of its presence to steady herself. It struck Thomasin that very soon, they were to drive away through the avenue of trees and this place would be only a memory. She had lain awake last night, thinking of it, as it came closer, but now the moment had arrived. By the end of the week, they would be in London and a new phase of her life would begin. The emotion rose suddenly in her chest, unexpectedly, threatening to betray her with tears. She had always found it difficult to keep such things hidden. It was all she could do now to turn away to conceal the sudden rush of feeling. After all, it wasn't as if she would never be coming back here. It was Cecilia who was getting married, not her.

"It's hard to leave this place." Her father spoke quietly at her side. "Whenever I am away from Eastwell it's always in my thoughts, as an ideal to return to."

Thomasin nodded, not trusting herself to speak in agreement with sentiments so perfectly in tune with her own. Her father understood her, though, without need for her reply.

"Although I do think your mother would be perfectly happy living permanently in London."

They watched Elizabeth, handing out orders for the arranging of the cushions and the loading of provisions into the carriage.

"Come," he added, "it won't be so bad. You might even enjoy yourself. Just two weeks, then we will be home again."

Thomasin sighed. "Cecilia looks very beautiful."

Her father nodded. "She does indeed. Sir Henry is a lucky man."

"She will make sure he knows it."

"She will indeed. And your mother hopes you will look kindly upon her cousin, Sir Giles. He has large estates and a pedigree going back generations, but you are young still. We've had no negotiations with his family, so look to see if you like him."

A sense of relief passed over Thomasin. She had known of her mother's wishes; in fact, they had been impossible to avoid. Sir Giles Waterson was constantly praised at the dinner table as a prodigy of learning, or family, or dancing, so that she was almost tired of hearing his name.

As if sensing the danger to her plans, Elizabeth turned and caught Thomasin's expression.

"It will be your turn next," she said pointedly. "We will have two weddings within the year, you mark my words. Now, into the carriage."

Thomasin turned and took a last look up at Eastwell Hall, with the children waving on the step, before she folded her skirts and climbed inside.

TWO

Lamps gleamed outside the gateway, even though dusk was still soft in the sky. The London townhouse of the Russell family sat in the centre of Thames Street, behind high walls, amid a plot of land that led down to the river.

The city had flashed past them in a whirl: tall buildings with narrow, crowded fronts, bustling streets and churches tolling the hour. The huge façade of the Tower had veered up before the carriage as it passed through the eastern gate, before they clattered along the rutted autumn roads that took them past colourful shop fronts and inns. All the activity made Thomasin's head spin. So many voices, carriages, such a great mass of humanity in all its forms, making such noise. Opposite her, Cecilia looked out coolly at the crowds, trying to appear above it all.

Once they had turned into the courtyard, servants in livery appeared, closing and bolting the gates, and lining up in welcome, to assist them out of the carriage.

"At last," pronounced Elizabeth, with a sigh of impatience, gesturing for her daughters to move, and reaching for the door handle.

Thomasin's limbs were stiff as she climbed out of the carriage into the cobbled yard. Before her stood Monk's Place, once an old lodge in the possession of the Bishop of Rochester, but now in the hands of her mother's family, the Russells. The huge building which enclosed her on three sides still had something of a monastic feel, with its heavy grey stones that had been set in place centuries before. Yet the east wing was more modern, with fashionable red brick decorated in the Flemish diamond style. Lights shone in its windows and the door stood open, invitingly. Two dark hounds with bright eyes came surging forward and pushed their wet noses up against the visitors.

"Caesar! Brutus!" A voice called after the animals, followed, in softer tones, with "Dear sister!"

A broad figure was blocking the entrance, arms spread in welcome. Thomasin had only met her uncle, Lord Russell, a handful of times, when he had ventured into the Suffolk countryside, but he was a welcome sight now. Her mother hurried forward to meet his embrace, as close as they had ever been, due to their constant correspondence.

"And Sir Richard, welcome Sir. I hope you are in good health."

Thomasin's father stepped forward to shake his brother-in-law by the hand. "We are in debt to your kindness, Matthew."

"No, you are not," smiled Matthew, "you are most welcome as my guests. I do hope your journey was not too arduous. Come dogs, off, off."

"Nothing we won't survive."

"And these surely cannot be your daughters?" Their host turned to Cecilia and Thomasin, and Richard stepped a little to the side to allow them to be admired. Cecilia lifted her chin in the anticipation of praise while Thomasin felt her cheeks colour. "But what have you done with those two little girls who used to sing songs to their poppets? These are young ladies, quite grown up."

Thomasin blushed to be reminded of how fond she used to be of her doll, a little raggedy thing she had named Nan. Goodness knew where it was now.

Matthew stepped forward and kissed each hand in turn. He was a large, jolly-looking man, his once-fair hair now faded to grey, although the short beard he wore was almost white.

"Oh yes," he laughed, seeing Thomasin looking at it. "We all wear beards at court now that the king does. It is the fashion. You will have to grow one at once, Richard."

"A beard? I suppose it is more convenient for those who dislike the barber."

"It is far more convenient. Well, come inside, eat and rest. Tomorrow we go to court."

Court. Just that morning, amid the Suffolk countryside, Thomasin had hardly believed that such a place existed.

Thomasin's uncle was as good as his word. The following morning, she awoke between fine linen sheets scented with lavender, in a chamber overlooking the garden. A maid was already lighting the fire and laying out her best clothes for the day ahead. As Thomasin stood waiting, while the laces on her bodice were tightened, her mind raced ahead to the people they could meet: King Henry VIII himself; his Queen, Catherine; Cecilia's betrothed, Sir Henry Kytson; and the man her mother wanted her to marry, Sir Giles Waterson. So many new faces in one place. Yet she had little time to dwell upon it on the way down to the hall for breakfast, as prayers were said, and the dishes brought out.

Sir Matthew Russell lived alone at Monk's Place, save for his dogs. He had been a widower for a decade now, with little inclination to replace his wife. Thomasin had a vague memory of her Aunt Bridget, Matthew's wife, and her kindness to a small girl who had grazed her knee, but a letter arriving at Eastwell one summer had brought news of her death in childbed. She had been much loved, and her memory was marked by a beautiful chantry chapel erected by her husband in her honour, at the nearby church of Our Lady. Their one son lived in the north, and was expected to arrive next week, in time to attend the wedding, with his wife.

As Matthew stood at the head of his table, in the long hall lit by wide, high, windows, he looked around at his guests with pride. "It is a joy to see this house brought to life again. For too long I have led the existence of a hermit, full of hard work and devotion. It is good to have young people here again. But, before we leave, I must inform you that the court has changed beyond recognition." He lowered his voice and gestured to the servants to leave the room. Once the doors were closed, he resumed. "You will not find the court to be what it was during your day."

At once Elizabeth was all ears. "The king is well?"

"Oh, quite well. Perhaps too well."

"And the queen? And Princess Mary?"

Matthew stroked his trim beard. "As well as may be expected."

"What does that mean? You may be direct with us."

Her brother nodded. "It is delicate. I would not raise it in front of the girls…"

"Cecilia, Thomasin, leave at once."

Thomasin rose obediently to her feet, although she was burning with curiosity, but her uncle stayed her with a hand.

"No, they must stay. Of course, I would prefer to shield them from any unpleasantness, but it is impossible for them to visit court and remain unaware of it; they should be prepared, to prepare for any … any discomfort."

"Good God, brother, you make it sound like the Sweat."

"No, not the Sweat. Some similar kind of scourge, though. It afflicts the king."

"Heaven help us." Elizabeth crossed herself dramatically.

"Please feel you can speak plainly," encouraged Richard, gently.

Matthew nodded. "You will recall some of my letters touched upon the king's conscience? In regards to his marriage."

"I do," Elizabeth agreed. "He has some scruple because of the queen's first marriage, to his brother. But that was settled years ago. I served the queen and she has always upheld that she came to the king's bed as a maid."

"Indeed so," said Matthew, "with a dispensation from the pope attesting to the fact, but now Catherine has passed the age of childbearing and the king has only a single daughter by her."

"He has my sympathies," smiled Richard. "It is a grief when a man only has one daughter when he might have the pleasure of more."

Matthew tolerated the interruption with an inclination of his head. "Still the consummate courtier?"

Thomasin felt the reply to be a little harsh and saw something in her father's face change; afterwards, he fell silent.

"The result of this," continued her uncle, "is that the king seeks means to put his wife aside."

Elizabeth's mouth fell open. "A divorce? Never."

"Not a divorce, an annulment, as he claims the marriage was never legal in the first place."

"But that would make the Princess Mary illegitimate?"

"It would indeed. Moreover, he seeks to replace her with a certain lady by whom he believes he will father sons."

For a moment, this information kept them dumb.

"He does?" asked Elizabeth, in a pointed, drawn-out way, with the wrath of all wives who had reached years of maturity. "He cannot. And what lady is this, pray?"

"The daughter of Sir Thomas Boleyn, whom he has installed at court in the position of his consort."

"The daughter of Elizabeth Howard? My old friend? But this is a scandal!"

Matthew raised his hands in a gesture of helplessness. "I only mean to prepare you for what you might see today. I know you were an old friend of the queen."

"And I am her friend still. Which daughter is it? What were their names? Mary, I think, was the elder, and Anne?"

"It is Anne. Mary has been wed these past six or seven years and is made a mother already."

"Anne, that dark little scrap of a girl! God in Heaven!" Elizabeth turned to her daughters. "Girls, compose yourselves; remember who you are and what you are worth. We are here for a wedding and we will conduct ourselves according to our position. Come, let's not delay. I will look upon this woman who thinks she can displace a queen of twenty years' standing."

Thomasin and her father exchanged an uneasy glance as her mother swept out and began issuing instructions to the coachmen.

THREE

The rushes were thick. Knotted. They smelt of wine and spices. Cinnamon, Thomasin recognised. Perhaps cumin too. But there was something else there, a sharpness she did not know.

They had gathered in the presence chamber an hour ago, a long, painted and panelled room with a dais and chair at the end, under a draped cloth of estate. They were told to be patient, as the chamber filled up with dozens of others; courtiers, supplicants, visitors, servants, gossiping, staring, coughing and scratching. The king had been out hunting since early morning and was expected back at any moment. Thomasin felt as if she knew every panel of the wood-carved walls, every stitch in the tapestries: now her eyes were fixed on the rushes underfoot.

Then, after all the waiting, there had been a sudden flurry of activity. A trumpet sounded, distant doors were flung open and feet shuffled as people sought their spaces.

"The king, the king! Make way."

Thomasin knelt, like all the rest, and kept her head low. Henry was moving towards them slowly, pausing to greet others and hearing their requests. Snatches of his voice reached her above the bended heads, low and rich. A voice resonant of power, of cloth of gold, of incense and spices, of jewels and palaces, and eternal memory. A man accustomed to getting his own way. Soon he would be before them, standing over them, looking at them.

She had spread out her yellow skirts carefully around her, so that the embroidered hem was visible. A dress she had adored, admired, and so longed to wear, but it seemed commonplace now, amid all this finery. Something about the king's approaching presence made her heart beat a new rhythm in her chest and her breath come short. Her hands trembled slightly. From under her lowered lashes, she squinted sideways at the gorgeous figure, broad of shoulder and studded with jewels; his shapely legs approached in their white stockings, feet encased in red leather with diamond buckles. Closer, closer.

"By our Lady, if it isn't Sir Richard Marwood!"

Thomasin saw her father raised to his feet, but she remained dutifully on her knees.

"God's blood, Richard, you have been absent a stretch, but your return is very welcome. It has been too long, too long, old friend."

"You do me too much honour, Your Majesty."

"You are in good health, I hope. What brings you back to us?"

"The marriage of my eldest daughter."

"Ah, your eldest daughter." The king paused as if this point required consideration. Then he spotted Thomasin's mother, still on bended knee at her husband's side. His voice changed when addressing a woman. "My Lady Elizabeth, still as radiant as you ever were, let me see you."

She lifted her head and for a moment, he scrutinised her face.

"And these must be your daughters?"

Thomasin raised her eyes for a moment, just a moment, not even a flicker, really. But it was enough. Her brown eyes briefly met those of the king. He had a broad, handsome face, the features small and regular, yet sensual, the expression conveying something of determination and insight. He was reputed to be very clever, quite the scholar of theology, and had been an excellent athlete in his youth, although she guessed that now he must be barely a few years younger than her father. His gaze seemed to penetrate her and she cast her eyes down at once, feeling his attention linger on her features. She felt that she had been assessed and the impression she made had not been an unpleasant one.

"Good," he said softly, "it is good to see you at court. I am in haste, but I will be dining in the hall soon, so stay and eat with us. It will not be long, an hour or so. There is to be a masque too."

Richard bowed. "Thank you, Your Majesty, we would be honoured."

"Honoured," echoed Elizabeth, her earlier indignation forgotten. "Honoured."

Her heart beating fast, Thomasin dared to lift her eyes again. As she had felt, his gaze was full upon her, from above, falling like a weight on the top of her head. The attention made her feel giddy. The thought that the king was a man like any other brought a blush to her cheeks and there was no other escape than to close her eyes.

"Are you praying?" Cecilia's whisper was sharp and to the point. "Whatever for?"

Ignoring her sister, Thomasin finally allowed herself to open her eyes, to find that King Henry had moved on and the rest of her family were on their feet. She scrambled up from the floor and followed them towards the gardens to while away the hour.

They paired off naturally, with Elizabeth and Cecilia following Matthew down to the river while Thomasin and her father decided to see the knot garden. She laced her arm through his as they headed along a walk lined with sweetly scented box. The fresh air managed to bring her to her senses again.

"The king remembered you fondly, Father, as if you had been a particular friend of his."

"Indeed I was, back in those days, when he was still a young king."

"Why did you leave court?" The question arrived on her lips without much thought. "I mean," she backtracked, "if you want to tell me. I know it was a long time ago."

Her father folded his hand over hers. "It was a long time ago."

"Forget that I asked."

She heard him sigh. They passed through a gate in a wall, into an enclosed garden, where little paths ran between beds of scented herbs. The flowers, fading into autumn, were a mix of reds, yellows and pinks.

"I suppose the short answer," he mused, staring above her head, "was that I was overlooked. There were plenty of ruthless young men at court in those days, willing to do whatever the king required, to make whatever sacrifice they had to, in order to get ahead. If you didn't keep up with them, you lost out."

Thomasin digested this for a moment. "What sort of things?"

"Things that you will hopefully never have to worry about. We argued, the king and I."

"You argued with the king?"

"More of a disagreement. It was foolish of me, I know."

"What happened?"

"We had differences. They came to a head when he wished to go to war with France. I believed it was better to sign a truce, to save lives and expenses. But Henry is not a man who likes to be told no."

Thomasin felt a little shiver run through her at these words. "No, I can see that."

"I should have reflected more. He was going to have his war anyway, whether I wished it or not. If I had kept quiet, I might have saved my career. As it happened, he found someone else who was prepared to give him his war."

"Oh? Who was that?"

"Thomas Wolsey, as he was then. He is Cardinal Wolsey now, although he was merely the son of a butcher."

Thomasin lifted her eyebrows in surprise. "Would you have wanted to be here, at court, all this time, under those conditions?"

"Sometimes I wonder what I have missed, but on the whole, I think not."

They passed by a bush of lavender, and Thomasin paused to pluck one of the purple flowers and raised it to her nose to breathe in its fragrance.

Suddenly she felt her father tense and draw himself upright. Two men had entered the garden from the far side and were making their way along the central path, deep in conversation. The first was in his fifties or more, his square-cut beard mostly grey but betraying that it had once been a vivid red, his slight body encased in a slashed doublet and padded sleeves. But none of this mattered beside his hooded eyes, which were shrewd and intelligent as he took in Thomasin and her father.

"One such man who has prospered at court," Richard murmured.

As they approached, the second figure came more into view. He was taller than the first, by half a head, his athletic build needing no assistance from the dressmaker. His chest was wide, his upper arms developed from exercise in the tiltyard and his legs were both strong and lithe, so that he walked lightly but conveyed a sense of easy power. He was dressed sombrely, in grey and black, with a little slash of red at his throat. Unlike the older man, he was bareheaded, and the sun caught his thick curly locks, showing them almost to be blue-black in their intensity. Thomasin arrived at his face last, aware that she was staring, but powerless to stop herself. His features were strong and well defined; the chin was prominent, the nose large without being obtrusive, and there was some sort of hint of passion and noble blood in his nostrils. The lips were full and sensuous, the forehead wide and the brows heavy and dark, but it was the eyes that caught her, a rich warm brown like chestnuts, set between long lashes, and unexpectedly sensitive, as if all his show of strength melted away at this most vulnerable point. He moved towards her with assured strides, as if the very path, the gardens, even herself, belonged to him entirely.

Her father made a reserved bow. "Sir Thomas Boleyn."

"Viscount Rochford."

"Viscount Rochford," Richard corrected.

The viscount looked at them coolly. "And you are?"

"You don't recognise me? It has been fourteen years."

Boleyn narrowed his eyes. "Enlighten me."

"Sir Richard Marwood at your service. And my daughter, Thomasin."

"Well, well, Sir Richard Marwood." His face softened a little. "Yes, I do see now. So you are back. I never thought to see the day."

Thomasin's father smiled. "Such days sometimes come around."

"Indeed, they do, and this is your charming daughter?" He swept a bow.

"One of them."

"And your wife?"

Thomasin sensed her father pause. "Elizabeth is here, along with our elder girl."

Boleyn's eyes opened wide. "So, she is here? Well!"

Something hung in the air between them. Thomasin tore her eyes from the young man's face to see the conflicting emotions twitch at the corner of her father's mouth.

"And this is my ward, Rafe Danvers," Boleyn swept on briefly.

Thomasin's lips suddenly felt very dry.

The young man nodded, as the occasion demanded, but he seemed not to see them, just as he did not see the insects on the leaves or the worms underground. He was in a world of his own, a dark, brooding, secret place, miles from that sunlit garden. Thomasin wondered at his secrets; what might entice those chiselled lips to curve into a smile?

"We must not tarry," said Boleyn. "The king expects us." But as he was about to pass them by, he paused and turned back, as if having been struck by an afterthought. His hooded eyes fixed themselves upon his old friend's face. "I recall your wife's allegiance to the Spaniard. I suppose we shall find ourselves on opposing sides now, when it comes to the king's business."

Thomasin thought of her uncle's warning over breakfast.

"The Spaniard?" Richard interjected at once. "Surely you mean the queen?"

"There is no queen in England; only the Dowager Princess of Wales. The marriage is invalid; the sooner you realise that, the better."

Richard was left spluttering out his indignation, as Boleyn walked briskly away without affording him the chance to speak.

FOUR

The masquers moved slowly, sensuously, through the hall. It had fallen dark outside, as the autumn days were already beginning to shorten. Tapers burned on the walls, casting long shadows and adding to the rising heat. They had dined well and drunk well; in fact, the spiced wine seemed to spread a warmth through Thomasin and loosen her limbs. She looked on at the dancers with a kind of envy, her foot tapping in time to the rhythm of the flute and shawm.

Their dance had been carefully choreographed, led by the king's own sister, Mary, Duchess of Suffolk and her ladies, in dresses of black and gold, their long hair set with sparkling stars, their trains bright with spangles. In pairs, they circled the room, white velvet masks covering their faces, although all eyes searched them, probing their youth and beauty. They were met on the floor by six men in silver and black, who were led, it was rumoured, by Mary's husband, the duke, as they each claimed a woman in the dance, and formed elaborate patterns, stepping, turning and lacing under the archways of arms. Thomasin was quite enchanted by the elegance of it.

On the dais, King Henry was sitting back and surveying the room, every bit as imposing as earlier. Since then, he had changed into a doublet of silver and red, adorned with gold chains and jewels. But even without it, he had a presence; he occupied the seat as if it was an extension of his limbs, and cast his eyes about the place as one who had the power of life and death over the dancers. He didn't look as old as Thomasin had first thought. He was broad, and wide, an imposing man who was no longer young, but he still had the air of the athlete he had been in his youth.

Around him, his courtiers looked on. There was Viscount Boleyn, and his brother-in-law, the stern-faced Duke of Norfolk, surrounded by a small knot of men, aping the king with their tight hose and garters, their furred coats and feathered hats. Impressive men of means and power, but none could rival the glittering figure on the throne.

Then, unexpectedly, Henry turned. He had been talking to an older man, with grey hair and a studious look, but their conversation now seemed to be at an end. He turned, surveying the room and fixing his gaze over at the bench where Thomasin sat with her mother. And he raised his hand, sparkling with diamonds, and gestured over the crowd, curling his fingers into his palm.

Thomasin blushed, looked away. Had he meant her?

But slowly, her mother rose at her side. The summons had been meant for her.

Thomasin watched as her mother crossed the floor. She moved with a deliberation that marked her out as important, and people moved out of the way for her. The king indicated a chair at his side, and she placed herself gracefully upon it, arranging her skirts.

And it was then, for the first time, that Thomasin saw the king smile. A wide, infectious smile of welcome, which made her mother appear to be the most important woman in the room. How must it feel to be on the receiving end of that smile, at the heart of the English court, amid all this finery?

Elizabeth inclined her head, listening attentively, as he spoke into her ear. He whispered again and she laughed with him, covering her mouth, almost girlishly. They had the appearance of old friends, and Thomasin realised how little she knew of her parents' former life, their allegiances and loyalties. For as long as she could remember they had simply been her mother and father, leading the family in prayers, riding in the park at Eastwell, supervising her education. She struggled to think of a time she had seen her mother's face wear that particular expression before.

Her view of the pair was interrupted by her father and Cecilia moving to take up their positions. The masquers were taking refreshment and a new dance was about to begin. Couples were rising, men leading out women by the hand, forming a circle around the masquers with their finely embroidered costumes. The musicians struck up a rhythm and in patterns, they began to move to a jaunty beat, seeming to concentrate all life and colour in the centre of the hall, and forcing the dark corners to recede. Yet each alcove and niche contained figures, whispering together, moving closer, watching or plotting in silence.

"May I partner you for this dance?"

It was a demand rather than a request. Thomasin looked up to see Viscount Boleyn looking down at her with a mixture of amusement and tolerance. His sudden appearance, and his importance, robbed her of words. But she knew the correct thing to do. Timidly, she held out her hand.

As he walked her into place, she thought of all the mornings she had danced in the great hall at Eastwell, under the supervision of Mrs Lascelles. The dance playing now was a variation of one she knew well, and the differences were not hard to pick up; the little lift, the run of three steps together, the coy turn. Sir Thomas Boleyn was still nimble enough, although he clearly expected her to lose her way and walked her through the steps slowly. She concealed her smile and threw herself into the dance, conscious of the king looking their way.

"You dance well," he said in appreciation, as they drew closer together. "And that dress suits you. However, let me advise you; your parents have been away from court too long. All the fashions are French now, not Spanish."

"French?"

"You should get yourself a little French hood; it would become you very well."

He turned away to follow the steps and Thomasin was briefly opposite her father. He looked at her with quizzical eyes before the music carried her away.

"So, your sister has found herself a husband?" asked Boleyn, as they came back together again.

Thomasin smiled. "She has, my Lord."

"And how old are you?"

"I am seventeen."

"Old enough to be married too." He stepped alongside her as the dancers formed new lines.

"Perhaps."

"Will you be looking for a husband next?"

"Are husbands easy to find at court?" The words slipped from her lips before she could think of what she was saying. At once she coloured, hoping she had not offended.

Luckily, Boleyn was amused. "You have a witty tongue; you are something like my daughter."

The dance carried Thomasin away from her partner again before she could reply, and she little knew whether to take his comparison as a compliment or an insult. Then the final bars played and he was back before her, dropping a low bow. She gave her best curtsey in reply and Boleyn thanked her, most politely, and moved away.

Her father had been watching, and was approaching her across the floor with two gentlemen.

"This is my younger daughter, Thomasin." Richard gestured her to his side, where he turned to introduce his companions. The first was in his mid-twenties, with a shock of very blond hair, the second older by a decade and slightly stooped, with a calm seriousness in deep-set eyes. "Thomasin, may I present Sir Henry Kytson and Lord Hatton."

"Sir Henry Kytson!" At once Thomasin focused in on the young man's face — Cecilia's intended husband — and offered him her hand.

"Charmed," he replied in a merry voice, "but this is Sir Henry. I am William Hatton."

Thomasin blushed as she realised her error and hid her emotion in a brief curtsey to the older man.

"My sister-in-law, soon-to-be," Kytson said in deep, measured tones, "I am pleased to meet you. We will soon be better related."

"Indeed the honour will be mine, my lord," Thomasin replied prettily, wondering where Cecilia was at that moment. What did she make of this man whose appearance could only have come as a disappointment to her?

"Come," said her father to Kytson, "Cecilia awaits you for the next dance."

"I pray you enjoy the evening," the groom urged as he was led away, leaving Thomasin with the firm conviction that Kytson was definitely not a dancer.

"Shall we?" asked Lord Hatton, turning the full force of his blondeness upon her.

"Why not?" Thomasin took his outstretched hand and stepped into the dance.

Thomasin's glass had been refilled once or twice more before she saw him. He stood in the shadows, his face untouched by any of the warmth of the dance, but she knew at once that it was him. Rafe Danvers, Boleyn's ward, the shape of his form instantly recognisable. His hair gleamed dark as ebony, and those sensitive eyes were merely two smouldering embers in the pale contours of his face. And he appeared to be looking her way. The realisation almost took her breath away. He was like something that had appeared from another world, unbidden into the room, with the brooding intensity of his gaze. She had not commanded his attention in the knot garden earlier, quite the contrary, but she was in no doubt that she had it now. Her fingers around the glass began to tremble. She felt rooted to the spot as if her feet had turned to stone.

"So, you danced? How very kind of that gentleman."

Cecilia had returned, her pale cheeks slightly flushed, her eyes already scanning the hall for her next.

"Earlier? That was Viscount Boleyn."

Cecilia's fair eyebrows were raised in genuine surprise. "Really? Where has he gone? I am sure he will want to dance with me too."

Thomasin could barely conceal her smile. "Of course, as there are no other women in the room."

"No," said Cecilia, with absolute certainty, "there are no other women in the room."

"And your betrothed?"

Thomasin saw an emotion chase across her sister's face, but it was so brief as to be barely recognisable.

"Is he not a refined gentleman? Such taste and poise. Is Sir Giles Waterton here tonight?"

"I believe not."

"Shame," Cecilia said archly. "So that pleasure has been deferred."

Refusing to take the bait, Thomasin shot a look back into the shadows but the dark figure of Rafe Danvers had disappeared. He was nowhere to be seen, as if he had just vanished into the shadows like a phantom. Realising that it was obvious that she was looking about, Thomasin returned to her wine. And yet, she could not escape the sensation of his presence, as if he was still close, unseen, able to come and go in the darkness. Or perhaps his face was just imprinted in her mind. Perhaps she had even imagined his presence.

She danced again, and again. Gentlemen of the court introduced themselves with a polite bow, a few words and she was once again drawn into the whirl of life. There was Nicholas Carew, tall and dark, William Compton with clipped tones but laughing eyes, and Francis Bryan, who wore an eye patch, and others whose names escaped her. Some of her partners kept their eyes fixed on her in appreciative silence while others asked about her arrival, or her life in the country. Once, the steps took her up towards the dais and she passed her mother and the king, their heads bent in reminiscences. Another time, she turned about on the same spot and found the king alone, his eyes fixed upon her.

More wine was brought out and glasses were filled. Little silver dishes bore pinches of spice or griddled wafers that snapped in the teeth and dissolved on the tongue. The tapers burned down. Thomasin found a seat and watched two imposing figures: the tall, stern form of the duke of Norfolk moving among the crowd, conversing, watching, listening, and the duke of Suffolk, with his red beard, standing back, beside his beautiful royal wife, taking it all in with wise eyes. Yet the hour was getting late. Soon it must be time to seek the carriages back to Monk's Place.

Suddenly the music was interrupted. All fell silent. The crowds fell away as a figure strode into the hall. It was a woman of medium height, yet slender and graceful so that she appeared taller, with her presence commanding a certain sort of authority. She was dressed unusually, daringly, with pearls around her throat and trimming her French hood, her long sleeves fitting close around her upper arms and flaring out to trail past her wrists. There was nothing conventional about her looks, but her face, her poise, and her lifted chin were somehow beautiful.

Without challenge, she claimed the floor as her own, holding out her hand to the nearest man, pulling herself towards him while she fixed her dark eyes upon the king. That was when Thomasin saw them for the first time, those black, flashing eyes that had the power to captivate and crush. And, most of all, she knew how to use them. The music resumed: a quick, new tune Thomasin did not recognise, and the woman began to dance. And what a dance it was, making all those who had gone before look like children who were still learning. She was slow and seductive, then swift and precise, with the air of an expert. She moved between the dancers, circling her partner without noticing him, as if she was the only person present. Just her and the king. Not once did she take her eyes off him. It created an intimacy, amid the crowd, that made Thomasin feel uncomfortable.

People began to slip away. Thomasin's mother rose to her feet, gathered Cecilia and edged around the side of the room to join her husband. The king was left alone, but he had undergone a transformation. He remained seated but he had lost his former air of easy comfort, and his limbs showed tension. Thomasin realised that the power had shifted; that someone had arrived who was able to put the king on edge. It was this dark-eyed woman who really ruled the hall at that moment.

"Anne Boleyn," Cecilia whispered at her side. "They have quarrelled again about the queen. She is furious with him."

"She is magnificent," breathed Thomasin, wishing she might possess one tiny amount of the hypnotic power this woman wore so lightly.

"But I had heard she was a beauty," Cecilia tutted. "What a disappointment."

"Disappointment?"

"Apparently, she learned to dance in France. Pray we never have to go."

"Come, girls," their mother tutted at the vulgarity of the show. "We must leave them to their business. Let us take a little air."

The gardens felt different under the cloak of darkness. Flares had been lit along the paths, but they only served to make the dark spaces recede further. The cold air rushed into Thomasin's lungs, bringing much-needed relief.

Anne's arrival had been seen by many as a cue to leave the hall and now they spilled out across the grass pathways, filling the space with noise and movement. The mood had changed swiftly, and people were on edge, recalling their allegiances. Voices muttered in agreement and condemnation. Bodies jostled impatiently. The wine had been flowing freely and while some tried to take up the dance again, under the trees, others were drifting away, or beginning to laugh too loudly, or too impertinently.

Thomasin followed her parents as they made their way through the gardens in the direction of the stables. Raised voices reached them from down the path, where two men had turned their disagreement into violence. One was a man with whom Thomasin had danced earlier, who wore the eye-patch, and he seemed to have taken offence at the other. As they jostled, a burning taper came crashing down between them across the path. The flames fell upon a bush and a handful of leaves began to blaze.

At once there was a ripple of panic. People pushed past as servants raced for buckets. Thomasin realised she had been lagging behind her family, who were walking at a faster pace. Now the fire separated them, and she could not see them, through it all. They might even have passed beyond the hedges, and be unaware of the fire. For a moment she felt the grip of fear in her belly.

"May I assist you, my lady?"

Rafe Danvers was immediately behind her. She was surprised she had not sensed him. As she turned, she could not avoid being drawn straight into the depths of his dark eyes. Words failed her.

"You will be safer over here, out of the way, until the flames are under control and we can reunite you with your family."

She allowed herself to be led. Down one of the paths, lined with late-blooming roses, there was an alcove with a seat.

"Please," he said, "you can rest here safely."

"Thank you."

"It's Francis Bryan causing trouble again. The king will hear of it."

He sat down beside her and they watched as a group of servants rushed past, in the direction of the glow. Away from the activity, it was shaded, quieter. Thomasin became aware of the scent of the roses around them and the rise and fall of her own breathing.

When they spoke, it was at the same time.

"You are new to court?"

"You are Boleyn's ward?"

They laughed, the sound breaching the divide between them. He inclined his dark head.

"After you."

"Yes, I am new to court."

She felt his eyes on her; for some reason, his gaze was heavier than any other she had experienced. It made her conscious of every movement, of the way she was holding herself, and unable to hide.

"But not a stranger entirely? Your father, earlier?"

"In the knot garden? Yes, my parents once served at court but I have not been here since I was an infant."

"I missed your name, before."

"Thomasin Marwood."

"Thomasin." It sounded different in his mouth. She could feel his eyes on her face, but she dared not look at him directly. Something in them was too raw.

"Sir Richard Marwood's daughter?"

"Yes."

"I saw you dancing. You dance well for a country girl."

"A country girl?" There was something about the lack of sophistication this implied that rankled with her.

"Are you not a girl? From the country?"

She pursed her lips. "From the country, I cannot deny. A girl? I am seventeen."

"Quite a matron, then."

She shot him a quick look, taking in the pale ellipse of his face in the gloom, with its strong lines and intense features. "Are you laughing at me?"

"A little."

"I might mind being laughed at."

"Do you?"

She threw him back his own words. "A little."

"So long as it is only a little. Perhaps this might make amends."

Rafe was holding out a rose, a deep pink that was still vivid in the darkness, quivering where he had just plucked it off the stem. She stared into the petals.

"You must take it," he urged, "or else I will have committed treason without cause."

"Treason?"

"Stealing the king's roses."

Thomasin took the rose carefully from between his fingers, with the slightest touch of skin on skin as her knuckles grazed his.

"See," he said, "more servants with water. The fire will soon be under control. You will be able to return to your family."

"They will be wondering what has become of me."

"They will be grateful that you are safe from harm."

Thomasin stood up. She held the rose between finger and thumb. "I thank you for your assistance; it was most timely. But I really should not linger here. My family will be worried." And yet, there was nothing that she would have loved more, than to linger there with him under the roses.

"Of course." Rafe was on his feet beside her. "But it is dark. Let me accompany you, until you find them."

"Thank you." She risked another look up into his eyes, the eyes she had noticed before as being alternately sensitive and burning. They were long, tapered at the edges, curved slightly upwards at the sides, lined with the thickest, darkest lashes. They seemed to drink her in. For a minute she was held by them.

"Thomasin! There you are!"

It was her father. Coming up behind her, he caught her as she swayed to her feet. "Are you hurt? We could not find you amid the crowd."

"I am quite well, thank you. This gentleman brought me to safety."

Her father shot glance at Rafe Danvers. "We are most grateful. Now, Thomasin, come, the others are waiting."

Rafe stepped aside to allow them to pass, back to the path, the rose still dangling between her fingers.

"Who was that?" her father asked impatiently as he urged her away.

"We met earlier today, do you remember? In these gardens."

"His name?"

"Danvers, I think. He is the ward of Viscount Boleyn."

"Boleyn." Richard snorted. "Then be warned, he is no friend of yours."

From his tone, she knew better than to question him.

At the gate, Thomasin risked a backward glance. The fire had been entirely put out, and even the smoke had gone. There was no sign of the earlier panic and danger. Rafe Danvers had disappeared, as if the darkness had reclaimed him.

FIVE

Their soft-soled shoes were silent along the stone flags of the corridor. This part of the palace was quiet, even despite the hour, quiet and cold. There were no braziers to ward off the chill, and no wall brackets to light the way. The few rushes strewn about the place had an unsavoury smell, brushed into corners and behind benches. Far removed from the hall, which had been warmed by last night's dancing and feasting, this wing had the air of neglect.

Thomasin paused. A small sound caught her ears as they passed an archway. There, perched on a stone ledge, sat a little sparrow who had flown inside and got lost. It noticed her attention, turned its head on one side. She pursed her lips to whistle, but in a silent spread of wings, it was gone, like a ghost.

The servant leading the way paused outside a heavy wooden door. Thomasin's mother drew up behind her, trying to ease her breath in and out, to conceal the effort it cost her. Cecilia rounded to a halt gracefully, with a swish of the skirts, brushing against her sister. Gone were the gold, white and yellow silks and the strings of pearls. Today their mother had insisted they dress in far more sombre colours, in grey and ash-coloured cloth, with their crucifixes about their necks. "It befits a Sunday," she had told them, "and does honour to the queen."

"Please wait here," spoke the serving woman, indicating a bench under a window. "I will see if Her Highness has returned from chapel."

Elizabeth took the seat gratefully. Thomasin turned over in her hands the gift she had been given to present to the queen:

a homemade pomander, of dried orange, cloves and ribbon. The oils released a spicy residue upon her fingers. She thought of the woman last night, the one they called Anne Boleyn, dancing so seductively, using her power over the king. Anne had once been here, waiting to be admitted to the queen's chambers, respectful, dutiful, wishing to serve the lady within, the lady whom she now mocked with every twist and turn of her enchanting head. Was it the king's love that had so emboldened her?

"What are you thinking?" asked Cecilia with typical directness.

Thomasin smiled. Usually she evaded her sister's demands to know her innermost secrets. "I was just thinking how fortunes can change, so swiftly and so completely."

Cecilia was surprised, but she brushed it off with her elder sister routine. "Well, of course, that is life. We rise and we fall."

"But must it be so?"

"Of course, that is God's way."

Cecilia's response, predictable as it was, made Thomasin feel a little chilled. But there was no time to reflect, as a waiting woman in a Spanish gown had appeared, in a waft of lavender and woodsmoke.

"Queen Catherine will receive you now. Please come this way."

Invisible hands held the door aside to allow them to enter. First, a corridor, then a waiting room and a little dark antechamber held clothing, religious artefacts and portraits of foreign-looking monarchs. Thomasin glanced over it quickly: guards sat on benches, pretending not to doze or playing at cards. Beyond, they reached the waiting chamber, which was larger, and brighter, with a dozen women sitting about sewing, and a boy playing upon a lute. His nimble fingers lifted the mood, and Thomasin's heart, as they entered, the subject of some scrutiny from all those who watched.

Ahead, Thomasin spotted the empty chair of state, used when the queen gave a formal audience. A canopy of silver tissue hung above and draped down behind it, embroidered with a coat of arms featuring a black eagle, with its wings outstretched, a reminder of the queen's Spanish heritage. Thomasin wondered about the occasions when Queen Catherine had occupied that chair, presiding over the visits of ambassadors, or masques and merriment, and wondered when the king had last visited these rooms.

The queen's chamber was at the far end, the ultimate prize after a series of closing boxes. The door stood ajar, barring, and yet inviting, the favoured few into the innermost sanctuary of the Queen of England. A Spanish lady at the door waved them through. Thomasin took it all in quickly: a large bed occupied the far side, and a fire lit the golden hangings and made them gleam; there was a cupboard of glittering plate, a shelf of books, a few chests, a round table, cushions.

Catherine of Aragon was standing by the table. By all definitions, she was a tiny woman, shorter even than Thomasin, and clearly, she had once been a beautiful woman with her round face and red-gold hair, but years of childbearing had made her stout. Nothing, though, not even the ravages of time, could detract from the regality of her bearing. As they knelt low before her, Thomasin could feel her presence, and how complete and consummate her power was. This was a woman born to rule, who would fight to keep that rule.

"Please rise, you do me great honour," she spoke softly, with her English still accented. "Come here, let me see you." She held out both hands, encrusted with rings. The gems were large and bright, in red, blue and green.

Thomasin's mother went forward to meet her, accepting the hands that were offered, and the kisses, one upon each cheek, the emotional moment of reconnection. Thomasin was close enough to study the beautiful adornment of the queen's person; the delicate blackwork cuffs extending beyond the furred sleeves, the tawny bodice embroidered with flowers in brown and yellow, the lace and pearls at the neck of her gown, the gable headdress with its flowing veil. Two perfect tear-drop pearls hung in her ears.

"It is so many years since I have seen my friend," Catherine said with emotion. "I am so happy to see your face again. Let me look at you. I am not so fortunate that I have friends to spare these days, and your return is most welcome."

The queen was studying Elizabeth's face intently, as if she could read her recent history there. Her blue eye seemed to plough and mine the contours of cheek and mouth, as if they were her property, almost making the guests uncomfortable.

"I am so glad to see Your Highness again," Elizabeth replied, "and regret that I never came sooner, but my daughters and illness kept me in the countryside."

"I hope you are recovered from any illness; you still look as well and fresh as in your youth. What ails you?"

"It is a malady in the breast, nothing that I hope a physician might not cure."

"I can recommend you my own doctor, here at court. Sir Thomas Elyot is a most sympathetic and learned man, with a great understanding of the humours, and the effects of diet upon the body, as well as being a good Catholic. His services are at your disposal. I will send him to you."

"I thank you, most humbly."

A movement behind her distracted Catherine, as one of her women was tidying some books. "Oh, it is you, Maria? Come here."

The Spanish lady-in-waiting crossed the room, with her demure, dark eyes and tidy person, dressed in the plain black of a widow. She gathered up the gifts in smooth, white hands.

"Oh, Maria," said the queen, "you must remember Elizabeth, wife of Sir Richard Marwood; Elizabeth, this is Maria de Salinas, who came with me from Spain when I was a girl. She was with me at my parents' court; she has known me longer than anyone. Her husband was Baron Willoughby, so she is a baroness now."

"Why yes, I do remember your good Maria," replied Elizabeth, her face widening into a smile, "who served you so diligently during those years."

"And still does," the queen smiled, as the two women embraced. "Sit with us, Maria, that you might hear all the news."

"Thank you, my lady. It is truly a good day when God has sent you to see us again, Lady Marwood."

Catherine smiled at Maria, then turned back to her old friend. "And these are your daughters? Let me see them. Come forward, girls, don't be shy."

Elizabeth stood aside to let Cecilia and Thomasin be seen. It was a strange sensation, Thomasin thought, quite unlike the heavy, hungry gaze of the king, which had roamed over them. The Spanish queen's dark eyes seemed to hold them in her embrace, with appreciation and a raw sense of emotion that Thomasin could not place. There was kindness, certainly, warmth, acceptance, appreciation, almost a vicarious enjoyment of their youth and looks.

Cecilia stepped forward to offer her gift first, then Thomasin. The queen cradled them appreciatively in her hands.

"Oh, Elizabeth, I remember them as babies. You have been so blessed, so very blessed. God has been good to you. And you know I have my own daughter too." She gestured to a servant. "Fetch Mary."

Elizabeth bowed again. "Cecilia is my eldest, and then Thomasin."

Catherine held out a hand, drawing Cecilia to her, as if enraptured by her beauty. "My goodness, she takes after you, Elizabeth. She looks so like you when you first came into my service, and about the same age, I should think."

The queen was very tactile, holding Cecilia's hand a long while, looking over her with a scrutiny that was born of her position, as she might examine a new piece of cloth or a beautiful vase. Cecilia bore it well, but the intensity of it almost became uncomfortable.

Thomasin had not been forgotten. "Here girl, you too, come close."

Thomasin stepped up to the queen's side, and accepted the small, dry hand that sought hers.

"Now, this one," said the queen happily, "is quite another fish entirely. She looks like she has just come striding out of the fields after milking a cow, or with her apron full of apples. Do you mind me saying that, child?"

Thomasin felt her cheeks grow red, as the queen encircled her waist with an arm and pulled her to her side. "Of course not."

"I hear you are marrying off your elder one. Let me keep this one, for my company, among my ladies. I like her looks."

Elizabeth struggled to conceal her surprise. "We do not plan to stay long. Barely a few weeks, before we return. I have four other children at home."

"Any sons?"

"Just the one, my Lady, and five daughters."

"One is enough," Catherine sighed, drawing Thomasin closer to her side. "It would be a grand start for her, should you wish to consider leaving her behind. A good way to find a husband. Who does your elder marry?"

"Sir Henry Kytson."

Catherine's face fell. "Kytson? For this beauty? What do you think of him, child?"

Cecilia knew the family line well enough. "I am honoured at the match, my Lady."

Catherine nodded as if she understood. "I know Sir Henry a little. He is an honourable man, and a fair jouster, although he has never been able to unseat my husband."

She said this with a glow of pride that made Thomasin wonder. Surely the queen knew what was whispered at court, and the influence of the dark-haired Boleyn woman? Perhaps she chose not to let it touch her, keeping scandal as distant as poison, like a true, dignified queen?

"Ah, here she is, the dear child of my heart."

Two small girls had entered the chamber, one a slight thing of ten or eleven, and a second, a few years younger, dark and captivating with great eyes. The taller one approached and Elizabeth bowed at once, realising that this was the Princess Mary, and her daughters followed her example.

The younger girl with the dark eyes went to stand by Maria.

"She has the look of my father," said Catherine, smiling, drawing Mary to her side, "and the intelligence of my mother."

Catherine's lineage was famous throughout the realm. She was the daughter of the warlike Isabella of Castile, Queen in her own right, and Ferdinand of Aragon, the military leader who won so many territories; they had been the most powerful couple in Europe, in the world, but their rule had not been without cruelty. Both were dead now, Isabella before Thomasin's birth and Ferdinand a decade ago, but their legacy was remembered, among the heretics and Muslims they had persecuted. Now they had one grandchild as Holy Roman Emperor, while another, young Mary, stood before them.

Privately, Thomasin thought that behind her velvet and lace, the girl's face was a mask; regular and pleasant, but with little to distinguish it. Perhaps she would grow to reflect the momentous history that had helped create her.

"What amusements have you been finding, my dear?"

"I grew tired of reading, so we've been playing chess, but Mistress Dashford is too cunning. She would win, but she holds back, to let me win, although I wish she would simply play and not try to flatter me."

Catherine laughed. "One day you will be able to defeat her, and then perhaps you will be the gracious one."

"Oh no, I will always play to win, whoever it might be."

"Even against your father?"

Mary did not need to think. "Of course, because he would take pride in my winning, would he not?"

"I am sure he would. Now, run along back to your game, and take these two young ladies with you, as I would talk privately with their mother. And take little Catherine with you."

Maria kissed her daughter and bid her go along with the princess.

Thomasin and Cecilia followed where the girls led, to a corner of the waiting chamber, where the chessboard was set up in the window, beside the place where caged songbirds hung. Little Catherine sat below them, upon a cushion, to watch them in their cages.

"Do you play?" Mary asked both sisters, with eagerness in her eyes.

"I do, a little," Thomasin volunteered, taking a seat before the board, releasing Cecilia to the contemplation of her lace cuffs.

The game was just finishing, a half hour later, when their mother emerged, walking stiffly, no matter how she tried to glide gracefully. She embraced and kissed the queen, and they took their leave.

"She isn't as I imagined," pronounced Cecilia as they headed back through the courtyard to the gate, where their carriage was waiting. "I thought somehow that a queen would be taller."

"Like you, you mean?" Thomasin couldn't resist asking.

"Why yes, now you mention it, yes, like me."

By the time they had reached Monk's Place, Elizabeth's breathing was laboured. The carriage rattled into the courtyard and the gates were rapidly closed behind them, shutting out the busy city. Leaning on her daughters' arms, the frail figure slowly made the journey inside to the door. Thomasin felt the slightness of her form, so much smaller than she remembered, like a bird, half walking on the earth, half in flight.

Gently, she guided her mother across the threshold, into the darkness of the hall. Wood, smoke and herbs hung in the air; the flicker of torches and the patter of dogs' feet. Their uncle's two hounds, grey, black and wolfish, padded out to nose them in eager welcome. Here, the Russell coat of arms was painted upon the wall, and swords of past battles were brightly displayed, the rewards of having backed the right side at the Battle of Bosworth, when the Tudors won the throne. Elizabeth paused, and held up a hand.

"Mother, you should lie down properly, in bed," Cecilia tried to insist.

"I will, I will," Elizabeth panted, "once I am able to climb the stairs. Please, give me a moment."

Thomasin was on the verge of calling for assistance when they heard the voices. Raised, men's voices, coming from one of the rooms down the corridor.

The women froze and listened.

It was difficult to make out the words, but one voice seemed to belong to Father, and another to Matthew, while a third, deeper and perhaps older, contradicted them. A third which had a particular timbre of insistence.

"Wait," she whispered, "listen, who is that?"

The dogs heard too, turned their heads, but knew better than to interrupt their master.

Thomasin and Cecilia caught her note of caution, standing absolutely still in the hallway, as still as mice in a field of threshers. Together, they breathed shallowly, haltingly.

"I have no desire to return," Richard was saying. "You know my reasons, both political and personal. Do not speak to me of duty."

The third voice spoke again, briefly and sharply. The owner was driving their argument home with a sense of urgency.

"Please," replied their father.

The third voice came again, mixed with the more mellow tones of their uncle Matthew, which they found hard to hear.

"No, I will not," added Richard. "I choose not to, no matter who commands it. I will retire to the countryside again in two weeks."

Again, the urged replies and the refusals, then the mystery voice spoke more softly, and at length, and there was a silence.

Finally, Richard gave his reply. The first part of it was muffled, but at the end, they clearly heard him say, in tones they recognised as forced, "I will consider your proposal."

There was a shuffling of feet and chairs, before three figures emerged into the corridor, approaching the place where the women stood. Richard came first, seeming subdued, closely followed by Matthew, and then a shadowy figure behind. The dogs surged forward to nose them.

"My dear," said Elizabeth, extending her hand towards her husband, "we have just this moment returned from our audience with the queen." The sentence took the entirety of her breath.

"Mother is unwell," added Cecilia, before Elizabeth could silence her.

"Not unwell, just…"

"She is short of breath."

Attention turned at once to Elizabeth, who sat passive and reluctant, furious at having her weakness exposed.

"Please forgive me for intruding at this time," spoke the third man, appearing close beside them. "I shall leave you, with my best wishes for your Ladyship's good health."

Thomasin looked up to see his face, pale and plain in the light of the entrance hall. He was a solid, coarse-looking man in his forties, with the physique of a fighter, although his sombre clothes and carefully controlled manner spoke of a quieter occupation. His cheeks were ruddy and pockmarked, as if he had recovered from illness. She noted that neither her father nor uncle answered him, and read volumes into that silence.

"I hope you will consider what I have said, Sir Richard," he added, on the threshold. "I will pass on your response to my master, and we hope to see you at court soon."

Her father bowed his head, but the man was already striding out, calling for his horse.

"Who was that?" asked Cecilia, who had also been observing the tension between them.

"Thomas Cromwell, a servant of Cardinal Wolsey — no one to concern yourself about."

"He wants you to stay at court?"

"It is no matter. I am not staying. Now, help me." Richard placed an arm about his wife's waist. "Let's get your mother up to bed."

SIX

The dinner hour crept up on them swiftly and quietly. With Thomasin's mother full of herbal draughts and asleep with the fire stoked and all the windows covered, they were to assemble for a modest meal when the hour of five struck.

Thomasin changed into a simple dark shift and let down her hair, relieved to enjoy her freedom after the formality the court demanded. As she brushed her dark locks through, she thought about the morning, and the Spanish queen, presiding over her ladies after chapel. The contrast with the night before, with its dancing and the fire in the gardens, could not have been sharper. And into her mind, unbidden, crept the image of Rafe Danvers with his dark, striking looks, and the way he had been so solicitous of her safety among the roses. Slipping her fingers under her pillow, she drew out the pink bloom he had plucked for her, a little crushed from the journey home, and pressed it to her lips. Its delicate fragrance could still be detected.

She followed Cecilia down the dark staircase. Her sister had chosen to keep on her ash-coloured silk gown and elaborate headdress, and cast a look of disapproval at her sister's deshabille.

"You didn't think it appropriate to dress? Or stay dressed?"

"I didn't think it necessary to wear court dress to dinner here."

"We're not at Eastwell now."

"No, but we are at home, so mind your business."

"Mind your own!" And Cecilia ran on ahead.

Thomasin felt a pang of shame. It was just like one of the squabbles they'd had as children, each full of ire and pent-up injustices, struggling to assert their individual selves against each other's difference. They were too old for such exchanges now, especially with their mother so ill. Perhaps, though, with the wedding only two weeks away, it might be the last.

Their father and uncle were already seated in the dining room, heads bent in conversation, brows heavy. As the sisters entered, they broke their serious mood and drew apart at once, welcoming them, and inviting them to be seated. It was a dark room, but not an unpleasant one, where the shadows were balanced by bright wall torches and silver candlesticks set upon the table. Jugs of wine and plates of spices stood waiting, as Thomasin seated herself next to her father, while Cecilia took the place opposite.

"A good morning at court?" asked Matthew, breaking white manchet bread and passing it among them. "You saw the queen?"

"We did," Cecilia replied, "and it was a surprise, in comparison with the previous night's entertainment. I had expected, I don't know, something more queenly."

"She was queenly enough in her bearing," Thomasin clarified. "You could not fault her there, although it is true that her rooms were quiet and modest."

"It is her circumstances," their uncle explained. "She has retreated from the court, and barely leaves her chambers when it is known that the Boleyn woman is present. They come and go with an awareness of each other; if one is out, the other stays away."

"But it should not be the queen's part to make way for the other," Thomasin could not help saying.

"I cannot disagree," her uncle nodded, "but it should be the king's part to protect his queen's position. He has had mistresses before, but always behind closed doors and he was discreet, even with Anne's sister."

"Anne's sister?" asked Cecilia.

"Yes, Mary Boleyn was his mistress some five or six years back; it is rumoured that he fathered her two children, but it cannot be proven. Even then, she showed respect for Catherine and never challenged her position."

"But Anne does?"

Matthew nodded. "Anne is brazen, she refuses to hide. Goodness knows what promises Henry has made her, how he has encouraged her to behave like this, as if she is a queen herself."

"It is also her character," added Richard, returning to the original subject. "Catherine is pious and austere. When placed under duress, she retreats into her religion, seeking simplicity, almost like one in holy orders, she is so focused."

"But she cannot be nun and queen," said Cecilia with perception. "She must choose one or the other."

Thomasin bit into her portion of the bread. It was soft and white, far better quality than what she was used to in the country.

The servants brought in plates, one after another in rapid succession, steaming from the hot meats and pies, straight from the kitchens. The air quickly misted with movement and heat as the plates were placed at intervals between the four diners, and the silent servers withdrew.

Thomasin's eyes widened at the delicacies set before them: chickens and quail, pheasant and roast beef, dressed and spiced, tender and flavoursome. And tonight, Mother was not there to chide her for her appetite.

"What exactly is her role at court, the Boleyn girl?" asked Richard.

"Well!" Matthew reached for a jug of sauce and stirred the thick, creamy substance. "That is a good question. This past year, everything has changed. For many years she was at the French court, but returned perhaps five years back, and entered the royal household. Catherine became aware of her husband's affections for her earlier this year and tried to send Anne away; she dismissed her from her service and called upon her father to return her to the country."

"Where is their residence?"

"In Kent, at Hever. But Viscount Thomas went straight to the king, who overruled it."

"So Anne is no longer a member of the queen's household?" asked Cecilia. "We did not see her there today."

"She is not. Catherine refused to have her back, and Henry was not cruel enough to push it — not that he can't be cruel, mind, if he chooses to be." Matthew turned to Richard. "You heard about Buckingham?"

Richard nodded, midway through cutting a slice off a roast chicken, dressed with cinnamon. "I did. That news even penetrated darkest Suffolk."

Despite the tenderness of the beef in mustard, Thomasin's curiosity got the better of her. "What happened to Buckingham?"

The men exchanged glances and Matthew indicated that Richard should be the one to answer.

"He was the king's closest male relative," her father explained, "the richest man in England, the next in line to the throne. And he knew it. Always trying to outdo the king, in his apparel, his jewels, his houses."

"And the king did not like it," concluded Matthew. "So he cut off his head."

Thomasin was agog. Across the table, she saw that her sister was too.

"For that? Really? How did he justify it?"

Matthew spoke confidentially. "Mind this goes no further than this room. Of course, there is more to it. Some trumped-up charge of treason was brought, five or six years ago. But the king can justify anything to himself; that's how he got into the mess he is in now, with one married wife and another in waiting. So Anne Boleyn lurks about the court, as his guest, with her own rooms, where he visits her, waiting for her moment."

Thomasin was puzzled. "But what can her moment possibly be?"

The candles flickered between them.

Eventually, her uncle answered. "Well, the king has had mistresses before. He even has an illegitimate child. However, he is not getting any younger, and this time he seems to think he might have a case to remarry. He has a queen living, but no son, so he seeks some grounds to put her aside. He has all his legal brains working upon it, to find an excuse, poring over theological texts."

"And that man who was here earlier," added Richard, "Thomas Cromwell, is secretary to the king's greatest servant, Cardinal Wolsey, who seeks to find him a French princess to marry, but I think the king does not want a Valois wife. He wants a Boleyn one."

"But what of Catherine, and Princess Mary? What would happen to them?" Thomasin thought of the gracious lady they had met that morning, already fearing the answer.

"The king wants an heir," said Matthew. "He has been quite open about it, and Wolsey wants your father to enter his service, to help resolve the matter to his satisfaction."

Both sisters looked up in surprise. Cecilia got her words out first.

"To work at court, Father? To help serve the king? But what an opportunity, you must take it."

"Oh no," qualified Thomasin, more sensitive to her father's mood. "You must not, absolutely not, sell your soul in this cause."

Cecilia was staring at her furiously, when there came a knock upon the door.

"Please, my Lord, two gentlemen have called."

Matthew rose to his feet. "Excuse me, this is unexpected. I will be back shortly."

Thomasin chose not to meet her sister's eyes. She reached instead for a dish of pottage, and spooned out a little of the meat onto her plate. Her father refilled his glass and drank slowly.

"Well," pronounced Matthew, in upbeat tones, as he re-entered the room. "Here's a surprise. Sir Henry Kytson and William Hatton have ridden out from court to attend us."

Thomasin looked up, but any surprise or disappointment Cecilia might have felt was concealed behind the mask she habitually wore.

The two gentlemen strode in, Hatton first, his fair colouring almost glowing, eyes bright and roaming about, dressed in an embroidered red doublet and grey hose, decked with gold chains. Kytson was more modest in green and brown, but with a nod to fashion, with a cap and white feather on top of his head. At once Thomasin regretted her change of clothes.

"Gentlemen, I bid you welcome," offered Richard. "We are honoured by your visit."

"We are indeed," Matthew added. "Will you not join us for our meal? Please, there is more than enough."

"Well, if you insist," said Hatton, jovially, his cheeks rosy and round as he smiled, "we would be most grateful. We've come from playing tennis with the king and we are starving."

"Who won?" asked Richard.

"Well," replied Hatton, "actually no, see if you can guess."

Richard laughed. "The king, of course."

"Of course, even though it cost me sixpence."

"And it was sixpence well spent," added Kytson, making the company laugh.

Hatton took the empty seat beside Thomasin, and Kytson, with a few quiet words of greeting, placed himself beside Cecilia. Thomasin knew her sister. They might be quite different, but having spent all their years together, she could sense her feelings just as easily as a change of wind direction upon her face. Cecilia smiled, in her perfect way, and returned Kytson's greeting with a few kind words; she did not move, even in the slightest, but she folded inwards in spirit. Her heart recoiled. Thomasin saw it in her eyes.

"I understand you attended court today?" Hatton asked, addressing the room. "I was present myself, in the king's chambers. I was sorry to have missed you."

"It was not myself," replied Matthew. "The women attended, visiting the queen."

"And how do you like court, ladies?" Hatton replied, turning a huge smile upon them.

"We haven't seen much of it yet," Cecilia replied, "one evening with the king and a morning with the queen."

"And I expect those were two quite different experiences," said Hatton, reaching for the plate that Matthew passed him.

"Like two different worlds," she replied.

"It seems very sad," added Thomasin, "that the king and queen do not dine and dance together."

"They did once," said Hatton, "not so long ago, before the arrival of the Boleyn woman."

"You are not of that faction then, no supporter of the Boleyns?"

Hatton put down his knife. "It is not as simple as that, although it may seem that way on the outside. There are bigger battles being fought underneath the dancing and flattering."

"Oh, I am sure the ladies do not want to be bored with all those intrigues, when they have only just arrived," protested Kytson. "We should speak to them of dogs and hunting and which ladies are the best dressed at court."

Cecilia smiled blandly, but this was a platitude that Thomasin could not let go.

"Why so? Are ladies not interested in intrigues? Are their minds so fragile that they can only bear light fare?"

Hatton laughed and raised his eyebrows. "Here, Kytson, you have uncovered a woman of the new learning, who refuses to know her place in the world."

Kytson was not able to produce any necessary fire. "I offer my apologies. I had no intention to offend."

"But what do you mean?" asked Thomasin, turning away from him to Hatton. "What is the new learning?"

"You have been all your life in Suffolk?" he replied.

"Most of it, yes. What have I missed?" She looked to her father, but he appeared content to let Hatton continue her education.

"Where to begin?" Hatton mused. "In recent years, we have begun to look at the world differently in all things, from literature and art, to philosophy and mathematics and astrology, inspired by the classical thinkers."

"But what other ways are there of looking at the world?"

"It's about perspective. Humanism turns the focus on the individual, and their actions and choices, in driving the world forward, acting instead of reacting, taking their own destiny into their hands."

"It sounds almost heretical," said Kytson, thinly, "to suggest that man may be his own agent instead of fulfilling the purpose ordained for him by God."

Hatton smiled. "Or perhaps it suggests more of a direct relationship with God, without the intermediaries of the Church and its saints. The world is changing, Henry, you must keep up."

"Hush," Kytson smiled, but he was also shaking his head. "You stray into reformist territory and will get yourself in trouble for your talk."

"You will see that the king is moving in my direction. The world is ours to discover."

"And on that note," said Matthew, rising to diffuse the tension, "please discover some of this delicious pie."

Hatton laughed, and took the dish, but Thomasin was lost in thought. She had known there was a physical world outside Suffolk walls, with cities, houses, palaces and gardens she had never seen, but the realisation struck her that there was an entire life of the mind, of which she had been ignorant. She ate slowly, listening as the talk became lighter, of tennis and bowls, and dogs and dancing, as Cecilia laughed and her father and uncle made jovial comments about this and that, but her mind was racing.

SEVEN

The tiltyard had been transformed into a pageant of people, movement and horses. Bright banners hung from the trees and the path was gravelled and railed in the Tudor colours of white and green. There was a nip in the air, and a smell of burning coals, mixed with the stench of horses. And, as Thomasin paused to breathe in deeply, the crowds ahead of her trailed an exotic thread, an unfamiliar perfume which caught her in its tail. It transported her momentarily to an imagined place; a princess bedecked with riches, an ornate foreign palace, across wild seas, before the scent was lost on the breeze.

Although the carriage set them down some distance away, Thomasin could already see the crowds moving, and the line of knights in red and gold, or blue and yellow, their horses walking slowly to display their golden bells and cloth of silver. They were too far away to be heard. She kept close behind her father, and Matthew and Cecilia, as they joined the line of people making their way along the path. There was no time to look around, to inspect the palace buildings behind them, or the trees rising to the sky, or else the crowd might part them. They followed the line of a tall, red brick wall, with pollarded fruit trees, towards the gate.

Her first glimpse of the tiltyard was one of immense space and activity. At the far end, a number of tents had been erected, canvas rooms made from gold or red cloth, embroidered and decorated with flags.

"Here we are," beamed Matthew, looking around. "Now we need to find a good spot in the gallery before all the space is taken."

They joined the line surging towards the wooden platforms, where braziers were lined up, blazing out heat. It was a crush among the spectators, jostling shoulder to shoulder, along the path and up the wooden steps. Thomasin had never seen so many people before in her life, not even at market day in the square at Bury St Edmunds.

"Here, along here," her uncle called back.

They gratefully sank into the empty seats at the end of the stand, with just one row of spectators in front of them. It was a good place, with a view right across the lists ahead, although on the right, their sights were a little restricted by the heavy hanging curtain.

"Oh, I don't mind that," said Cecilia, arranging her skirts around her. "It will help keep out the chill."

Thomasin sat beside her, pleased to see that the wooden benches came with flat, dark cushions and the draughty floor had been scattered with rushes and herbs. They had barely settled, when the trumpeters began to blast out their notes into the air, and the crowd looked round eagerly, hoping for a glimpse of the riders.

"See across there," indicated Richard, nodding to the stands opposite, across the other side of the lists.

Thomasin followed his gaze and found the royal section, where the canopy was gold and rich hangings made a private little room for those within.

"There's the queen."

Catherine was seated to the left, in a large chair with carved arms, under a red and gold cloth. She was wrapped in furs, but even at that distance, Thomasin could see her sparkling with jewels as she sat still and intense, holding herself erect like a marble statue. Beside her, her daughter Mary, dressed in royal blue, stood up in her excitement, while her ladies sat in rows either side.

"The queen loves a joust," Matthew added, handing them wooden cups of hot, spiced wine. Thomasin curled her hands around hers, feeling the warmth rise up to her face. Cinnamon, she could identify, and mace or nutmeg, and a strange, star-like thing floating on the top among the peppercorns. Too hot to drink yet, though.

Cecilia had been watching the tents. "Look, they're almost ready."

The riders were assembling, as men were milling about in bright costumes, carrying pieces of armour and long lances. One figure was standing in the entrance, while the others tied his laces, and checked his helmet and breastplate.

There was something familiar about him; Thomasin was sure she recognised him, although she could not place him.

"It's the duke of Suffolk," supplied her father, as if he could read her thoughts, "the king's brother-in-law, whose estates lie not too far from our own."

"Oh, yes." Thomasin nodded, recalling having seen the duke and his wife, Mary, who had formerly been Queen of France, dancing in the masque.

Suffolk was being helped into the saddle of a horse trapped in gold.

"They say he's second only to the king," added Matthew, "but I do not see who his opponent is yet."

Thomasin looked to the other end of the lists, where a matching set of tents fluttered lightly in the breeze. A man in black and green, with silver armour, was inspecting the lances.

"He waits on the far side, see him?"

"Yes, but I can't make him out."

As they all stared, trying to identify the mystery man, he climbed onto a white charger with flowing yellow ribbons and set his face towards the lists.

At that moment, Thomasin's sharp eyes spotted movement in the queen's gallery. A figure had entered from the right side, into a space left vacant by the ladies-in-waiting, which had perhaps been deliberately left. Thomasin recognised her at once; a woman, above average height, dressed in flaming scarlet, with a gold hood and pearls. A cluster of waiting women followed her, closing in about her, protectively, if a little hesitantly. The woman stood for a moment, surveying the scene as if she owned it, and all the people in it, before her ladies carried forward a special chair, and she lowered herself slowly into it, commanding the right-hand side of the gallery.

Thomasin felt an acute sting of pain. Although she was new to court, and new to the ways of the world, she felt strongly that Anne Boleyn should not be there, in the other half of the gallery occupied by the queen, as if she was herself entitled to the space, by blood. And she saw that, although Catherine did not move an inch, she was aware of Anne's presence, painfully aware. The little princess looked on, her hands clasped in excitement, oblivious to her mother's situation.

Movement drew Thomasin's eyes again, this time to the far end of the lists.

The black and green challenger on the white horse had begun a slow ride about the circuit, his visor up, as he waved to the cheering crowd. Thomasin watched him approach. His face was barely visible from that distance, and even as he rode past them slowly, gathering a little applause, his features eluded her.

"George Boleyn," Matthew informed them. "Her brother."

As soon as he said this, Thomasin understood that this lap was just the preliminary. As George rode round the rim of the yard, and approached the royal gallery, his sister came forward to the edge of the stand to meet him. She stood for a moment, visible to all in her bright dress, before he bent the top of his lance towards her. About the end, she tied a silk favour, in the same shade of flaming scarlet that she wore. Some words passed between them and Anne laughed, throwing back her head to reveal her long white throat. It was quite a performance, staged for all the crowd to see.

And then, as George rode away, wearing her colours, Anne tossed her head and threw a look over at Catherine, to see if she was watching. But the queen was not. Just metres away, she had fixed her eyes straight ahead and her face was impenetrable.

The trumpets sounded and the two riders took their positions at either end of the lists. As the signal was given, they began the charge towards each other, thundering closer and closer until they passed in a blur, with a shattering sound as their lances clashed. Thomasin blinked, tempted to look away, but they continued unhurt, taking up fresh lances for the next round. A squire had picked up the scarlet silk from the ground where it lay, and returned it to George Boleyn. He rode again with it, and again, as his sister looked on, and the crowd cheered in anticipation. The pair ran again, and again, breaking lances but remaining seated, until it was time to change the competitors.

Thomasin drank her wine.

"Oh," said Cecilia nonchalantly, "there is Hatton."

Thomasin turned to see William Hatton pass, walking down the side of the lists towards the tents where Boleyn had dismounted. He stood out with his bright hair and light, jaunty walk, but he was easily overshadowed by his companion. A second figure walked beside him, tall and broad-shouldered, in black and purple velvet, his dark head turned to look out across the tiltyard. Her heart beat harder for a moment. It was him, Rafe Danvers, whom she had last seen in the gardens after the fire, whose pink rose was still under her pillow. She became conscious of her breathing, of her body, sitting there upon that spot, as he approached, knowing that he just had to turn his head a little, look up towards the seats, and she would be discovered. And she couldn't drag her eyes away from him, as if she was transfixed, or under a spell. It was not just his looks; there was something in the way he was shaped, and how he moved, that made him the most beautiful man she had ever seen.

"Thomasin, you're staring."

Cecilia's voice shocked her out of her fixation. "No, I'm not."

"Yes, you were. At the tall one."

"I was just looking at the crowd."

Her sister laughed. "You don't have to hide it from me. Just make sure you look your kindest upon Sir Giles Waterson when the time comes."

"As you do upon Henry Kytson?"

"Ah, but you see," Cecilia replied swiftly, "Sir Henry is not here to look upon."

The trumpets announced the next challengers. When Thomasin looked back, Hatton and Danvers had reached the far tent and were conversing with George Boleyn. The woman in scarlet opposite had disappeared from the gallery. Queen Catherine was sitting there alone. The sound of horse hooves thundered down the lists and the lances crashed again.

Spices upon Thomasin's fingertips: hot, sharp, sweet. The dust was brown, red, grey. Thomasin licked them off, feeling the warmth spread through her mouth.

A banquet had been spread out on tables set up under the trees. The galleries around the lists had disgorged themselves of spectators, who had crossed the lawn to observe another uncomfortable sport. Below an embroidered canopy, two chairs had been placed upon a wooden dais. Henry sat in one, resplendent in silver and grey velvet and on his left side, Catherine occupied the other, as separate and detached as if the other seat was empty. Above the heads of the crowd, Thomasin could only glimpse them in the distance, but she could be certain that Anne Boleyn, in her scarlet silk gown, was nowhere to be seen.

Before the king and queen sat a small table, covered in a carpet woven in red, grey and blue and spread with plates and goblets. Members of the court were taking it in turns to select a dish from the banquet and offer it to the royal couple. On the side, a group of musicians, with their recorders, viols and lutes, were making a fast-paced tune, and some couples had stepped up to dance on a little square of grass, rolled flat for the purpose. Thomasin watched as she licked each finger in turn, tasting each difference, wondering which exotic part of the world had grown them.

As she wondered, she became aware of two gentlemen who were moving closer to her. But they were not aware of her, their bodies bent towards each other in frames of conflict.

"You would not dare say that again," said one, in controlled and menacing tones.

Thomasin turned, in surprise, suddenly on edge. A chill of fear surged through her, but she saw at once that she had not been the cause of the comment. Two men in expensive doublets were squaring up to each other, their eyes full of anger.

It was George Boleyn, the black and green jouster, who had spoken, his anger towards the other plain to see, as he pushed his finger into his adversary's chest.

"I dare you. Say that again, say it to my face, go say it before the king."

The other man, an older figure with a greying moustache and the air of easy affluence, was refusing to be riled. He merely looked at George, as if he were a puddle to be stepped over.

"Then admit you are a coward who will not stand by your words."

"I will do no such thing. Nor will I be sent down from court for brawling with an upstart child."

"Upstart child! Stand your ground, Sir!"

At close proximity, Thomasin could see his face reddening, this young brother of Anne's, whose handsome looks were clouded with rage and impetuosity.

"I stand my ground, but I have no intention of engaging with you."

Boleyn's hand went to the hilt of his sword. "Stand and fight, Sir, for the sake of honour."

"There is no honour in it," replied the other, reaching for a wine glass, "only dishonour, which I do not wish to incur as a result of your arrogance."

George was just reaching boiling point when his father intervened. The viscount had been summoned by one of his circle and hurried over, taking his wayward son by the arm at once and turning him away, in a smooth gesture that placed him between the two adversaries. The Boleyn men were now facing the spot where Thomasin stood, her fingers licked clean of spice. A short way behind her, Cecilia and Hatton had been conversing, but they fell silent.

"Cool your ire," breathed Boleyn through clenched teeth, so that none but George, and Thomasin, were close enough to hear. "You do your family harm with such a display, in earshot of the king. Why would he honour us when you behave thus?"

"I suggest," said George's cool adversary, still behind them, "Viscount, that if you cannot control your children, you do not bring them to court."

"You should mark your words, Sir," Boleyn replied, his teeth still clenched, "for you will find that the king welcomes them with open arms, and also their friends."

And Sir Thomas Boleyn marched his son away, his eyes briefly meeting those of Thomasin as he passed: rich, dark pools of intrigue, that both compelled and terrified her.

The gap left in the crowd soon closed. She heard Cecilia resume her conversation with Hatton and, across the field, Richard and Matthew were presenting their dishes to the king, apparently unaware of the disturbance. She stood, alone, feeling the tension that had gathered in her chest.

EIGHT

"I hope that little scene did not alarm you," Rafe said softly at Thomasin's side.

She knew who it was at once, without turning. She felt it. She dared not look up into his face, but one glance at the black and purple velvet sleeve beside her confirmed it.

"Not at all," she smiled. "I suppose that happens often."

"When George is around, yes. It's my fault too, I was supposed to be watching him."

He came forwards, so that she could no longer avoid him. The strong chest, the broad shoulders. His proximity made her feel hot, and she caught the scent of his leather boots and a muskiness coming from his person. She lifted her eyes and met his; dark, wide and full, tapering into thick lashes at the sides. The intensity in them made her feel weak.

"My Lady?"

She nodded, unable to reach for the right words.

"You are quite well?"

She nodded again, not wanting the moment to end.

"Did you watch the jousting?"

"Yes, I did."

"I am one of the challengers for tomorrow. Will you be here to see it?"

She was flattered, but flustered. "Oh, I'm not sure. We had no plans to attend a second day."

"You are not staying at court?"

"No, with my uncle at Monk's Place."

"The Monk's Place in Thames Street? I know it. I have taken messages there. It's not so far."

"No," she said softly. "Not so far."

Rafe looked around. The crowd was starting to move. She saw from the vacated chairs that the king and queen had left their places. He offered her an arm. "We are heading inside. Might I conduct you in?"

The temptation was too strong. Light as a bird, Thomasin let her hand rest on his sleeve, feeling the pressure of muscle and bone beneath her fingertips, then let it slip down and round, so they were linked by their arms. He began to lead her forwards, and her heart longed to follow, but a sudden remembrance of family and duty summoned her and she sought her father in the crowd.

Richard was not so far off, walking with Matthew towards the red brick gateway, as all the others were. Sir Henry Kytson had appeared to accompany Cecilia and the pair were walking coldly together, with Cecilia listening as he spoke. And in spite of all her concerns, her father had seen her, understood her situation, and gave her a brief nod of approval. It flooded her with unexpected feeling, and she felt herself blushing hotly, so turned her face away.

Rafe led her forwards. It was a strange sensation, having been chosen by him to walk at his side, among the court. It was the feeling of being seen, recognised, for the first time. Of complete and utter immersion in the moment, of every second being precious, a shining jewel in her mind, which she would take out and relive later.

Their walk was brief, and the press of people on all sides made conversation difficult. At one point, he stepped aside, to let her pass first, and on another, he steered her over to a less muddy patch of path. Her arm touched and retouched him, and once or twice their eyes met, and he gave a gentle smile.

But silence seemed to hold them both quite happily, without the need for words.

As they joined the queue of people heading into the main courtyard, he drew her closer. "I don't want to lose you among the crowd."

Thomasin was unable to hide her smile, beaming at his words, hoping he had not seen how easily she was pleased.

They passed through the red brick gateway with its carved rondels, into a cobbled yard, with decorative brickwork and windows on all sides. A stone fountain stood in the centre, topped with gilded beasts. More coloured banners and streamers had been hung up for the occasion. Crossing from one side to another, their path lay through a half-open stone corridor and up a flight of steps. At the top, a pair of wooden doors stood open to reveal a large hall with a vaulted ceiling, quickly filling up with people. The walls were adorned with heavy tapestries and curtained portraits, open to reveal the painted faces of the king and queen, and others she did not recognise.

Thomasin heard the music at once. Without a word, she took the lead and brought Rafe forwards, seeking out the source of the song. At the top end of the hall, where a little crowd had gathered, Princess Mary was playing the virginals, and singing a song in French. Her voice was sweet and high, just as was fitting from a young girl, in perfect tune. The king and queen stood a little way off, but apart, listening to their daughter.

The music danced on, sometimes light, sometimes melancholy, like a child's dance or a leaf caught in the wind.

"She plays well," whispered Rafe, and Thomasin was torn between wanting to answer but not wishing to lose a moment of the performance.

When the piece came to an end, the room erupted into applause. The sound fairly rang from the rafters, in praise of the little princess. Thomasin let go of Rafe's arm in order to join their clapping, and her eyes wandered to the king and queen, united in their pride. Henry, tall and majestic, in his late-thirties, with the physique of an athlete dressed in grey velvet with cloth of silver and red laces, his neck hung about with gold chains and a jewelled collar about his throat. Catherine wore a dress of dark green and tawny orange with pearls and jewels, and tissue of gold. For a moment, they gave the impression of a happy couple, a happy family, surrounded by their friends, clapping and laughing together.

But as she looked closer, as the applause died and the princess rose from her seat, Thomasin saw that the queen's face was downcast. Catherine went to meet her daughter and drew her into her arms, kissing the top of her head. Then she turned her face away, towards the shadows, as if to hide tears.

"The queen is sad," Thomasin whispered, unguarded, before thinking what she was saying, and to whom.

"Yes. She has to say goodbye to her daughter today."

"Goodbye? But why?"

"Mary must return to her household at Ludlow."

"Ludlow?"

"A castle on the Welsh borders. As Princess of Wales, she has her own establishment there. She will be back again for the Christmas season."

"She can't stay here?"

"It's tradition. All royal heirs do it. Shall we get some wine?"

Thomasin accepted a glass, watching as Cecilia and Kytson took up their positions, for the musicians were about to play.

A messenger was making his way through the hall, dressed in Boleyn livery, heading for the king. His movement had a sense of urgency about it. Thomasin and Rafe both followed him with their eyes. Waved forward by the king, almost as if expected, he approached and spoke his message into Henry's ear.

A cloud chased across the king's face. He waved the man away, but he shifted in his seat, unsettled. Thomasin drank her wine and watched the dancing begin. Cecilia was very graceful, her limbs lithe; Kytson kept up with her, and proved a proficient partner, but his performance lacked the colour she emanated. When it was finished, the couples bowed to each other and a second tune began.

"Shall we?" asked Rafe.

Thomasin followed him gladly. The men formed one line, the women another, mirroring each other. Standing facing Rafe, she felt a strange conflict in her body; a sense of self-consciousness and shyness, matched with the thrill of excitement and desire. But she was ready, ready to begin, her body surging with energy, waiting for permission. In time with the chords, she took two steps forward to meet him, trying to be light on her feet, and two steps back again. All the time, he held her with his dark eyes. But she was growing bolder and dared to meet his as they drew closer. Following the others, she turned away, walked in a circle, until they came face to face again. This was the moment when he was supposed to take her in his arms, hold her close, turn her around.

His arm was tight about her waist, warm and strong. He pulled her body to his. His face was only inches from hers, his mouth just above hers, but the intensity was too great. She gave him her cheek instead, her eyes seeking safety beyond his shoulder. So she was perfectly placed to see the figure appear in the doorway. Flaming red in gown, her long dark hair streaming down her back after she had discarded her hood.

The dance continued, but the dancers had noticed. The king had tensed in response. Queen Catherine was absorbed in her daughter.

Thomasin felt the moment that Rafe noticed the new arrival, as he turned her round in the dance, then came to a pause.

"Anne Boleyn?" she whispered.

"Now we shall have trouble. It was not needed today."

They continued to dance, choosing not to break the formation and disrupt the other dancers. Separating again, they joined the large circle of all participants, hand in hand, about the floor. Then there was a pause, and each dancer linked arms with the person beside them. Thomasin found an elderly bearded gentleman swinging her in an enthusiastic circle.

But between the dancers there was a flash of scarlet. Anne was walking in a straight line down the centre of the hall, heading for the king, so that the couples needed to move aside for her. There was whispering and stunned faces watched her path as the dance steps were forgotten, or altered. A little way away, closer to the king, Rafe had brought his partner, a matronly lady, to a halt, and was watching intently. It was just a matter of moments before Anne reached the dais where Henry sat as if impaled, his face dark and glowering, yet unable to tear his eyes from her.

It was at that moment that Catherine turned, and saw the approaching figure. Thomasin had never seen such dignity, as the queen lifted her chin and looked above Anne at the ceiling, with composure and strength. With the arm already laced about her daughter's shoulders, she pulled the girl closer, making a fortress of her body. And she waited.

Anne was almost close enough to speak, when the unexpected happened. Rafe broke out of the circle of dancers and stepped into her path, bowing low, so she was forced to stop. Thomasin stared, transfixed by the scene.

"Might we dance?" he asked in clear, firm tones, "my lady?"

Anne was interrupted. Knocked off course like a bird in the wind. The entire room waited to see what she would do. "I came to speak with the king. He is expecting me."

Her voice was low for a woman, and had the rich, nasal notes of one who had lived in France. There was something both refined and animal about it.

Rafe half turned, reluctant to concede, but Henry had already stepped down from the dais, and the crowd was parting to let him through. Mindful of the queen and her daughter, Thomasin wished he would send the new arrival away.

But instead, the king held out a hand to Anne. Sensing a victory, a sort of strength seemed to ripple through her lithe body, magnetic and compelling, outshining every other woman in the room. With a toss of her dark hair, she placed her hand in his. Rafe stood aside. The previous song was forgotten as the musicians struck up new notes. The circle melted away to allow the king and Anne to take the centre of the floor. Slowly, at first, with eyes locked, they began the sequence of steps.

"He is utterly obsessed with her." Cecilia had shaken off Kytson and appeared at her sister's side. "He cannot take his eyes off her."

Nor could Thomasin. They moved, back and forth, together and apart, tense with the strength of their feeling. It was an uncomfortable public display of passion, of intimacy.

Catherine stood frozen upon the dais, heavy with humiliation. Then, taking her daughter by the hand, she walked firmly and decisively down the steps towards the dancing couple. Those people she passed on the way, dancers and spectators, bowed and curtseyed, or moved aside. Head held high, the daughter of Isabella and Ferdinand maintained her straight path, directly towards the far doors, through the sphere of the dancers. Anne may have seen her first, and pretended otherwise, but Henry could not avoid her. By some chance, or by his clever control, he twirled his partner round to the side, out of the queen's way, so she and her daughter were able to continue, unimpeded, straight out of the hall and beyond. A number of ladies and gentlemen followed in her wake. Those remaining in the hall erupted into a wave of whispers but the couple on the floor danced on, as if nothing else mattered.

Thomasin breathed deeply. It had been a remarkable statement from Catherine; an amazing act of bravery and status. Judging by the crowd's reactions, the Boleyn faction did not have as much support as she had believed, and Catherine's victory had impressed many.

Cecilia turned away, finding their father, but Thomasin was compelled to watch the dance to the end, when Anne sunk in a breathless curtsey and Henry bowed low. Everyone else in the hall had been forgotten. Even Rafe had melted away.

"Such a vulgar display, such degeneracy," commented Richard, as he shepherded his party towards the door. "Time to leave."

But despite her sympathy for the queen, all Thomasin could think was how it must feel to be loved like that. Such raw intensity between man and woman. All through the carriage ride home, and back into the courtyard at Monk's Place; all the while they ate a quiet supper, while she played at dice with her father, and while she washed her face in a bowl of rose water and undressed for bed, she could only think of the passion in the king's eyes. Only with love like that, could a person be truly alive.

NINE

"You have tired yourself," said Dr Elyot, standing over the bed where Elizabeth lay, heaped under blankets. She had been bled, after her thin veins had eventually yielded up their harvest. "And, I suspect," he continued, "you are not following the recommended diet. Being of a phlegmatic humour, you should eat foods that are hot and dry: spices and red meat, mustard and cloves. Drink rich, dark wines and avoid watery foods, no soups or vegetables."

"I have very little appetite," she replied, speaking weakly from the lace pillows.

He waved away the dish of blood, dark and ominous, as the servant lifted it.

"Meat," he said, turning to Richard, "she must eat red meat, any game, and older beasts, not the fresh young ones whose meat is tender and wet. Old venison and beef are perfect."

"Meat," Richard echoed.

"I will make up a poultice for her breast and send it tomorrow, and you must ensure there is a constant fire burning and no draughts, at least until she is back on her feet again."

"But there is a wedding to organise," said the patient, feebly from the bed. "A dressmaker is coming this afternoon."

"Cecilia is more than able to take care of it," her husband reassured her, "and there are almost two weeks — plenty of time for you to rest in advance of the ceremony."

"And then you return to the country?" asked Dr Elyot.

"That is our intention."

Elyot nodded. "I will return in three days and see how you fare."

"I will show you out," offered Thomasin, hovering in the doorway.

They walked down the long staircase, with its three turns, made of polished oak. She thought of it as the dark, oppressive heart of the house, spiralling up, with its carvings of fruit and vines. On the final turn, a little square landing halfway between the first floor and the ground, Thomasin paused.

Elyot stopped too. He was a sombre-faced man in his forties, wearing a flat, dark cap.

"Is there anything else I can do to help Mother?"

He nodded. "Ensure she rests. No trouble or drama at home; I know what you girls can be like."

Thomasin frowned.

"Fear not," he added, "I am in jest. I am all admiration for the fair sex, so much so that I am compiling notes for a book in their praise."

"Really?"

"It will be called *A Defence of Good Women*, or *In Praise of Good Women*, or something like that. I doubt you need my advice about how to take care of your mother."

He continued down the stairs into the hallway. Thomasin followed, intrigued.

"Please, Sir, do tell me, in the eyes of a man of the court, what are the qualities that make a good woman?"

He smiled. "Ah, now that might take some time."

"In short, as much as you can. I would appreciate the advice. If a man at court was looking to take a wife, what qualities would he seek in her?"

"Ah, I see." Elyot pulled on his fur cloak. "You are, perhaps, considering marriage?"

"Well," she replied, deflecting the blow, "as you know, my sister is marrying and I am not so much younger than her."

"And you would like to choose your own husband?"

"Oh, I didn't mean... I just wondered..."

"Goodness," he smiled, "virtue, honesty, charm and wit make up a good woman. Chastity and cleanness, fruitfulness and a merry disposition."

Thomasin nodded at the uninspiring mix.

"But," he continued, "men are simple creatures and they look to like with their eyes. The more you can please a man's eye, the easier he is to please in other matters. You are young and charming; be virtuous, obedient to your parents and they will have no trouble finding you a husband."

But Thomasin was not satisfied. The doctor saw it in her face.

"What? You would have more?"

"I would not have just any husband, I would have one to my liking. My sister has to marry a man I think she does not like."

"Has she said as much?"

"No, she is too proud and obedient, but I know her. I want a husband to please my eye. Is that so wrong?"

"I do not think so. Next time you go to court, bestow your smiles wisely and your beauty should perform the task. Here." He reached into a pocket hanging inside his coat and pulled out a little cloth pouch. "This is a mix of spices and rose petals, with a drop of musk and civet, brought from merchants in the east. It is thought to contain special elements that create attraction. I was to give it to a widow in Cheapside, but I can make up another for her."

Thomasin received it delicately between her fingertips. "Thank you. This is not magic, is it?"

He laughed. "Not magic, no, no, unless medicine is magic. Wear it against your skin and the heat of your person will allow the scent to rise."

"But I have no coin."

"Never fear, it is a gift. Be modest in your demeanour, God-fearing and honest, and I am sure that all will be well for you."

"Thank you, doctor, thank you so much."

"And look to your mother; be quiet about the house while she sleeps, entertain her with gentle pastimes while she wakes and watch that she eats properly."

"I will do."

"I must away. My carriage awaits outside. Farewell."

Thomasin watched him climb inside. The coachman spurred the horses into life and they sped away, through the far gates out into the street. She caught a glimpse of people and horses outside, passing before the house fronts opposite. But instead of closing, the gates admitted another carriage, a shabbier, smaller one, painted in dark colours but hung with long pink and white ribbon. She waited in curiosity as it drew close, and the single grey mare came to a halt. A lady and gentleman climbed out, dressed with the affluence and cut of city money.

"My Lady? This is the residence of Sir Matthew Russell?"

"He is my uncle."

"We are the cloth merchant and dressmaker, Mr and Mrs Jankin, summoned to prepare for the wedding. Your wedding?"

"Oh no, it is my sister Cecilia's wedding. Please come inside."

Thomasin pulled gently on the thin green strand and held it to her nose. Its scent was complex, slightly lemony with earthy notes.

"Sometimes I find it difficult to tell rosemary from thyme," she explained to her father, and held up her fingertips for him to smell.

"Definitely thyme," he said. "If you are in any doubt, it will be thyme, because you will always know rosemary, it being so distinctive."

They had left Cecilia choosing from different swatches of fabric that had been unloaded from the merchants' carriage and ventured out to explore Matthew's long gardens at the back of Eastwell Hall. The sun was daring to peek out from behind autumnal clouds and the ground was dry underfoot. Following the recent fashion, the long paths had been railed and the small gardens enclosed with low walls. The herb garden lay close to the back of the house, but Thomasin's attention was already fixed upon a wooden roofed passage that led down to the water's edge. The sight of the Thames, a strip of grey-green at the far end of the lawn, intrigued her.

"Come," she summoned her father, "let's walk down."

He obeyed, as he did in most things, and they entered up a few steps onto the platform, which was walled on the boundary side and open to the garden on the other. The roof above them was trailed over by the climbing tendrils of that summer's roses and a young vine, with tiny leaves, feeling its way towards the light. At intervals on the way down, sat stone urns, statues and the occasional bench.

"I suppose this is to allow access to the river in all weathers," Thomasin suggested.

"In the old days we used it a lot," confirmed her father, "coming back late at night from court, at Greenwich or Westminster."

"What was it like then?" she asked, with a readiness to absorb the romance of it all.

"Brutal," replied her father. "But beautiful. I scarce know how to describe it."

"Brutal? How so? It's not a word I would have imagined you to use for it."

"Perhaps it was not the right word. Perhaps relentless is better. It required endurance."

"The endlessness of it?"

He sighed. "It felt endless. There was always something, day or night, that you had to give yourself to: dancing, feasting, council meetings, business, entertaining guests or ambassadors, riding, hunting, masques, schemes, and just waiting, and endless acts of service."

"It must have been exhausting."

"Yes, but I was a young man then. I had the stamina for it."

They were approaching the end of the walk and the salty tang of the Thames rose up from the silvered line ahead.

"Then what was it?"

"I think it was the absoluteness of it. It demanded that you give everything, not just your time, or your possessions, but everything of yourself, even your soul."

Thomasin turned to look at her father.

"I know that sounds dramatic, but it could take everything from a man and leave you crushed. It happened to my friend, Edmund, and I should have taken notice then, and left, but I stayed a year or two more, until I was in danger myself."

She stopped, the river forgotten. "What happened? Who was Edmund?"

Richard's eyes misted over, as if he were looking back into the past. "You recall me telling you that I came up to court as a young man in the last years of the old king's rule?"

"Henry VII? Yes."

"I joined the household of the prince, our present king, when he was fourteen or fifteen, and I a few years older. I was no one important, just a page. I played him at tennis, I cared

83

for his hounds, I waited upon him in the chamber, along with a dozen other young men, but I did not feel that I belonged there. I missed Eastwell and Suffolk too much. Edmund, Sir Edmund Dudley, became my friend, an unofficial mentor, as he was older and had experience of the court. It was Dudley and Sir Edward Guildford who helped me find my place."

"Sir Edward Guildford?"

"He is currently out in Calais."

"And Edmund Dudley, what happened to him?"

"Well," Richard sighed and crossed himself, a gesture his daughter did not see him perform often. "The old king died, and the new king, just a boy, decided to make an example of him. The old king's taxation had been very unpopular, and Edmund had helped enforce it, so he was executed, in the year of your birth, in fact."

"Executed? Like Buckingham? For displeasing the king?"

"It was so. And then the king went on to spend all the money raised by his father's taxes."

"Oh, Father."

Richard nodded. "I was horrified. I should have left court then, but it took me longer. I was inexperienced, and your mother had a position with the queen which she was loath to leave. And she was in good favour. But three years later I saw it again, when he wanted to invade France. Good men, wise men, advised him against it, but he would not listen." He stopped and looked around carefully. "What I say is criticism of the king. It amounts to treason; you must not repeat it anywhere, to anyone. If I were to be overhead, it would be a disaster, you understand?"

Thomasin shivered. "Of course. I would never speak of it."

"But be warned. This king gets what he wants."

Richard offered her his arm and they walked the final distance together, to the edge of a wooden platform that overhung the river and the stone steps that descended into the rapids. There was an incredible power and energy about the body of water, surging closer to them and then falling back, sloshing and crashing, with the power to break and kill. Alongside, the boat house contained Matthew's barge, which was rising and falling, and bumping against its moorings due to the high tide. Some craft had ventured out; mostly little vessels, but the odd barge or two, heading up stream. The distant bank seemed green, dotted with trees, although Thomasin saw the roofs and towers of a few grand houses.

"On a clear day you can see the duke of Suffolk's house in Southwark from here," Richard explained, looking away to the left, in the direction of the bridge, "but not today, I think."

"And what of the current situation?" Thomasin asked. "The king will get his way again?"

Richard raised his eyebrows, although he was used to his daughter's questioning ways. "He hopes. Although this time he has set his sights upon something far more difficult, outside his own rules. Divorce is one thing, as is annulment, but divorce from the aunt of the Emperor is another entirely. Not even the Pope will support him and he is furious. So the question is not whether Henry will get what he wants, as I have no doubts about that, but how he will achieve it."

"Is such a thing easily achieved?"

"What makes it worse is that the Pope granted his sister, Margaret, the former queen of France, a divorce only this spring. But her husband was not as important and did not have the connections of the queen."

"And that man Cromwell, who came here the other day?"

"Wants to enlist me to the service of his master, Thomas Wolsey, Cardinal Wolsey. We have been invited to a dinner tonight at York Place, where I am sure he will make me an offer of a post at court."

"And you will refuse?"

"I will hear what I am refusing, before I refuse it. But in the meantime we will enjoy the cardinal's hospitality."

They walked back to the house slowly, Thomasin's head swimming with all the information her father had revealed. When they reached the end of the wooden platform and stepped down into the herb garden, Cecilia appeared, her gown unlaced and her hair streaming, in quite an unusual state of undress. Thomasin's first thought was of fear for their mother but as she came closer, it was clear that Cecilia was smiling.

"Look," she stated, offering up her hands. Inside them lay a rich blue jewel, pale like the sky, cut and faceted into a rectangle, and set in silver with small pearls.

Richard stared down at it, impressed by its size and obvious value.

"A gift from my betrothed," Cecilia explained proudly. "A servant just brought it from Henry. Look at the size of it. He writes that it matches my eyes."

"It's a goodly sapphire," her father confirmed, "and the exact shade of your eyes. He has obviously had a good look into them."

A small frown chased across her brow. "He has not yet, actually, but if he continues to give me such gifts, I shall certainly feel more disposed to allow him to do so."

"You should wear it tonight," said Thomasin, "when we attend the cardinal at York Place."

"I had already planned to," Cecilia snapped, unwilling to allow her sister ownership of the idea. "Now I just need to pick out the right dress to wear it with." She turned and hurried back up the path, holding the jewel out before her, as if her hands were cupping holy water.

"I am glad," said Richard. "If I am honest, I had experienced a few doubts about Kytson's ability to please our Cecilia, but now that he has discovered the effect of jewellery upon her, I believe they will live very happily together."

TEN

Thomasin pulled her furs tighter about her shoulders. It was not really a cold evening, but chill vapours rose from the river, and it was comforting to be wrapped up warmly. It also allowed her to feel the little cloth bag of petals and musk, which Dr Elyot had given her, tucked inside her bodice.

The journey from Monk's Place was short, especially with the tide in their favour, but Thomasin was unaccustomed to the rocking motion. It was a shame that her stomach was twisting and churning in knots, because there was such a huge, beautiful yellow moon hanging overhead and a sky full of bright stars, which she would usually have enjoyed. Richard and Matthew had amused themselves the entire way by pointing out the different constellations, but she could not partake of their talk. It was with relief that she realised their journey would soon be ending.

Torches burned on the steps at York Place. Their long yellow tails made blurred reflections in the river, dancing and leaping as the barge drew nearer. The building loomed large across a wide expanse of river, dark on both sides where it was surrounded by gardens. Thomasin looked with interest at the house-front, red-brick and half-timbered, overhanging the water's edge, with the roofs of other buildings rising up behind. There was maybe a hall, and beside it, a chapel. Hidden lights and shady walls and corners promised a vast complex, full of places to discover.

The boat bumped up against the quay, where the waves lapped constantly, with a sucking and swishing sound. Servants were lined up to help, holding the vessel fast and offering their arms and hands in support as Thomasin shakily stepped to shore, followed by Cecilia.

"I am so thankful to be off the water," Thomasin admitted. "It was a most peculiar sensation, I liked it not."

No witty retort was forthcoming from Cecilia and, looking at her pale face, Thomasin realised her sister had also suffered from the motion of the boat.

"Yes, I am sure it will soon pass," Cecilia confirmed. "I am feeling better already with my feet on dry land."

They were conducted in through a hallway, so bright that it made them blink after the darkness outside. Thomasin could make out pillars of marble, and alabaster carvings, painted walls and Italian-style statues. Underfoot, the floor was laid with tiles in terracotta, black and white, in diamond patterns.

"This was all part of the improvements made by the cardinal," their guide was explaining. "After he acquired York Place, he spent over a thousand pounds expanding and modernising the property, employing the master mason of Westminster Abbey, to reflect the classical style."

The young man showing them around took off his cap to reveal scruffy brown hair. He smoothed it down at once with a hand.

"And here, on this side, we have the Council Chamber, but on that side, look, you must see the gilt chamber."

He pushed open a door to reveal a room where two or three tables were set with gilt plates, jugs and other items, and a wide cupboard on the wall held pieces made of gold, gleaming bright.

"I have been in the cardinal's employ for five years," said the young man, "as a gentleman usher, and this room never fails to impress guests." He moved in closer, to speak more confidentially. "Henry Percy was a page here too, back when it happened."

Thomasin looked at him, then at her father, whose confusion reflected her own.

"Henry Percy?" asked Richard. "Is he one of the Northumberland Percies?"

"The very one that Anne Boleyn wanted to wed, before the king had sight of her. Did you not know?"

"We are just up from Suffolk," Richard explained. "Such gossip does not reach us there."

"Well, I am happy to oblige." The young man gave a short bow. "There was a secret engagement, entered into by the couple without the consent or knowledge of their families. Anne was already intended for the Butler family, and Percy had been matched with a daughter of the Earl of Shrewsbury. It was quite a scandal. Anne was banished from court and Percy was forced to wed against his inclination. It was my master who insisted upon the match."

"Is that so?" asked Richard with sudden interest at the last piece of information. "Wolsey prevented Anne and Percy from marrying?"

"Anne was nothing then, and Percy had his obligations, and was living under my master's roof. But she has never forgotten. Nor forgiven. She hates him with a passion. Which is why you will see none of her friends here tonight. Whoever loves Anne gives a wide berth to Wolsey."

And it immediately occurred to Thomasin that, if their guide spoke true, there was no chance of seeing Rafe that evening.

"Thank you," replied Richard, "you have been most illuminating."

"Here is the hall. If there is anything else you wish to know, about people, in particular —" he gave a wink — "then ask for

George Cavendish, at York Place. I have many tales to divert the ladies with."

Stepping aside, he waved them forward, then disappeared about his duties.

"Strange young man," commented Richard. "I would not keep such a tongue-flapper in my household."

"I expect he knows everything about everyone," agreed Thomasin, fascinated by the possibility of further conversation.

"Exactly!"

"How different things might be," Thomasin mused, "if Anne's match with Percy had been allowed."

"And," her father added confidentially, "there is nothing quite so determined as a woman who has her desires in love thwarted by those meaning well. Your mother's family were against our match at first; they did not go so far as to forbid us to marry, but they tried to dissuade your mother from joining the Marwood family. We were not as grand as the Russells back then."

Thomasin was agog. "I had no idea. What happened?"

"I got a position at court, and your mother insisted. She could usually convince her father to let her have her way in most things."

"And you married, of course."

"Eventually."

The hall was, perhaps, half full. Thomasin's first impression was of it shining like a shrine, with gold and silver cloths hung the full length of the walls and the dozens of wax branches mounted upon brackets. Servants in the cardinal's livery brought plates of wafers and gilded marzipan and poured glasses of wine.

"What is this?" Cecilia asked, staring down at a silver plate with biscuits topped by a strange, sticky confection.

"Preserved syrup of green ginger, my Lady," replied the server.

"Green ginger?"

"From the West Indies, my Lady."

Cecilia tried a piece, chewed and winced. Thomasin took it from her and bit into the strange, crystalline substance, part liquid, part lumps. Her taste buds recoiled at the textures and flavour.

"An exotic treat, but not for us," laughed Richard, refusing a piece.

"My dear Marwood, we are honoured that you were able to attend."

They turned to see Thomas Cromwell, the thick-faced man who had called before at Monk's Place. The mood became immediately more sombre, in spite of his warm greeting.

"Cromwell," replied Richard, briefly.

The other smiled as if he noticed no slight. "And you have brought your lovely daughters."

"Indeed. Cecilia and Thomasin. Unfortunately, my wife's doctor has urged her to rest."

"Please convey to her my good wishes. I trust your time back in London has been fruitful so far?"

"So far, but there is still much to do."

Cromwell raised his eyebrows as if in hope.

"In planning a wedding," Richard insisted, "there is so much to do in planning a wedding."

Cromwell made a small, formal smile. "Of course. If there is any way the cardinal may be of service, please do not hesitate to speak to me."

Something in his reply made Thomasin uneasy.

"Thank you," replied her father, "but I think we have everything we need."

It was at that point that Cardinal Wolsey entered the hall. A tall, wide man, with a stern, square chin and short, clipped, grey hair, he paused to survey the room. The crowd bowed before him, but he waved them at once to rise. There was something very controlled, very measured in his manner, not in a sinister way, but in the sense that he considered every step before he placed it.

"Please, my friends, be seated, for the masque is about to begin."

There was a strange drawl to his voice; that of a man who had lived long in London, travelled overseas, but never quite shook out the country burr.

Thomasin had expected him to be dressed in robes, either red or white or black, or whatever colour the ecclesiastical season dictated. She was surprised to see him apparelled almost as a king, in an ermine coat, a silver and tawny doublet and white hose, hung about with gold chains and jewels.

"He is not what I expected," she whispered to her father, but broke off short as Wolsey approached them.

"Now," he said, with long vowels that Thomasin seemed to recognise. "This is a face I have not seen in many years. I was glad to hear you had accepted my invitation tonight, gladder still that you are back at court after all this time, although your departure still baffles me. I escaped Suffolk as soon as I could, yet you bury yourself away there. Come, kiss me."

Richard embraced Wolsey as he requested, tolerating the man placing his lips to his cheek in a kind of blessing.

"I hear you have been thriving since my absence, as this place confirms."

"A few pieces I have collected. It makes a difference. The property belongs to the Church, of course."

"And these are my daughters," Richard explained for the second time. "Cecilia, my eldest, and Thomasin."

"Charming, charming," Wolsey nodded. "Come, take your seats. The masque is about to begin, but we shall speak more anon."

They did as he bid, finding places upon the trestles at the side, allowing for the front half of the hall to be cleared.

Thomasin hadn't noticed the minstrel's gallery. It lay above the entrance, behind them as they had come in, but the sweet notes of the lute drew her attention now. She noted the ornate wooden carving, of fruits and flowers, coats of arms and devices she did not recognise. In the centre, though, was the carved form of a cardinal's cap, recognisable by its broad brim and laces, symbolic of the property's owner.

As the lute played, and instruments joined them, the gold wall hangings opposite parted and, through a secret door, the masquers appeared. Twelve in total, six gentlemen and six ladies, they came forward in curious moves, waving their arms, with strange steps that took them round in circles. Their visors were made of gold and their clothing was black and yellow, with gold and scarlet laces and capes, and golden bonnets that looked exotic, perhaps from the east. Each lady had a jewel set upon their forehead and it seemed to be the task of the men to woo them and win it.

Through the main doors, with a great rumbling of wheels, came a large carriage pulled by servants. As it drew closer, coming to a stop in the corner, Thomasin saw it was the representation of a mountain, covered over with green cloth, and painted roses and bushes, their leaves and fruits made of silk and jewels. The masked women formed a group and, in rhythm with the lute, made a show of trying the climb the mountain, stopping to gather flowers and fruits along the way. Coming close behind in pursuit, the men inched up behind them, using fine words and promises, to draw them to them. Thomasin sat and watched this game of love in fascination; this representation of courtship that touched her closely and represented her secret desires. Love, and images of love, were everywhere in court circles, with the tall lady at the front taking her beau by the hand, and the gentlewoman seated on the mountain, whose lover offered her a rose.

And Thomasin thought of Rafe. That night in the gardens, he seemed to have been playing out a love scene, not wholly dissimilar to this. He had snatched an unknown young woman out of danger and presented her with a pink rose. To what end? To what purpose did the lovers pursue the women up the mountain?

As she sat watching them, an uncomfortable question occurred to her, leading to more questions, so that she felt foolish. Rafe barely knew her. Were his attentions sincere, or just part of the game of courtly love that the young courtiers played? Had she been naïve to take him seriously, to let him affect her feelings? Should she have remained calm, aloof, like these masked women? She watched them turn away, rejecting advances that only became more ardent. Was cold disdain the way to win a man? She realised how little she knew of ways of the heart, and how quickly and warmly she had responded, without thinking of the consequences. Must she play the game, and conceal her true feelings?

The masked women on the mountain had gathered together at the top, where a sort of platform, entwined with roses, had been erected for them. Creeping their way up the sides, the men prepared for the final onslaught, while the music's pace picked up and the women pelted them with fruit and rose petals.

"Oh, this is silly," muttered Cecilia at her side.

Thomasin checked herself. It was always sobering to see how differently her sister viewed things. Yes, in some ways it was silly, but it was also a symbol, a pattern of the endless dance between men and women. There was much to be learned from silly things, if only one chose to look carefully.

The victorious men, having each claimed their sweetheart, led them down the mountain to bow or curtsey before the guests. At the front, one of the tallest gentlemen pulled off his gold visor to reveal a familiar face.

"The duke of Suffolk," Richard whispered to his daughters.

At his side, as they might have anticipated, the lady's mask revealed the face of the king's sister Mary, Suffolk's duchess these past twelve years, after her brief tenure as Queen of France. Thomasin looked at her with interest, knowing her to be reputed as one of the most beautiful women at court. There was no doubt that she was a Tudor, and somewhat like her brother in her red-gold colouring and strong features, but they were moulded with such nobility and grace in Mary that she was quite captivating.

As the other masks came off, the servants wheeled out the mountain and gathered the scattered petals.

Cavendish appeared again, to conduct the guests through to a smaller chamber where the banquet had been laid out. Here, in silver, gilt and glass, were crystallised fruits, syllabubs, gingerbreads and tartlets, rich dishes of strawberries despite the season and thick clotted cream. Thomasin picked up a strange biscuit, made with candied peel and almonds.

"Florentines," whispered Cavendish at her side, "from Italy. They are quite delicious."

One bite into their firm stickiness was enough to convince Thomasin. She revelled in the syrupy mix of fruits and nuts.

"And that is orange peel. Have you tasted oranges before?"

"Why no, I have not. I suppose they are foreign?"

"The queen brought them from Spain," he said knowingly, as she navigated the citrus morsel around her tongue.

"My Lord," spoke Wolsey, appearing through the crowd. "Here is someone I think you would like to meet."

Richard turned around in expectation, to see a young man in his mid-twenties, with an earnest face, medium height, and dark hair, dressed as one of the masquers. At his side was a woman of similar years in a grey gown, open-laced to accommodate the child she was carrying. For a moment, he was baffled, unable to place them.

"I will leave you to it," said Wolsey discreetly, dissolving again into the evening.

"My Lord Marwood, I am humbled to meet you," the young man began. "The cardinal leads me to believe you were a friend of my father. My name is John Dudley, and this is my wife Jane, who was Jane Guildford."

At once Thomasin recalled the names her father had spoken of in the garden at Monk's Place.

"John Dudley?" Richard replied, with some warmth. "Son of Edmund?"

The young man nodded. "Although Father's name is rarely mentioned these days."

"God be praised, I remember you as a boy at court. Your father was such a good friend to me. And Jane, daughter of Edward Guildford? Come, come, let us find an alcove where we can speak uninterrupted. It is such a great pleasure to see the children of my old friends, and married too!"

Thomasin and Cecilia were left at the banquet table. Having filled their plates with sweet treats, they returned to the hall and ate quietly, seated on one of the benches.

"Look, there is Uncle," noticed Cecilia eventually, nodding over at a group in the corner. Thomasin followed her direction and saw Matthew, deep in conversation with Thomas Cromwell and another man she did not know, an older man with a close-shaven face and intense eyes. The matter looked serious, and not entirely amicable. Following a few more exchanges, Matthew made a curt bow and strode away. He spotted the girls sitting alone and joined them.

"You are enjoying the evening?"

"It has proved most enlightening so far," said Cecilia haughtily, before returning to her syllabub.

"You have had a pleasant evening yourself?" asked Thomasin, reluctant to ask him directly about the conversation.

"Yes, mostly. Well, until Cromwell appeared again. I was conversing with an old friend, Sir Thomas More, until then. You know More educates his daughters? Teaches them Latin and Greek, theology and medicine, would you believe? How would you like that, you two?"

Cecilia rolled her eyes at the imposition, but Thomasin thought of her own lessons at Eastwell Hall, with the old tutor Harefield making her recite passages from the Bible.

"It sounds fascinating. Theology?"

"The study of religious doctrines and the nature of the divine."

"Really? To study and explore that, instead of just reading and accepting it?"

"Yes, indeed."

"Ordinary men and women discussing the word of God? Instead of a priest? But what if … what if that might lead us to, I don't know, to question it?"

Her uncle laughed. "Thomasin, you are as bright as a button. That is exactly what the reformists would have you do."

"The new learning?"

He nodded. "You see why it is causing so much debate? More tells me of reformist books entering the country that are being burned as heresies. It is becoming a world where the king holds up a mirror to his subjects' souls."

And the thought of that chilled Thomasin, the fear that her inner thoughts, half-resolved and emergent, might be drawn out of her and subject to scrutiny.

"Don't be so serious," chided Cecilia, holding up a silver dish full of white froth. "It's hardly something you need to worry about. Have some syllabub."

Thomasin was relieved when her uncle announced his intention to return by carriage, instead of barge. The hour was past midnight as they stepped out into the courtyard of York Place, and the stars were still bright as earlier, the night much colder. As they waited for the horses to come round from the stable, she shivered and watched her breath form clouds before her face.

"Please, come again, partake of my hospitality and kindly remember me in your prayers," said Wolsey on the steps behind them. "Since I returned from France, I find I have fewer friends than I thought. The Boleyn faction has quite taken hold at court."

"Hopefully he will tire of her soon," Matthew tried to reassure the older man, "just as he did her sister."

"Perhaps, but he has another purpose now, as the queen will never give him a son. You know, he insists that she sit with him, during my private interviews with him? That is change, mark me, a sign of real change. He has given her power, unprecedented power."

The carriage rolled around and drew to a halt.

"God speed," added Wolsey. "We shall meet again at court, sometime soon."

"Farewell, and thank you," echoed Matthew and Richard together, ushering the girls into the carriage first.

It was a wide, luxurious space, bearing the cardinal's arms, lined with crimson velvet and padded with cushions.

Cecilia snuggled down into the corner. "I could fall asleep here."

"Well, do not," instructed her uncle, "or else you will end up back in the cardinal's stables!"

There was a crunch of gravel as the horses pulled them away, down the long drive that led to the main road back into the city.

"He's a strange fellow," mused Richard. "I cannot make him out, where his heart truly lies, whether his friendship is genuine, or if it is all in service to some intention. I know not what."

"He certainly showed us signs of favour," replied Matthew, "and with a figure as high up as that, ours is not the cause to question why. We accept whatever he offers, with gratitude, for he can open doors."

"True enough. Only I am no longer sure it is his doors that lead back to the king."

"The Boleyn girl?"

"Yes. It feels as if the stage is being set for an ugly struggle. We do not want to find ourselves in the cross-fire."

"Well, you will be safe back in Suffolk by the end of the month, so no need to trouble yourself. Not unless you intend to accept Cromwell's offer?"

"No," said Richard, turning his face to the dark window. "I do not."

Monk's Place was flooded by torchlight as the cardinal's carriage rolled in through the gates. They climbed out wearily, ready for their beds, and the release of sleep.

Thomasin came last, turning back to retrieve a lace she had almost lost from her dress. She was about to head inside when there came a rustling noise, and movement from the darkest part of the shadows. Her heart leapt into her mouth. The others were already within, having their cloaks stripped off their shoulders by servants.

"Thomasin!"

The sound of her own name made her jump. One instinct told her to flee through the safety of the open door, but another had her intrigued at the direct appeal.

He stepped out of the darkness behind statues. Rafe Danvers, dark as the night, and tempting as the banquet.

"What are you doing?" she hissed, terrified and delighted.

"I had to see you." He threw up an anxious glance at the house.

"You can't come in, not at this hour. I must go in."

"I have been waiting."

"But why?"

"I heard you were leaving. I wanted to see you."

"We are leaving, but not until after Cecilia's wedding next week."

"Can't you let me in? In secret?" His dark eyes gleamed insistently.

"This is madness!"

"I would hide in your chamber, steal out before the light."

Her body flushed hot with the realisation of what he was suggesting. And how desperately she wanted to accept.

"Go home, this is too much. You know it is folly."

"Thomasin?" Richard called from within.

"My father! Now go, go!"

"You don't want…"

"I do." She let the admission burst from her. "But we can't. Please go."

She hurried over the threshold into the bright hallway, without waiting to see Rafe fade away into the shadows. As the servants removed her cloak, her heart was pounding so loudly in her chest she was certain it must be heard.

Her bedroom overlooked the gardens at the back, but halfway up the staircase, she paused to peer out of the diamond pane window, across the front courtyard. It was dark and silent. The moon hung huge above. The statues at the side were motionless. Rafe had disappeared into the night, as suddenly as he had appeared.

She lay in bed, sleepless, restless, but her mind was racing. Even after the whole house was still, and all the candles snuffed, sleep would not come. Once or twice, as she drifted, she imagined Rafe beside her, his hand upon her arm, as he leaned over to kiss her lips, and then she was wide awake again. And questions came to plague her, all through the small hours. Had he really expected to be admitted to her uncle's house at that hour? What were his intentions? And, most of all, what might have happened, if she had agreed?

And she thought of the words of William Hatton, on the night he had come to dinner, that the new thinking encouraged people to act as individuals, to shape their lives and take their destiny into their own hands.

It felt like she had only just drifted off to sleep when the sound of church bells woke her.

ELEVEN

Elizabeth whirled round to face her daughters in the alcove outside the queen's chapel. Having risen after four days of rest, and a diet of wine and meat, she had regained a little of her strength and adamantly refused to miss such an important occasion as Cecilia's formal betrothal dinner.

"Let me have a final look at you."

Cecilia stopped and posed at once, lifting her chin for inspection, knowing her beauty could bear scrutiny. She wore on her breast the stunning pale sapphire sent to her by Sir Henry Kytson, which gleamed like rainwater in the daylight.

Elizabeth looked closely at Cecilia's face for smudges; her deft fingertips pinched her cheeks to make them rosy, poked in her hair, brushed a strand from her shoulder. Thomasin ducked out of the way as her they came towards her next.

"Thomasin!"

"I am well, I need no attention. It's not me getting married, anyway." She had already spent the morning being laced into a new gown of green velvet and cream silk, delivered by a London dressmaker at the crack of dawn. It fit her snug and tight about the body, pinching her waist before flaring out in huge, voluminous skirts that required lengths of green willow wand inside, wrought into hoops. "I feel like I am walking inside an eel trap!" she added, as her mother tried to eye potential places of imperfection.

"It is the Spanish farthingale; you do the queen honour by wearing the fashions of her homeland. We can never repay her great kindness in hosting this betrothal dinner, but you can at least look as if you are enjoying it."

Thomasin hoisted up her sleeves. They were tight at the elbow, but the ends were wide and heavy with fur. "I don't know how I am supposed to eat in these."

"It is the latest style," said Cecilia condescendingly, pleased with the many folds and pleats of her new silver gown. "Try and become it."

For all her complaints, Thomasin did feel that the gown became her. Her long hair, thick and chestnut brown, hung down below her plain bonnet and she wore a simple string of pearls about her neck. Stopping by her chamber before they left, her father had nodded in praise, "Aye, you do look bonny in it."

And she had not forgotten to slip Dr Elyot's little perfume bag in her bodice, perhaps out of some new superstition or just plain vanity.

"Are we all set?" asked Richard, approaching with Matthew and John Dudley. "The guests are arriving and the queen is asking for you."

"Is she?" Elizabeth patted the new Venetian gold trim on her bonnet. "Then let us go at once."

Taking Cecilia by the arm, she sailed back along the passage to the queen's rooms and through the open doors. Thomasin followed, amused at the sight of the pair of them, trailing their silks and laces.

Queen Catherine's large waiting chamber had been set for a feast, with a great table down the centre of the hall, fire blazing in the grate and red streamers strung from the rafters. A group of boys, dressed for the choir of the chapel, were singing sweet and high, a lament about love and loss. A number of people had already gathered, adorned in furs and jewels, listening to the singers, talking and partaking of wine and spices.

Catherine came gliding out of her private entrance at the far end, a most regal sight in black and tawny, set with diamonds. Lady Willoughby stood at her side, her black gown relieved by a white collar and cuffs and her little daughter, the queen's namesake, was dressed in blue and a cap with yellow ribbons. Thomasin noticed the absence of Princess Mary, who was on her way to the bleak Welsh marches and Ludlow Castle.

Behind the queen came Sir Henry Kytson, in a disappointing grey doublet, quite without adornment, an older lady in brown and gold, her bodice strung across with chains and her white headdress set with gold beads and a long lace train. Her lower sleeves were made of brown silk, folded and refolded, slashed to reveal the white linen which erupted in a froth at her wrists. A third lady was behind them, young and pale, dressed in dark red.

Elizabeth bowed low, easing herself down slowly. Her party followed suit.

"Lady Marwood." Catherine came forward in greeting, asking them all to rise. "And your daughters, and this must be Sir Richard, whom I have not seen in these many years."

"My Queen." Richard kissed the hand she extended. "We are so grateful to be received by your grace."

"And Sir Matthew Russell, whom I know, and John Dudley, you are both welcome. Dudley, how fares your wife?"

"She is making preparations for her confinement, My Lady. Her hour approaches."

"I will send her some remedies I used during my travails, and some books to help pass the time."

"You are very generous, thank you, My Lady."

Catherine turned to the group beside her, with the chain-decked lady in the centre. "Here we have both bride and groom, Sir Henry and the lovely Cecilia, soon to be wed. And this is Lady Honoria Kytson and her daughter Lucy."

The Kytson women bowed low, eyeing the Marwoods with interest.

"It is such an honour to finally meet you," said the matriarch, whose white hair and brows gave her a distinguished look. "Henry has spoken often of your daughter's fine qualities, and through all our negotiations, it has always been my wish to unite our children, to the advantage and happiness of both families."

"The honour is ours," replied Elizabeth. "We have been anticipating this day with the greatest of pleasure. And we are so glad that your estates lie on the Essex border, so we shall not be too far apart, given the happy events that will surely follow."

"You are all welcome at Eastwell at any time," chimed in Richard. "We are quite at your disposal."

"I wish to thank you also," added Honoria, "for the fine brace of pheasants you sent us. They were much enjoyed."

"As were the plums and apples from your orchard," smiled Elizabeth, "which made for many fine tarts and pies. Such sweet tasting apples, we enjoyed them heartily."

"Come," said the queen, "let us continue these pleasantries at table."

With Cecilia and Henry seated together, her mother and Honoria deep in conversation, and her father and uncle speaking with John Dudley, Thomasin found herself placed at the end of the table. On one side, she had Lucy Kytson, whom she guessed to be in her mid-twenties and somewhat reserved, and on the other, a young man with mid-brown hair and a merry face. White linen had been draped across their places, where a folded diamond-patterned napkin sat beside a silver plate and goblet.

A small army of servants in red and gold brought up the dishes from the queen's private kitchens below her apartments. Thomasin watched eagerly as they placed each plate around her: a leg of pork in mustard, larks in thyme, beef chewets, orange and lemon tarts, saffron sauce.

"Shall we share?" asked the young man on her right, who had already dug in with a large spoon and was breaking the leg of pork apart. "You'd better let me serve you first or else I might gobble it all up, it being my favourite dish."

Thomasin smiled at his frankness. "Please do act to avoid such a disaster."

He spooned a generous portion onto her plate. "You like mustard? It's not too hot, lots of honey in it."

"I do."

"There we go then. Which dish is your favourite?"

Thomasin looked around the table. The beef pieces floating in a rich gravy drew her with their salty, savoury smell. She pointed, hoping that he might pass the dish along to her.

"Right, the beef," he nodded. "Now you must serve me first."

Thomasin laughed. "I must? Where is it written?"

He pretended to look surprised. "It is the way of good manners, from the modern European courts. I surrender my favourite to you, so you do the same for me."

Thomasin looked at her plate. It was true, he had been most generous with the pork, which was steaming on her plate, savoury and inviting. But then a thought struck her, and she laughed.

"What is it?"

"This could all be a cunning trick on your part. What if, in fact, you don't like pork at all but your favourite is the beef?"

He took up a second spoon at once, dug it deep into the beef and, before she could stop him, heaped almost all of it upon her plate.

She gasped and held up her hands in a vague attempt to stop him, but he had made his point.

"And now I," he laughed, "for the sake of my good manners, must content myself with gnawing upon bones and wet vegetables. I shall dwindle away to nothing and become of a melancholy disposition, while you, plump and pink with so much meat, will visit me on my sick bed and say prayers for me."

Thomasin laughed, amused by him, but unused to his brand of wit. How far, exactly, was he going to take this joke? She knew she was able to outsmart him, too.

"Well, then," she added, reflectively, loading up her spoon, "since I have all the food, I shall be the one to feed you." She held it up towards his mouth. "Come now, open up, like a babe, so I shall not have your dwindling upon my conscience."

The merry young man looked at her in appraisal. "A right witty retort. But I do not think I should allow you to spoon-feed me yet, as we have not been introduced."

"You are right. As I am neither your nursemaid nor your wife, I do think your modern European manners might be outraged at the thought of me putting a spoon into your mouth."

He laughed again, revealing a small, neat line of teeth. "I feel I have met my match today. Allow me to backtrack, to before the pork and beef so rudely interrupted us. I am Sir Giles Waterson."

"Oh!" Thomasin almost dropped her spoon.

"My name gives you some offence? I can change it if you like. After today you should call me Sir Mustard Pork."

She could not help smiling. "No, no offence. It's not that. I believe my mother wants me to marry you."

"Indeed?" He raised his eyebrows. "Then she must have heard about my sharp wit, my expertise on modern manners and my excellent serving skills."

"No," urged Thomasin, "she really does intend to make a match between us. This is my sister's betrothal party. I am Thomasin Marwood; I think we are distantly related."

"Oh, yes, I believe so," he said, his manner changing in recognition. "I think my late father and your mother were cousins. So, how on earth are we going to manage our wedding feast?"

"Well, I fully intend to eat mine," concluded Thomasin, new ideas racing through her mind. "I hope you will share my plate."

"I suppose it is best to start as your mother intends us to go on," he shrugged, and dug his spoon into the mustard.

They ate contentedly, clearing the plates, until the end of the first course. Servants removed the dishes and the musicians played again. A huge subtlety, in the shape of Cupid, carved from sugar and marchpane, covered in gold leaf was brought out as a centrepiece, to much admiration.

"You are pleased by this match?"

Lucy Kytson had spoken softly beside her, from the depths of her reservations and grey coloured silks.

"If my sister is pleased, then I am too, very much. Your brother seems a goodly gentleman."

"He is," Lucy agreed, "he is a very good man. He has always looked after us well."

"I am sure he will continue to do so."

The corners of Lucy's mouth twitched but did not form a smile. "I think we will be quite bereft."

"Your mother is a widow?"

"These past ten years. And I have been so for two summers."

"Oh, I had no idea, please accept my condolences."

Lucy nodded and sniffed, as if acknowledging her dues. "It was the sweat, you know. He was in London and we were in Essex. He was dead before we even knew he was ill."

"I am so very sorry."

"Thank you."

Thomasin wanted to say something reassuring about the new marriage, but could not think of anything suitable, so she erred on the side of optimism. "You will gain a sister in this new match. I am sure Cecilia will be most kind towards you all."

"We hope they will stay often with us in Essex, when they are not at court, but Henry hopes he has a chance to be appointed as an usher to the king, so they might be resident here a lot, more than Mother would like."

Thomasin looked down the table to where Lady Honoria was listening politely to the queen.

"I am sure they will make the effort to see you as much as they can, or you can always visit them in London."

"He seems very fond of her," sighed Lucy, watching her brother. "I think he is almost in love already."

"Surely that is a good thing and will help their marriage thrive."

Lucy sighed again as if the thought was too much for her. Thomasin noticed she had little on her plate, just some bread and a lark, half picked at.

"Might I pass you something?"

"No, thank you, I have a complaint. Well, I have many complaints, but I should not eat rich foods. Mother will chide me."

"Your mother can't see what you eat from over there. I am sure the queen's hospitality would be an exception to her rules."

"Well, I don't know, I am quite a martyr to my complaints..."

"How about some tart?"

"So long as it is not cheese or quince, or else I shall be up all night."

"I think this one is simply curds. Have a little."

"Just to be polite."

Thomasin cut a slice and slipped it down onto Lucy's plate, turning away so as not to be watching her eat. On her other side, Sir Giles was recounting a most humorous hunting story about a time when he became lost in the forest, making John Dudley laugh out loud. And Thomasin could not help thinking what a contrast there was between her two dining companions.

After the feast, the trestles were swiftly cleared away, leaving space for dancing. The minstrels played heavy, formal music that seemed to belong to the past, and spoke to Thomasin of the queen's former glory. She did not recognise any of the steps either, tripping over her father's feet when he asked her to accompany him.

"It's an old Spanish dance," he whispered, as they passed each other by. "I remember the queen dancing it as a young woman."

Thomasin looked over to the chair of state, which Catherine now occupied, with her ladies about her.

"She doesn't dance now," added Richard, as he took his daughter by the waist and turned her around. "John Dudley says she practically lives in these rooms and barely leaves, except when she is commanded. She takes comfort in her faith and her daughter."

"And now her daughter is sent away."

Thomasin tried to imagine the scene, of a younger queen, in happier days, being visited in these apartments by the king, laughing and dancing together, before retiring into her inner chamber. The court must have felt very different then.

She danced with her uncle, with John Dudley and the merry Sir Giles, laughing their way through all the steps. Giles, was a neat, deft mover, she could not deny that. Not too tall and not too short, he was about her own height, powerfully built but on a smaller scale, and well put together. His rust-coloured doublet became him and fitted snugly. There was a grace of movement about him that seemed to place him at perfect ease in the world, and such a light in his blue-green eyes. His nose was short, but not too short, well-modelled and slightly turned up at the end, his lips full and sensuous, his chin firm and jaw square.

When the music changed, and another song began, he did not let go of her hand, and so she danced with him a second time, quite gladly.

"I think we have made up for that silliness with the food," he said as they walked together, arm in arm, in the group of couples.

Thomasin smiled.

"I think," he continued, "perhaps we should decide what we are going to do about our families' outrageous plan?"

"Outrageous plan?"

"To marry us off. We should go hunting or riding or something, to keep them happy."

Thomasin laughed. "Sadly, I am not at court for long."

"Then we should make it soon."

As the dance drew to a close, the doors at the far end opened to admit a figure in ecclesiastical robes. Short, plump and dark, he had the look of someone deeply immersed in thought, as he moved with focus and direction, but making slow progress. He put Thomasin in mind of a diligent beetle.

"The Imperial Ambassador Bishop Inigo de Mendoza," announced a herald.

The final dancers parted to allow him access through to the queen. Catherine rose from her chair and held out both her hands to him. When he attempted to make his bow, robes skimming the floor, she drew him up at once. They exchanged a few words in what Thomasin assumed must be Spanish, before withdrawing into the private chambers beyond. The door closed behind them.

Unsure of what to do next, in the queen's absence, the minstrels struck up their chord again. Kytson led out Cecilia to dance, but after having partaken of the last four rounds, Thomasin went to sit with her mother.

"I see you have met Sir Giles," Elizabeth opened, straight to the point.

"I was placed beside him at dinner."

"So you were," she replied, smiling. "And was he to your liking?"

Thomasin could not lie. "He is a most pleasant and merry gentleman."

"Isn't he?" Elizabth said, nodding as if this only confirmed her suspicions. "And he has a goodly leg."

"Mother, I am hardly likely to judge a husband by the shape of his leg."

Elizabeth did not reply, but sat smiling to herself as if she had won a victory.

"Oh, Mother, you are vexing. I shall fetch us some wine."

But barely had Thomasin risen from her seat when a great cry was heard from the queen's chamber. A long, heart-wrenching, wailing cry that tapered into a sob. The music and dancers stopped at once. Conversation fell silent. All eyes turned to the far door.

Catherine's remaining ladies hurried down the hall at once, into the chamber beyond. The guests looked around, uncertain of what to do, and some took their leave.

Within minutes, Maria Willoughby reappeared in her dark widow's weeds, urging all those remaining to depart.

"The queen is quite well, the king and princess are well; she has merely received some news and wishes for quiet contemplation."

Quickly, the chamber emptied.

Elizabeth grasped Maria by the hand. "Please give the queen my fondest regards. I will stay a little while, in the gardens, in case she wishes for me."

Maria nodded, her mind occupied. "It is the king. He has begun the formal process of separation."

Thomasin heard her mother's sharp intake of breath and saw her eyes narrow.

"I will wait. Our gracious Lady can be assured of my entire devotion and discretion."

"Thank you. That will be of comfort to her. But please, do not linger in the cold, it will not be good for you. The queen will send for you at Monk's Place when she needs you. Now I must return."

At that moment, the doors burst open again and the king stood there, his face red with fury, his eyes narrow. Those left in the hall immediately scattered, as he strode down the floor, through the debris of the party.

"Madame?" he called, seeking his wife. "Entertaining, I see? Where are you?"

Catherine's door opened slowly and she appeared, her face pinched with pain, but composed. "My Lord, your arrival was unexpected. We were celebrating the forthcoming nuptials of…"

"You should not be entertaining, and indulging yourself at this time, Madame. You should be kneeling in prayer, asking for guidance for your soul."

"But, My Lord, I … I have sought guidance. The path of my soul is clear, as is my conscience."

"Your conscience? As clear as when you took my brother to your bed?"

"I was his wife in name, but never in deed. I am your true wife, as you know well. We were joined together in the eyes of God and your desire to separate will go against his wish."

"Against his wish!" roared Henry.

"Quickly," ushered Thomasin's father, "we must leave, at once."

The doors closed abruptly behind them. Elizabeth lingered at the point where the passage divided. The red brick arch folded in above them and branched out to left and right. The way to their carriage lay ahead, through the service corridor and round to the stables, but cold air blowing up from the other passage indicated that the garden door stood open.

"The poor queen. It has quite taken my breath away to see her treated with such harshness."

"There is nothing you can do now. We must away," Richard urged.

"Very well, but let me pass through the gardens. I have a desire to see them and a need for some air."

"You can see them another day, when it is not so cold and you have not already exerted yourself."

Elizabeth sighed.

"It is wisest to hurry home," added Matthew, "but perhaps we might walk through the gardens in order to reach the stables. It only takes us a little out of our way."

Richard frowned, but his wife brightened at once.

"Very well," he agreed, irritated at being overruled, "but no stopping, straight on to the stables and straight home."

Taking his wife briskly by the arm, he led the way down the cold passageway and the others followed.

Cecilia and Thomasin walked side by side, the hems of their skirts rustling together.

"Did you enjoy dancing?" Cecilia asked, but Thomasin could only think of the queen and shook her head to dismiss the question.

They came out upon a little gravel path that ran around the outside of a courtyard, planted with flowers and shrubs, and railed with green and white. Statues of heraldic beasts, painted or gilded, stood at intervals throughout. The effect was both majestic and playful, and the air turned out to be milder than they had thought. Walking at a slow pace for the sake of her mother, Thomasin had time to look around and appreciate her surroundings. Leaded windows on three sides overlooked the little space, where late roses bloomed and the leaves were turning from green to brown. On the far side, a servant girl was sweeping away debris from the path, while another walked with a basket on her arm, plucking at the plants.

Passing along the central gravelled walk, they headed for the gate at the far end. It led into the great gardens, which Thomasin had briefly seen on the night of the little fire, with its long walks, leading to the open park beyond, where the king loved to ride. As they turned towards the stables, the sound of laughter and dogs barking reached them. Halfway down one of the walks, people were approaching, preceded by hounds, who came racing up to the Marwoods' party. Matthew could not resist, cradling a soft muzzle in his hand and patting the backs of those brown and white dogs that came pushing up to greet them.

Three figures emerged from the end of the walk, onto the main path. Thomasin knew them at once: the distinctive woman in a green outdoor habit, with the proud set to her head and the elegant, dignified walk; her brother George, full of fire and energy, and the tall, broad-shouldered Rafe with his blue-black hair. Thomasin's stomach clenched. She both longed and feared to encounter Rafe here and now, after his strange appearance at Monk's Place. He had spoken to her then with such urgency, such desire, but she had heard nothing from him in three or four days since. Nor did she wish to encounter Anne Boleyn, who was the cause of such suffering to kind Queen Catherine.

Anne stopped, turned and stared. It was clear that a meeting could not be avoided.

Elizabeth was set to stride off straight away, but Richard held her by the arm, with all the precautionary air he could muster. To depart now would be to slight the woman, and by association, to slight the king.

Calling to her dogs, Anne moved across the grass towards them, with a lithe, sinuous motion that seemed to necessitate little effort. Thomasin was aware of Rafe, at George Boleyn's side, falling into step with him. Although there had been signs, she had not appreciated he was so close to them.

Now, they could see Anne's particular charms closer at hand. She wasn't conventionally beautiful, but more handsome and striking. Her face was well-modelled; lean and sophisticated, with an air of knowledge and sensuality, qualities that had a kind of exotic air, no doubt picked up from her years spent at the court of France. While the most arresting of her features were her dark eyes, the rest of her face was regular enough, the mouth wide, the nose straight, but those large dark eyes, flashing, expressive and intelligent, could easily captivate. Thomasin was surprised to feel a twinge of jealousy.

"My lords, ladies," Anne said, in a curiously lilting tone, as she approached.

Thomasin followed her father's lead and bowed low. Anne and her group came to a halt before them.

"Our dogs favour you," Anne smiled, with unexpected warmth, "but I am not sure we have met."

"My Lady," replied Matthew, with the polish of a seasoned ambassador. "Sir Matthew Russell of Monk's Place at your service. This is my brother-in-law, Sir Richard Marwood, and my sister Lady Elizabeth, from Eastwell in Suffolk, and their two daughters Cecilia and Thomasin."

"Enchanting," said Anne, eyeing them in turn as they rose. "And you are visiting court?"

"For the marriage of our eldest, Cecilia," supplied Richard, sensing that his wife would not speak.

Thomasin felt Rafe's eyes upon her and briefly raised hers to meet them. His expression was unclear, and though she thought she read interest, there was no chance for them to speak.

"How lovely," replied Anne. "I adore a wedding. What will your title be, when you are married, Cecilia?"

"I will be Lady Kytson," Cecilia managed to stammer in reply.

"And how soon do you wed?"

"Next week, my Lady."

"Next week!" Anne looked around at her companions. "I will soon be seeking ladies when my chambers are upgraded, and I love to have beautiful young people around me. I wonder how your daughters would like that, Sir Richard?"

"It was our intention to return to the country once the ceremony has been conducted," he replied with restrained certainty.

"But intentions change, I believe," laughed Anne. "Come to my court for dinner tomorrow, both of you girls, and I will see how I might persuade you."

And with a whistle to her dogs, she strode back in the direction of the palace.

Thomasin caught a last look from Rafe's black eyes but he gave her no sign, no recognition of what had happened the other night. Instead, he turned and quickened his pace to catch up with Anne.

"Intentions change," muttered Elizabeth, through gritted teeth, "they do indeed, but loyalties never."

As they found their carriage and settled, Thomasin found her feelings beginning to cloud. Rafe had barely responded to her and had hurried away at once after Anne. The elegant, sophisticated Anne. Of course he would prefer to spend time in the company of a woman like that, rather than a young girl up from the country. She should not be surprised. Yet as the carriage turned out of the palace gates, she found it hard to suppress the stinging sensation behind her eyes.

TWELVE

"Well, we cannot accept them," said Thomasin's mother tautly, looking at the two bonnets that sat on the table in the parlour at Monk's Place.

It was mid-morning, with a glimmer of sunshine daring to break through the diamond-paned window.

"But they are so beautiful," said Cecilia, picking one up and admiring it. "Look at that exquisite work, I've never seen anything like it." She turned it from right to left before lowering it carefully down onto her head. A half-moon shape, it was made from back silk, edged with pearls and gold Venetian lace. The veil at the back was snowy white, trimmed with more gold. "I've never owned anything like this; it's the latest fashion. It's not the bonnets' fault who sent them."

Thomasin looked at the other, identical to Cecilia's, which sat waiting for her on the table, still part-wrapped in cloth.

"But from Anne Boleyn? You understand these are not just a gift," replied Elizabeth. "If we accept them, we accept the connection; we put ourselves in her debt. We are obliged to her, we are choosing her over Queen Catherine."

"I don't know if we need go that far," qualified Richard. "We need not compromise any existing loyalty we have, but we do need to consider the consequences of refusing them. We must keep them, surely you see that? Otherwise we slight Anne."

"Mark me," said Elizabeth, growing angry, "she had some purpose in sending these. Just as she said in the park, when she would have our girls for her household, there is some intent behind this gift. I like it not."

Richard eyed the table. "But we are due to depart in a week, and Cecilia will be a married woman, Anne knows that. Surely there is little harm in a bonnet, and such a pretty bonnet?"

"There is harm, you know it. I don't know why you pretend to be ignorant of it!"

"Now, come, my love, it is not worth you getting upset about. Do not let this be the cause of strife between us."

"I like them not," insisted Elizabeth. "I do not want them in the house."

Slowly, Cecilia began to remove hers.

"Anne will be expecting to see the girls in them at dinner," Richard said.

Thomasin thought her mother might be on the verge of explosion. Instead, Elizabeth became very still and composed.

"You are not thinking of accepting that invitation?"

Richard looked sheepish. "How can we not? It would be a slight to the king."

"To have our girls dine in the private chambers of that … of that … whore!" The word fell from her lips and created a stunned silence. Elizabeth was trembling with rage.

"My love," said Richard, after a pause, "you will make yourself ill over this."

"I am already ill."

"I fear we must face the reality of the changes at court."

"What do you mean?"

"The king seems determined to put Catherine aside and marry Anne. He has sent his envoys to the Pope for that purpose. Whatever our loyalty and friendship for the queen, it may be the case that she now represents the past, sad as that is. No, do not rail at me," he said, seeing her grow enraged, "it is pragmatism, realism, that makes me speak. Anne and her family are in the ascendant. They will be the ones with the power, the gifts and patronage to give. However distasteful it is, we must look to the future, for the sake of our family. We have been favoured by Anne. We should see it as an opportunity."

A long silence followed. Thomasin stared miserably at the bonnet sitting on the table.

Finally, Elizabeth spoke in a quiet voice. "I never will. I am retiring to bed."

Thomasin paused to adjust her new bonnet, which pinched a little at the back of her ears. Cecilia had refused to swap, even though hers was slightly larger across the span, because she thought the pearls on hers were better.

It was already dark outside, as the autumn evenings were drawing in closer each night, but the corridors in this part of the palace were brightly lit. It was their first time visiting the further side, the north wing, far from the cold space occupied by the queen and her chapel, and no doubt deliberately arranged that way, to prevent the two women meeting as far as was possible.

Thomasin had a curious sensation in the pit of her stomach, part nerves, part guilt, and something else she could not identify. In spite of it, though, she felt that behind the doors ahead, lay a new world so exciting, and full of such promise, that she dared not turn her back upon it. Mother might protest, Queen Catherine might sit alone, but blood pumped through Thomasin's veins, blood and life and passion, ready for an adventure. She was young and her father's words earlier had resonated with her. The Boleyns were the future.

The door burst open to reveal a scene of chaos. The chamber was full, but it felt more crowded due to the whirl of activity, of chasing and dancing and laughter, as if the whole place itself was alive. A mix of words, broken chords, and footsteps greeted them. Arms circled through bright light, coloured skirts flared out, lines of song and poetry chimed together. A handful of young men and women were playing some kind of game of catch, while others clapped and sang, and dogs jumped up to follow and gave chase, and a frantic rhythm was eked out on a lute. The chasers, perhaps five or six of them, were in pursuit of a woman, a slight, dark-haired woman who raced about dizzily in blue, dancing and spinning around the room, trying to avoid the grasp of the men, whose hands reached for her as their voices called her back. And in the middle of it all, stood Anne, blocking one woman's path, catching at the sleeve of another, swinging a third about on her arm. And laughing. All the while laughing, as if the world was hers. Those dark eyes, that long white throat, that wide mouth. She was the still point, the pivot, at the heart of it all.

They stood in the doorway, open-mouthed. Transfixed.

"Oh Mary, Mary, look!" Anne laughed, wiping her eyes. "Guests. Stop, everyone, stop, they will think us quite the infidels. Stop!"

The music ceased, courtiers flopped aside onto cushions and Anne came forwards. Someone picked up a lute while another began to sing. Wine was being poured. The woman in blue came up and laced her arm through Anne's, smiling and out of breath.

"My sister, Mary Carey," Anne explained. "Mary, I hope you have not frightened our new guests."

Mary laughed. "It is good that they are warned!"

Anne poked her in the ribs. "You are scandalous." She turned back to the Marwoods, suddenly gracious. "Forgive us, we are playful tonight. It is nothing more than high spirits, and you are such a welcome addition in those beautiful bonnets."

Cecilia and Thomasin curtseyed low.

"You did us too much honour with such a gift," replied Richard from behind them, more formally than usual.

"Nonsense. Pretty girls must have bonnets. French bonnets. Otherwise, what is the point of beauty?"

He stammered, unsure of how to answer. It was the first time Thomasin had seen her father lost for words.

"Now, my dear friend here, Tom Wyatt, would have an answer for that." Anne turned away, to a handsome dark man with a neat-clipped beard. "What say you, Tom, what is the point of beauty?"

"Why, to catch a king, of course," he replied at once, and the room roared.

"Hush now, hush, you are a terror," Anne laughed. "Are you coming in, or have we scared you away? Sir Richard, I promise to return your daughters in the same goodliness of mind and body that I see them now."

Thomasin felt her father bristling and regretting having brought them. "It's all right," she turned to reassure him, hoping her tone would convey that they would be sensible.

"Well," he said in quiet, controlled tones, "I am going to call upon Cromwell, then I shall return. If you wish to leave sooner, you may summon the carriage."

"Thomas Cromwell?"

"The same. You are not the only ones with an invitation."

"More?" asked Mary Carey, refilling Thomasin's glass, without waiting for her answer.

Food had been served on a banqueting table, and a multitude of sweetmeats, but little had been eaten. Thomasin had taken a white manchet roll to chew on, in the hope of soaking up the wine she had already drunk, which was starting to make her feel dizzy. Cecilia was talking with Anne Boleyn, seeming to compare notes about their dresses, while Anne's elder sister had settled beside Thomasin.

"How are you finding court?"

"Different to my expectations, I think."

"Oh?" Mary sucked upon candied lemon peel. "And what were your expectations?"

Thomasin thought for a moment. "I'm really not sure."

"How old are you, if I might ask?"

"Seventeen."

"Still young enough. Well, everything is changing. It's exciting. In five years' time the English court will be the most dazzling in all Europe. Once a few inconveniences have been seen to."

Thomasin wondered if she meant Queen Catherine and decided to play ignorant. "A few inconveniences?"

But Mary would not be pinned down so soon. "Change is coming, all across Europe. You would not believe the things I saw in France."

"You were in France?"

"Oh yes, before my marriage, I was with the Duchess of Suffolk, when she was Queen of France, as part of her household. It did not last long, of course, as old Louis died, but the things I saw there; the chateaux, the art, the tapestries, the dresses. They quite put us to shame. I felt such a misfit there until I bought a French gown."

"Really?"

"The French are the leaders in fashion, surely you know? Their manners might stink, but they know how to dress. And how not to pretend."

"Not to pretend?"

"Oh, there's such an honesty about them. About Francis. If he wants something, he takes it. There's none of this worrying and fussing about the legality of things. He's such a powerful king, he makes his own rules. At least, that's how he used to be, when I knew him. He's quite a broken man now."

"Why so?"

"I suppose these things don't always reach the country; I forget how it is when you don't live at court. Francis was the prisoner of the Emperor for a year, and he came home a broken man. But now Henry will be his friend again, because he hates the Emperor."

Thomasin could hardly keep up. She had heard her father speak of the Emperor once; a young man more powerful than a king, who ruled the entirety of the Holy Roman Empire, stretching all across the Netherlands and down into Spain.

Mary continued, as if anticipating her questions. "Because the Emperor is the dowager's nephew and he is so powerful, he will prevent the Pope from granting the king a divorce."

"The Emperor is more powerful than the Pope?"

"Why, of course. He's the ruler of the whole of the Roman Empire. And he was betrothed to the king's daughter, Mary, and then, last year, he broke his promise and married someone else."

"Little Mary? But she is just a girl."

"She has royal blood. They settle these things early. It's a lot to take in, you'll catch up. But make sure," she said knowingly, "that you choose the right friends. It's good that you are here tonight. Here, let me fill your glass."

And more of the strong, dark wine was poured.

"More song!" cried Wyatt, picking up a lute. "A new composition from Thomas Wyatt, poet to the Gods, celebrating the matchless beauty of Lady Anne Boleyn. Our brunette, with her dark hair, her dark eyes, and her dark ways."

"Dark ways?" laughed Mary. "Mr Wyatt will end his days in the Tower if he is not careful."

"No, no!" he cried, strumming a chord. "Forget the dark ways, it was my jest. A celebration of her eternal beauty, renowned through Europe, captivating young and old alike, winning the heart of a king."

"No," Anne replied, "enough, enough. I am so tired of hearing your doggerel about my beauty that I shall scratch my face off with my own fingernails."

"No, you won't," he said, leaping up, "because then you won't be able to marry the king and you'll have to marry me instead."

"Tom," she said, rolling her eyes, "you have forgotten you are already married."

"No!" They were interrupted by a cry from the corner. George Boleyn jumped up from his seat, knocking over the gaming table. Playing cards scattered on the floor. "Oh no, that cannot be. You must have cheated."

His partner, a stout young man with a red beard, shook his head. "You always say that when you lose. You're a bad loser."

"I am not! Tell him, Jane, tell him I am not a bad loser!" George called to a sleepy-looking woman in the corner, who showed little interest in their games. She nodded obligingly. "There you are, Will," continued George. "I am not a bad loser. My wife always tells the truth."

"This is a strange gathering, is it not?" asked Cecilia, coming up beside her sister. "I am sure Mother would be in an apoplexy if she were to witness such conduct."

"I am sure you are right. We should not stay long, in that case. Just long enough not to be ungrateful."

Cecilia nodded. "I find them strangely unsettling somehow, especially that Wyatt."

Thomasin agreed. She could not help but be overawed by the company, and excluded from their talk and jokes by her newness. Their boisterousness unsettled her slightly, and she did not wish to be thought staid or dull, but she was aware of the rising heat in the room and the effects of the wine, which she realised too late had been strengthened with sugar.

At that moment, the door burst open behind them, and in came a group of revellers, perhaps a dozen, dressed in the brown and green of huntsmen, with silver visors covering their faces. In unison, they made low, elaborate bows to the company.

Anne jumped up and clapped her hands. "Oh, wonderful, who have we here?"

One by one, she went from man to man, removing their masks with her bare hands. There was something intimate, possessive about the way she revealed them, untying their laces and exposing their faces. Thomasin felt it was not quite chaste behaviour but stopped short of being indecent. However, she then reminded herself these were far more sophisticated, experienced people than she was used to.

She recognised the first man, who wore an eye-patch, as Anne revealed him.

"Francis Bryan! I might have known you would be behind this, it smells of you. Who else do we have? Ah, my cousin Nicholas Carew, and of course, our dear Henry's shadow, William Compton. Who is next? Funny Henry Norris, and your brother John, William Hatton and Rafe Danvers. What naughty men you all are to surprise us like this. I suppose you will make us dance, however much we protest?"

At the sound of Rafe's name, Thomasin looked up, finding the room very intense and bright with all the people. He was there, among them, dressed in costume, his dark hair dishevelled. He had not seen her yet, as he greeted his friends, clapping the men on the back and kissing the women's hands.

"Is the king not among you?" asked Anne, disappointedly.

The huntsmen looked from one to another.

"He was with us in the hall, and will come, by and by," offered Francis Bryan. "He had some business to attend to."

"What business?" she asked sharply. "You mean the dowager? Has he gone to see her?"

Francis placed a kiss on her forehead. "Do not worry, cousin. I have no idea where he is, probably in his close stool."

The room erupted in laughter at this, and music started up again. Some of the huntsmen took partners and started to dance. One, with a long fluffy beard and hairy hands, reached for Thomasin but she waved him away. Cecilia was taken up by William Hatton, who put his arm right about her waist and pulled her close, twirling her about the room. Thomasin heard her laughing with pleasure in a way that was most unlike Cecilia.

"You? You are here?"

Rafe had seen her through the crowd. She struggled to her feet, but the room was shaking, revolving about his dark-lashed eyes.

"How do you fare?"

"This is a merry company."

"It is. I am glad to see you among it."

"Are you? I was not sure. I nearly did not come."

"You were invited by Anne, were you not?"

"Yes, in the park the other day. And she sent us these bonnets."

"I must say…" he began, but the dancers lunged towards them, pushing them aside. "I must say … not here, come…" He took her by the hand and led her to an alcove, out of the way of the dancing. The light was dimmer here, and they had a degree of privacy. "I must ask your forgiveness for my impetuous behaviour that night, when I came to your uncle's house. It was rash and foolish. I don't know what I was thinking. It was a stupid risk; I might have compromised you."

Thomasin nodded. "I was surprised."

"I had heard a report that you were about to leave London, for Suffolk. I wanted to speak with you before your departure."

"What did you wish to say?"

He looked down into her eyes, his blue-black hair falling forward, leaning towards her, so that she could smell the musky, spicy scent of him. And, recalling the little bag she wore tucked inside her bonnet, Thomasin could not help leaning in to meet him, in the hope that he would catch her scent.

"So much," he said, meeting her eyes. "So very much I have wanted to say, since we first met. I didn't mean anything by it. I know it must have seemed as if I was asking for … for what I should not, but it wasn't my intention — well, not at first, no, not at all. I just … I don't know. It was the moment."

Thomasin felt her cheeks growing warm.

"Please forgive me."

"I do," she replied, far too quickly, already regretting the ease of it.

"Thank you."

She took a deep breath. "I had not realised you were so closely connected to the Boleyns."

"As the viscount's ward…"

"I meant Anne." Thomasin surprised herself with the words.

"I suppose so. We are of an age. They have been kind to me, given me a place in her household."

"She gave me this bonnet."

He looked at it appreciatively. "It's a very pretty bonnet."

"My mother thinks it obligates us."

"What do you think?"

"It's a very pretty bonnet."

"I'd prefer to see you without it."

"Oh, but I cannot, surely."

Taking up her hand again, he pulled her further back into an antechamber that was lit only by a single candle. And she knew, in her belly: she knew his intentions, and could not stop the smile creeping into the corners of her mouth.

"Here." Carefully, he took hold of the pearl band and lifted the entire bonnet off, leaving Thomasin bareheaded. It was a strangely intimate act, but liberating. She shook out her hair and it fell across her shoulders.

"That's better."

He nodded. "Much better."

He put the bonnet gently down upon a chest, then his hand was drawn to her hair. She felt the sensation like a jolt, as his fingers wove through the strands and cupped her face. In the gloom, his dark eyes smouldered with a new intensity. His face was close.

"What I really wanted, when I came to your uncle's, was to kiss you. I could not bear the thought that you might leave court and I would not see you again, and yet I had never had the chance to kiss you."

He was closer now, his face just above hers, and the warmth of his hand moved round to the back of her head, pulling her gently towards him. She felt a sudden thrill of expectation rush through her. And then his lips were hot upon hers, drawing her in, soft and responsive. His other arm wrapped about her shoulder and her head tipped to the side, out of an instinct she had not known she possessed, as he kissed her deeper.

She relaxed into his arms, with a sense of release, wanting to give herself to him, as another wave of excitement ran through her. Her hands found his chest, flat against the broad stretch over his heart, firm and muscular. And something inside her responded, eagerly, came to life, as she returned his kiss. Feeling her passion, he grew hungrier, more urgent, and she felt the hot dart of his tongue upon hers.

"The king, the king!"

They broke apart, stunned and dazed. Rafe recovered first.

"Come, quick."

She followed him through into the chamber, realising it had fallen quiet, and all those within were kneeling. They fell to their knees in the doorway, as Henry surveyed the room, hands on hips.

"I see you began without me," he was saying, raising Anne to her feet.

"We did not know you were coming," she replied sulkily, turning away and indicating for the music to continue.

"I had told you that I would," he said, watching as she idly picked over the dishes left on the table. "You should have waited."

Anne shrugged, recklessly. "I thought perhaps you had gone to her. So, we have been making merry, to prevent me becoming melancholy at the thought of it."

Thomasin rose, with the others, but a wave of dizziness came over her. She stumbled a little to the side and Rafe caught her.

"You are unwell?"

"A little, but it's the wine."

"Come, sit here."

He led her to the settle, where gold cushions were spread. Thomasin felt the need to retreat into her mind, pushing the rest of the room away.

Anne and Henry were talking, close and intense, across the crowd, seeming not to care who might hear. Suddenly everyone else was an irrelevance.

"No," they heard the king break out, "you are wrong."

"Wrong?" she said, quietly and ominously. "Am I not to take appearances as they seem?"

"You must take things as I tell you."

"While you visit her, still treating her as your wife?"

Heads turned. The mood of merriment was already broken, but now the courtiers were in the way. Thomasin spotted Cecilia sitting with William Hatton, who was whispering in her ear. The discomfort of nausea rose inside her.

"I think I should like some fresh air," she whispered, "and to go home."

"Are you sure? You are unwell?"

She nodded once, dizzily, not trusting herself to do it twice.

"Here, let me help you." Rafe gave her his arm, and somehow, she made it across the room to gather up her sister. Cecilia pulled a face at having to leave and whispered something into Hatton's ear, before she rose and came away. Others were starting to melt away as the king's responses to Anne became more urgent and hers were rising in tone.

"You can't treat me this way," Anne said, clear and cold as glass. "Not even as the king: the man Henry can't keep me dangling while he visits his wife."

"She is not my wife," the king insisted. "I went to tell her that we were not man and wife in the eyes of God."

"Yet you continue to treat her as such, with constant kindnesses, while I am left alone."

"Hardly alone," Henry snapped, "you have had all your playfellows here tonight."

"What else am I supposed to do? Sit and sew? Or say my prayers? You would make a nun of me."

"Oh, no, Madam, that is the path you have chosen yourself, with your constant denials."

Neither the king nor Anne noticed as Rafe led the sisters out into the corridor. The walk down to the gate seemed very long, and very dark, with the floor uncertain, but soon the cold air was rushing up against them. It brought Thomasin back to life.

And there, standing in the shadows, was her father.

"I was on my way to collect you," he explained, although he seemed distracted. "My business is conducted. It is high time we departed."

Thomasin barely noticed Rafe disappear into the shadows, beyond the warm pressure of his hand upon her arm. She scrambled into the waiting carriage behind Cecilia in relief, her mind a muddle of the past hours, her body longing for her bed. It was far too late when she realised the new French bonnet had been left behind in the anteroom.

THIRTEEN

"It's nothing that a good rest and two days of a bland diet will not repair," said Dr Elyot, looking down at Thomasin, as she lay propped up on her bed cushions. "And let this be a lesson to you not to drink too much sugared wine."

"There is no fever, then? No infection?" asked Elizabeth, hovering by the fireplace.

"Nothing but a bout of overindulgence. It is common in the young. Call me again in three days if she is not fully restored to herself, and take care of yourself in the meantime."

"I will see you out," said Richard, gratefully, leading the doctor down the stairs.

Thomasin turned her face away from the window and closed her eyes. Her head throbbed with pain and her stomach churned; she had not managed a single mouthful of the white pudding her mother had been trying to tempt her with.

"I knew no good would come of this," Elizabeth complained. "I told your father not to take you, but he knew best, and now you are returned to us in a suffering state. What other terrible indulgences did you witness in there? What did you do? How did she behave, this Anne?"

"Nothing," Thomasin repeated, having already reassured her mother several times. "It was the wine. I did not realise its strength."

"You are not used to drinking so much and I suspect it was not usual wine, but something fortified. They are an indulgent, irresponsible group, Anne and her circle, to ply a young girl with drink like that. Has she sent word this morning, to enquire after you?"

"She was not aware that I was unwell."

"Neglectful too, then. Was she too busy cavorting to take proper care of her guests?"

"No, Mother."

"Well, your behaviour is an absolute disgrace. The first time you visit court alone, you disgrace yourself. What does this say about your good name, our good name, behaving like this? You cast doubt on the good reputation of the Marwoods and you have acted far below the expectations of a lady, of your father's daughter."

Her mother continued talking, speculating and complaining, but Thomasin shut her out. Her mother only knew half the story. She returned to that bright, hot chamber, swimming with people and merriment, where the colours seemed more intense and the laughter louder and longer. There, the world revolved around Anne, with her friends and admirers, directing the company, all of whom basked in her light. And into that enchanted space came Rafe, beautiful Rafe, with his tapering dark eyes and his soft, urgent lips. Had it really happened? The way he had pulled her towards him and enfolded her in his arms, kissing her as if it were their last day alive?

"These might help pass the time." Matthew had entered the room and set down a pile of books upon the table. "I have been downriver to Chelsea, to visit my friend Thomas More. He has some very wise and witty daughters, who very kindly permitted me to borrow some of their books. So we have Thomas à Kempis's *The Imitation of Christ*, a Greek primer, an old romance called *Richard, Coeur de Lyon*, a book about the stars and a translation of Herodotus. You can improve your mind while your body rests."

"That is most thoughtful of you, brother," smiled Elizabeth.

"More speaks so highly of reading, of its spiritual benefits and the training of a woman's mind. I told him about your interest and he let me have free choice of his shelves, barring the most valuable editions, of course. So I picked a few at random. They will be as good a place to start as any, if Thomasin is to become one of these new learned women."

Thomasin managed to mutter her thanks but the thought of reading, with the words jumping before her eyes, made her head ache more.

"I don't know how much of this new learning we want to put inside her head," mused Elizabeth, "not if it's going to encourage this type of behaviour."

"It's just youth," said Matthew. "You remember how merry the court was back in the early years, when you were Catherine's maid?"

"I remember well enough," she replied, "and the fortunes that were spent and the marriages that were made as a result."

"Including your own, I seem to remember."

Elizabeth frowned and batted him away. "It is a woman's duty to be a good wife and mother, that is what Queen Catherine always taught us and what she strived to be. Nothing else matters, which is why it is so cruel the way the king is treating her, now that she has reached advanced years."

"Take care what you say about the king," Matthew warned. "You are always safe with me, but never let anyone else hear you speaking criticism of him."

"I have known the king since before he took the throne, when he was a youth of sixteen or seventeen. He would never move against me and holds me in high esteem."

"I am sure not. Only remember the duke of Buckingham, who was the king's own kin."

But Elizabeth shook her head. "You don't understand. Henry…" But she trailed off.

"Henry what?"

"It's nothing."

"I am going now, Mother," said Cecilia, passing the doorway.

"Wait!" Elizabeth turned. "Remind me where you are going."

"To see Lucy Kytson, to discuss our dresses, as I mentioned this morning. I will go straight there in the carriage and back."

"I do not like you going alone. I would prefer to go with you."

"But Thomasin needs you. It is no distance and I shall not be above two hours. There are things I wish to ask her."

Their mother frowned. "You might always ask me things. Did I not bring you into this world?"

"But I want to speak with a young woman, a woman close to me in age. You understand, Mother, surely? Particular things," she said with emphasis. "It must have been the same for you, when you were about to be wed?"

Elizabeth fell silent, as if in contemplation.

"I will be back before nightfall, or else you can send for me."

"Can your uncle not go with you?" Elizabeth turned to Matthew, expectantly.

"I am afraid I am expecting a visit from the clerks of my guild."

Cecilia did not wait any longer, but hurried down the stairs. Presently they heard the grinding of wheels on the stone cobbles outside.

Sleep came for Thomasin. Blessed, peaceful sleep, to soothe her head and heart.

FOURTEEN

"Here they are," said Matthew, looking through the window into the front court, in which a carriage was pulling up. It alighted before the entrance, showing off its impressive black and gold lacquer work, and the Russell family crest. The dogs surged out, to inhale the scents of the countryside it had recently passed through, yelping in excitement. "Quick, into the hall."

The family had gathered to welcome Matthew's son and his wife, who had travelled down from Derbyshire for the wedding. Married for ten years to a Yorkshire woman, Barnaby Russell ran an estate outside Buxton, and only returned to London occasionally, to deal with matters of business. Having lived exclusively in Suffolk for the last fifteen years, though, the path of the Marwoods had not recently crossed theirs.

Thomasin stood beside Cecilia, trying to see these cousins she had never met, and had heard so little about. Her mother had rarely spoken of Barnaby, hinting once that he had had a difficult youth, on another occasion that he had run up debts, and on a third that he was too proud for her liking. She had pleaded the need for rest that morning, retiring to her bed in anticipation of Dr Linacre's visit, placing her conveniently out of the way of the new arrivals.

Matthew called back the hounds, who came trotting reluctantly. "Caesar! Brutus!"

Out of the carriage climbed a dark-haired, plump young man of thirty, or slightly older, in the dark furred robes of a gentleman, with leather riding boots and a cap beset with jewels. His doublet, though, was a most striking peacock blue, chosen, perhaps, to contrast with the gold chains that hung draped across his chest. He held himself so erect and precise in every movement, as he steadied himself and turned back to hand down his wife, that he appeared almost ridiculous. The woman to whom he offered his hand was small and round-faced, neatly but simply attired in a brown frock with a lace collar and a plain, old-fashioned bonnet. She climbed out of the carriage, beaming widely, looking over to the group on the step, as if everything pleased her. And then, unexpectedly, Barnaby offered his hand again, and a second woman appeared, a thin, pinched-faced woman, who looked drawn and weary, despite the magnificent headdress she wore, trimmed with handmade lace.

"By Jove, there is the sister too," muttered Matthew under his breath, as the trio approached.

Assembling themselves into a line, the women on either side of Barnaby, they moved forward in unison and bowed at the same moment, as they had clearly planned beforehand.

Thomasin tried to hide her smile, imagining how they had rehearsed this before their departure. Their mixture of clothing, with family heirlooms set on top of their country simplicity, showed how they had made the closest approximation they could of suitable court attire, but also that, until he inherited the Russell fortune, Barnaby was not a wealthy man.

"My son," boomed Matthew, drawing the young man into his open arms. He came, awkwardly, as if he was more comfortable with distance. His wife, though, felt no such qualms and sprung forward to kiss her father-in-law upon the cheek, followed by Richard, then Cecilia and Thomasin.

"Ellen, my dear, I trust you are well? This is my sister's husband, Sir Richard Marwood and his two eldest daughters, Cecilia and Thomasin."

"From Suffolk? How lovely it is to meet you," she said, with sincerity. "I am glad not to be the only outsider here, although I always feel a little that way. I do hope we shall become good friends."

"And Lady Dorothy Springe," added Matthew, with a little rise to his voice, "what an unexpected pleasure."

Thomasin heard the undertone in her uncle's voice and did not see anything in Dorothy's face that suggested her capable of giving pleasure. Her skin was sallow and, although her features were regular, even pleasant, there was something cynical in her gaze that was most off-putting. She bowed low without a word.

"I do hope you don't mind sister Dorothy too," added Ellen. "I would have asked Barnaby to write and tell you she was coming, but it was a last-minute decision, and the letter would have arrived after we did. I did not wish to leave her behind alone, as she would have been so melancholy, and she is such a martyr to her teeth."

"You are all most welcome," said Matthew graciously. "I hope your journey was not too arduous?"

"We broke the journey at Nottingham and Northampton," replied Barnaby, very formally as he stepped across the threshold, as if the floor was littered with hot coals.

"Well, do come inside and take some refreshment."

"Do you have a chapel here?" asked Dorothy.

"A chapel? At Monk's Place?"

"I thought all large houses had a chapel."

"It did once, as it was in the possession of the Bishop of Rochester, but that was converted long ago. We use the Church of Our Lady, further down Thames Street."

"Then might I be conducted to my chamber?" Dorothy asked, her face prim and closed.

"Why, of course." Matthew summoned a servant. "Shall I send up some refreshment?"

"No, nothing."

"Do ask for anything you might need."

She inclined her head, as if she deserved such favour, and followed the servant up the stairs.

When they were seated in the parlour, taking wine, and Ellen was bubbling over with enthusiasm about everything, Barnaby took his father aside and Thomasin overheard the conversation.

"Do not mind my sister-in-law's poor temper. She has been most ill for the entire journey. I would imagine a good sleep will restore her to her usual self."

"And this is the bride," Ellen was saying, standing back to admire Cecilia, who usually enjoyed admiration of a more subtle kind. "Are you prepared? Your dress is ready? And is the bridegroom wonderful? Are you very much in love?"

Thomasin knew her sister well enough to know that behind the mask of her face, she was struggling to control her laughter.

"I was so very much in love with my Barnaby, it's the only reason I married. I always swore that I would not. But it is not so long to go now, just a few days. You must tell me everything."

"And have you been much at court, Sir Richard?" asked Barnaby, in a clipped voice.

"A little. We have been received by the king and queen, who kindly hosted the formal betrothal dinner."

"And we are to attend the king today, at four," added Cecilia, desperate for any escape from Ellen's questions.

"This very day? How convenient. We shall accompany you, and have the opportunity to do honour to the king."

There was an awkward stillness, to which Barnaby was oblivious.

"Of course," bowed Richard, "as you wish."

The carriage brought them right up to the palace gate. Sunshine lit the red bricks on either side, creating a warm arch of welcome, although the heraldic beasts and the warlike symbols around them were thrown into fierce contrast. Dismounting, they made a small party for the inspection of the guards in red livery, Thomasin and her father and sister, Barnaby and Ellen. Dorothy Springe had elected to remain in her chamber, with the daylight blocked out and a fire blazing in the grate.

Thomasin had put on her white and yellow silk again, with a brown velvet cloak lined with fur. In the middle of their second week in the city, her wardrobe was already wearing thin and she could not touch the dress she had set aside for the wedding itself. That must be new; untouched, unseen. But an audience with the king demanded something special, so she had braided up her hair, although there was little of it visible beneath the French bonnets from Anne Boleyn, which their father had insisted they wore. Thomasin's had been sent back to Monk's Place, after she had left it in Anne's antechamber.

The air was heavy with the smell of woodsmoke and horses as they passed through the gateway into the courtyard, on the opposite side to the gardens. Smooth cobbles made patterns underfoot. On either side, the brickwork rose up two or three storeys, patterned with white and black diamonds set among the red, and large windows of paned glass, all below stacks of twisted chimneys. The sky above was striped with pink and grey, ahead of the sunset in about an hour's time.

Ushers conducted them to the king's entrance and up the steep flight of steps. At the top, they had barely a moment before their presence was announced and they were shown in.

Any fears Thomasin had that the meeting was going to be uncomfortable were immediately dispelled by the atmosphere inside the hall. A good number of people had gathered; mostly young people in bright costume, who appeared to be rehearsing a dance. In their midst, Anne Boleyn and her sister Mary were conducting proceedings, showing the dancers their steps, calling upon the musicians to play, and watching them repeat the motions.

"Yes, yes," Anne was crying, "you already have the cross-step, but you go too slowly into the turn. It must be neat, tight, like this." And she stepped and turned sharply, with an elegant rustle of her damson-coloured skirts.

Around the outside of the hall, other courtiers were seated, or talking, playing at dice or cards, or reading letters. Thomasin saw Viscount Boleyn, his son George, the duke of Norfolk and others she recognised, although she quickly ascertained there was no Rafe. William Hatton was reading a passage from a book to the young, fair lady-in-waiting, but he let the book drop in his lap as he saw the Marwood girls. Further down the hall, past the dancers, Thomasin recognised Thomas Cromwell, sitting like a statue, hands folded as he watched the scene. The king was further on, standing on the edge of the dais, deep in discussion with another man, with his back to them.

Across the floor, Anne called to them. "Girls! Girls! There, you must come and join us. Mary Norris has two left feet and I swear my cousin Bryan is deliberately doing the opposite of what I tell him, just to annoy me."

"I am improving the dance!" protested the man with the eye-patch. "I am a connoisseur of dances and this one has areas of weakness. It has been designed by an amateur."

"You see how he provokes me? Surely you two lovely ladies must be light of foot and quick to learn a step. We need you to join our masque."

"No, Anne." Her voice had drawn the attention of the king, who now summoned them forwards. "They are here at my invitation. You can have them afterwards for your dance."

"Very well, but do not leave it too long!" Anne replied, slightly vexed, as she turned and threw herself back into the planning. "No, Norris, you come forward, and Mary there, too. So, Francis and I should be here, and there, then we link arms and pass under your archway. Lift your archway! Here, no, now, like that!"

Thomasin and Cecilia walked steadily down towards the king, bowing low at the point where they met. As always, Thomasin felt a sense of unease in the king's presence, either a fear of saying or doing the wrong thing, or of his unpredictable response. She bowed her head low, until she was certain it was safe to look up. King Henry was standing before them, hands on hips, in a slashed doublet, with white linen pulled out between murrey velvet and cloth of gold. His cheeks were flushed and his small blue eyes gleamed down at them.

"Sir Richard, and your lovely daughters."

"My Lord," replied Richard, rising. "Might I also present my nephew, Barnaby Russell, and his wife Ellen, who have just arrived from Yorkshire for Cecilia's wedding."

"Ah, yes, the wedding," said the king, paying the others no attention. "Come, Cecilia, let us talk of it." He offered her his arm, and the astonished Cecilia took it and followed where he led, up the steps of the dais and into the alcove made by an oriel window.

"You do not think that was a mark of disfavour?" asked Barnaby, turning to Richard. "He did not acknowledge us at all."

Ellen looked down at her plain brown dress, which she had done her best to trim with ribbons and lace. "You do not think we are dressed too humbly for court? That we look too country?"

"It is my honest opinion," reassured Richard, "that the king sees only what he wishes to see. Right now, he wishes to speak with Cecilia, so nothing will stop him, and he sees nothing else. Your time will come."

Thomasin seated herself with Ellen upon a bench and watched the room. Anne was still conducting her dancers, quite unaware that two ladies were available, but neither did Thomasin wish to intrude. William Hatton had joined them, and was laughing most amiably with Norris and Bryan, although Thomasin noticed he was frequently looking towards the king, perhaps from fear of displeasing him.

She allowed herself to watch King Henry with Cecilia, wondering what he might be saying to her. Letting Ellen's chatter wash over her, she noted the way he was speaking, gently and appreciatively, then waiting for her response, as if he was asking a series of questions.

"Perhaps he wishes to make her a particular gift for the wedding," suggested Richard, following Thomasin's gaze, "or else promote Sir Henry."

They saw Cecilia nod, and the king smile and place his hand over hers.

"They say he has many mistresses," whispered Ellen, far too loudly. "I heard that he had Anne Boleyn's sister in his bed before her, and that he married her off, to keep it a secret."

"Hush!" replied Richard, sharply. "You are too loud and you speak impertinence. What if you had been overheard?"

"I don't say anything that is not already known."

"Known? You have been here barely an hour; you cannot know anything of the sort."

"I'm sorry." Ellen flushed, and looked as if she might spout tears.

"Come now, no harm was meant," replied Barnaby, although Thomasin noticed he turned away from his wife as he spoke.

"Sir Richard." Cromwell had approached noiselessly and bowed before them. "It is good to see you at court."

"My daughters were summoned to attend the king."

The minister shot a look over to where Henry and Cecilia stood in the oriel. "Ah, of course." Then he added, with greater significance, "Of course."

"It is because of Cecilia's wedding, which takes place next week."

"Yes," Cromwell nodded. "It is fitting that he honours the bride in some way. And yourself, Sir Richard, have you yet spoken with the king?"

"Not yet, it is not long since we arrived."

"Well, I do hope you will get the chance, and that you find yourself in accord with him."

Richard sighed.

Cromwell inclined his head. "If you will excuse me."

"Our good Mr Cromwell," said a voice as the minister departed. William Hatton had come up behind them, waiting for a chance to speak. "Needed by the king, but beloved of no one."

Thomasin looked in surprise at his shock of blond hair, his bright eyes. "You do not like Mr Cromwell?"

"My dear," he smiled, "no one in this room likes Mr Cromwell, save for himself."

"Why so?" she asked, curious, as the minister worked his way around the room.

"Well, they say he was raised in a forge. Now, you know my ideas about learning; I am all for men making their own way in the world. Women too, lifting themselves above their origins with education, but there must always be proportion, and humility, and Mr Cromwell could afford a little more humility in his dealings."

"You think him an upstart, Hatton?" asked Richard.

"I do not think so, I know so. I do not hold his rise against him; he is a man of ability, and useful, too, except he must behave as if the rest of us owe him respect."

"Is that the entire basis of your dislike of the man?"

Hatton laughed. "That is merely the beginning, but I came here to be merry with the ladies, not to take the man's character apart."

"Indulge me," pressed Richard. "I have particular reasons for asking."

Hatton needed little more encouragement. "Well, I dislike him as an upstart and a braggart, as a thoroughly unscrupulous man, who would do anything, betray anyone, to achieve his aims."

Thomasin thought of the king's pursuit of Anne Boleyn. "But what if his aims are the king's aims?"

"Then the king knows he might stand back and let Cromwell sully his hands in the dirty work a monarch must rise above."

Her father raised his eyebrows. "Those are strong words. You are bold to speak so."

"I have personal experience of him. I have a sister, a widow, living in impoverished circumstances because Cromwell refused to grant her the rights to her late husband's estates, as it was earmarked for the Boleyns."

"Anne took it?" Thomasin asked.

"No, I doubt that she was even aware. But when the king lavishes her and her family with gifts, those gifts have been taken from somewhere, or somebody. And it was the job of Mr Cromwell to find those estates. No matter how I pleaded with him, he would not reconsider."

Thomasin watched Anne whirling round amid the dancers, her gold-edged skirts forming a circle.

"So my sister suffers in order that she might dance."

"Can you do nothing for her?"

"I would have her live with me, but she is infirm, and unwilling to travel. Before the winter grows harsher, I will go and fetch her, even if I have to pull the litter myself."

Cecilia's interview with the king had come to an end and she was making her way down the hall, back to her family, her face all smiles.

"He would see you next," she hissed at Thomasin. "Smile like me and you might be given some jewels too."

"Jewels?"

"Wedding gifts. For when you marry."

Slowly, Thomasin approached the king. He was standing back in the alcove, a vast and impressive figure, still athletic, his eyes quick and his face sensual. It was hard to believe that he wished to speak with her, and her alone.

She made her curtsey and he beckoned her to sit by him in the window seat which overlooked the park.

"Thomasin Marwood," he said gently.

"My Lord."

He was sitting facing her, with barely any distance between them, and she felt his proximity almost painfully, overwhelmingly. This was the King of England!

"What should I ask you, Mistress Thomasin? How well you like court? Whether you like dancing? Whether you have enough dresses?"

"I hardly know, my Lord."

"I have been speaking with your sister. Tell me, is she an obedient daughter?"

Thomasin had not been expecting the question. "Yes, my Lord, yes she is."

"She strikes me as a girl with spirit."

"Ah, well, yes, that too, I think."

"And do you think she is happy in this forthcoming marriage?"

Thomasin thought for a moment. "She has not said anything to make me think otherwise."

"Hmm," the king mused. "I could not get her to tell me what it is she most wants. Was she being coy with me, or does she have few needs?"

"I cannot imagine Cecilia being so unforthcoming. She likes dresses, jewels, of course, but most of all I think she would like to remain at court."

"Truly?"

Thomasin nodded, looking round to where her sister was conversing with William Hatton. "I think she is happy here, and once she is married, she will not wish to return to a quiet life in the country."

"Well, that is a gift I will gladly bestow upon her. She will have a place in Mistress Boleyn's household. And what of you,

Thomasin? What are your wishes? Have you thought of marriage yet? Or a place at court?"

She dropped her head, full of sudden thoughts of Rafe Danvers. "I've not really thought much…"

"I understand. You are young. Although many of your age are already wives and mothers."

"Oh, I do not think…"

"Do not concern yourself. I am not about to urge you to marry, unless it is your parents' wish." He nodded towards the dancers. "I do believe Anne has developed something of a fondness for you and would like you to be part of her masque. And after that, after the wedding, perhaps you might like to stay on at court? We like to have young, pretty faces about us. And, I understand from your sister that you have a ready wit, and are capable of much thought, so I promise to show you my library."

"Your Grace is too generous. I don't know what my parents intend for me, although we had all planned to return to Suffolk."

"Suffolk would be the richer for it, but I might speak with your father, tempt him to return more often. And your mother, how is she?"

"Not so well, my Lord. Perhaps less unwell than annoyed today, but she remains in bed."

"Annoyed?"

Thomasin felt a twinge of panic, realising the root cause of her mother's annoyance was the unfolding situation between the king, queen and Anne. "Oh," she stammered, "wedding arrangements are tedious and lengthy, I think."

"Of course. I do hope that once she is satisfied, Lady Elizabeth will visit us again. Many years ago, when she was about your age, and I was not much older, she was one of the brightest ornaments to our court. Do pass on my regards to her. Now, look, here comes Anne to claim you."

Anne Boleyn was heading towards them, her dark eyes mischievous. "Now, Henry, you have had my young friends for long enough, and I must have them. How else am I to complete the masque for your entertainment?" She held out her hand to Thomasin, who felt obliged to take it. "Now, promise you will dance in this masque tonight with me. It will be wonderful; I have all the seamstresses hard at work and we will deck you head to toe in gold. What say you?"

The king laughed. "That sounds like an offer you cannot refuse."

Thomasin felt the truth of his words. She dropped a small curtsey. "Of course, my Lady."

Anne led her away to where Cecilia and William Hatton were already walking through the steps.

"Here," she said, summoning a handsome, older man with a head of chestnut curls. "Mistress Marwood can partner Harry Norris. Now watch, carefully: one, two, three and then turn to the left, and walk, walk and cross and stop. Do we have it? Again, again."

FIFTEEN

The gold headdress with its flowing train felt unfamiliar on Thomasin's head. She shivered as she waited in the narrow servant's corridor, hidden behind the tapestry, with the other masquers. She could not deny that her costume was magnificent, far more than she had ever dreamed of wearing, or probably would again. The gown was of gold tissue, set all over with gold braids, sewn with gold and scarlet spangles, which shimmered each time Thomasin moved. The men's costumes were of purple velvet, set all over with leaves of gold, and borders embroidered in gold satin. In the gloom behind the scenes, Thomasin whispered excitedly with the others; Anne and her sister Mary, George and Jane Boleyn, Francis Bryan, Henry Norris, William Hatton, Cecilia; gleaming bright, awaiting the summons of the music.

Mary could hardly restrain herself. "Anne! Stop tickling me! Stop it!"

"It's not me," her sister laughed, quickly swapping places. "It's Harry Norris, look at him, see his face! He was pretending it was me."

Norris held up his hands in despair, but Mary convulsed again.

"Anne, you are the most shocking liar. I know your tickles of old, you jab in the ribs like a rapier, whereas I think Mr Norris would be more…"

"More?" he asked.

"I don't know," she replied coyly, "caressing."

"Caressing!" laughed Anne. "My goodness, that is quite an assumption. I think he would not dare to tickle you anyway, so you will never find out."

"Oh, wait!" interrupted George. "Do you hear it?"

The masquers fell silent. Music was playing in the hall.

"That's it!" cried Anne. "Everyone ready? In we go!"

She pushed through the service door and between the gap in the tapestries. The warmth and heat of the hall struck them at once. Guests were lined up around the sides or seated about the dais where King Henry took centre stage, filling his chair of state with its golden canopy and padding, matching the dancers. Thomasin slipped in behind her sister, filled with awe at the moment. It had taken only a little persuasion for their father to allow them to stay; he had promised to return later, to fetch them home, but Barnaby and Ellen had remained, and were sitting among the group by the hearth, their eyes wide at this unexpected treat. Taking her place in the line, with Henry Norris's hand in hers, Thomasin thought how little she could have guessed, upon waking that morning, just how exciting her day was to become.

They moved forward in formation, as they had practised. Keeping level, with their eyes facing front, they took up their positions. Thomasin was third in the line of women, behind Anne and Cecilia, and their partners Francis Bryan and William Hatton. In his purple velvet suit, Henry Norris began the steps.

"And one, two, three," counted Anne, softly.

Thomasin followed the others, and then turned, before joining the women's line again. Then they followed the same pattern the other way.

All the time, she was conscious of eyes upon them, upon her, watching every move. The sensation of their attention seemed to fill her limbs with energy, coursing through her veins. As she danced, feeling part of a charmed circle, Thomasin realised it was such a thrill to perform. She hadn't expected to enjoy being the centre of attention, but at that moment, following Anne Boleyn's lead, with Norris at her side, smiling as they passed and linked arms, she knew she was born for it.

The first part of the steps concluded and the masquers rearranged themselves into formations of four. Thomasin and Norris were paired with Cecilia and Hatton, who had the routine perfectly. As they spun about together, with the music quickening in pace, she felt the greatest rush of excitement pass through her, swirling past the faces of the crowd. Ahead of her, Anne's group broke apart, and Thomasin followed, keeping her eyes on the Boleyn girls' graceful moves, and emulating them as best she could. And she realised this was what she wanted, always: to be at court, to be dressed in spangled tissue of gold, dancing with all eyes upon her.

When the routine concluded, the masquers took their line and made their final bow. The minstrels made their final flourish and the hall erupted in applause, led by an enthusiastic king.

"Oh, such a success," beamed Anne, turning back to the group. "Well done, everyone, you were all just wonderful."

And her black eyes shone, and her voice was full of genuine praise, and Thomasin felt that yes, she had indeed been wonderful.

"Come on, come on," urged Anne, "we're first to the banquet!"

Thomasin looked about for Cecilia but she seemed to have disappeared into the crowd, so she followed Norris and the others towards the table at the far end, which had been set with tarts, pastries and candied fruits.

"How fare the dancers?" asked the king, approaching, with eyes only for Anne.

"Very well," she replied prettily, "and hungry after our exertions."

"You lit up the hall magnificently, both the dancing and the arrangement. It took much skill to arrange."

"It was something I did often in France," she replied, "at Queen Claude's court, to entertain her during her confinements. I have danced my way through all the chateau of the Loire."

"I don't doubt you have," he replied appreciatively. "I hope you will give me the benefit of your expertise later, when the dancing resumes."

"If it please you, my Lord."

It was while she was listening to the chatter of the masquers, that Thomasin spotted them. Standing behind the torches, perhaps thinking themselves unseen, their faces partly in shadow, and partly flickering with bright light, were Viscount Boleyn and Rafe Danvers, who must have arrived during the dance. Both were looking towards the masquers, and speaking in a confidential way, with heads together. Rafe's darkness was exaggerated by the play of light, but his black eyes shone like coals. Then, abruptly, as if a light was shone upon them, they drew apart. Thomasin might have been mistaken, but she thought that it was her observation of them which broke up their conversation. The viscount gave Rafe a brief nod, and Rafe set off around the outside of the room, approaching the spot where she stood at the table.

Thomasin turned away, unsure of what she had seen pass between the two. Sure enough, Rafe was soon at her side.

"I saw you dance," he said quietly beside her.

She half-turned towards him. The memory of his lips upon hers came flooding back.

"You did very well. I had not known you were to be included, or else I would have joined the group."

"It was only decided this afternoon. Mr Norris was an admirable partner."

"I am glad to see you looking well, after the other night. I was hoping to see you again."

She waited, just breathing, to see what would come next.

"When does your sister marry?"

"Next Thursday."

She chanced a look at him. His eyes were directed towards Cecilia, whose head was bent towards that of William Hatton. For the first time, Thomasin saw through his eyes, saw the laughter between the pair, and wondered if there was a spark between them. It gave her a moment of unease.

"Let's take some air, in the gardens?"

"But are we allowed to leave? Do we need to ask?"

"No, it's fine."

"Won't we be missed?"

He held out his hand. She allowed herself to be led, in hope, in trust, still thrilled by the success of the dance, by the feeling that she belonged.

The steps and corridors down to the gardens were busy. Courtiers lingered, whispering rumours, waiting for lovers. The dark walkways outside were lit with flares, burning bright in the night air, and a number of people were taking advantage of a milder night. Thomasin felt the cool rush of air upon her face with pleasure.

"Isn't that better?" Rafe asked, smiling to see her response.

"I hadn't realised how hot it was in there."

"And you were dancing, building up a heat. Dancing very prettily."

A couple walked past them on the path, and Rafe drew her closer to him.

"Have you been thinking about the other night?"

Thomasin smiled, knowing he referred to their kiss. "I have."

"And do you think you might be wishing to do it again?"

She laughed at his directness. "You are bold, Sir."

"And I would be bold again, if you allowed it."

But they were too close to the palace, and people were nearby. She smiled and turned away.

"I had heard," he continued, "that you might be staying on at court."

"You did?"

"Is it not so? I thought the king suggested it?"

His words confused her. "It was suggested only this afternoon. It is not something I have given much thought to, and I am unsure what my parents would say. We had planned only to stay a few days more."

"And then back to the country?"

"Yes."

"But your sister is staying on?"

"Yes, I suppose she is."

Thomasin realised she had given little thought to Cecilia's life after next week, but she supposed there was a London house, where the Kytsons were currently in residence. She tried to picture Cecilia there, in strange rooms, with Henry, and perhaps with Honoria and Lucy, too, but she could not.

"Would you consider a place at court?"

Thomasin felt torn. "It is difficult. Queen Catherine also favours me, and has asked for me to remain with her, and now the king asks for Anne, I do not know what to think. I should be loath to disappoint anyone."

"But the choice is clear, surely," Rafe replied. "The queen is old; no matter how pious and worthy she may be, her court is quiet and dull, and the king will soon set her aside. She will be queen no longer, but Anne will. You would be following a misplaced loyalty if you went anywhere else."

Something about his words needled her, not least because there was truth in them.

"But it seems so unkind."

"Is it not unkind that the king lacks a son?"

"No," she replied, thoughtfully, "I do not think that can be considered an unkindness. It is unfortunate, but it is unfortunate for both the king and queen."

"It is a mark of God's displeasure with their marriage, don't you think?"

And despite his beautiful eyes, and the thrill of being with him in the gardens at night, Thomasin felt a twinge of doubt in Rafe.

"I would not presume to interpret the pleasure, or displeasure, of God."

At that point, a figure appeared along the path before them, and Thomasin recognised Viscount Boleyn, walking with Thomas Cromwell. They were in conversation, but both men's eyes were upon Thomasin and Rafe. It made her feel uneasy, as if their appearance was somehow connected to the moment earlier, with Boleyn and Rafe in the alcove, behind the flares.

She looked into his face, searchingly.

"What is it?"

"I don't know. I don't know, I can't put my finger on it, but I must go."

"Don't go." He put a hand upon her arm. "Stay a while."

"No, I can't. My father is coming for me."

And she walked away, in the opposite direction from Boleyn and Cromwell.

Just as Thomasin was approaching the gateway that led into the courtyard, there was a loud bang, followed by another. They seemed to be coming from the sky. Her heart leapt into her throat. She spun round. Above her, above the trees, were flashes of red, green and yellow in the sky, shooting up and splitting into pieces, which faded out and fell to the earth.

"Did the fireworks startle you?"

It was Giles Waterson, his handsome face all smiles. Thomasin was surprised to see him, as he didn't appear to have been in the hall before, for the masque.

"Oh, Sir Giles, good evening. I confess they did startle me, as I had not been expecting them."

"While I have been expecting them all evening, so when they arrive, they feel something of a disappointment."

A blue shower lit up the sky behind them.

"I have never seen anything like it," Thomasin replied. "What makes them?"

"Oh, all sorts, a mixture of chemicals and gunpowder. It's quite a skill, so I'm told. What brings you to court tonight?"

"I was dancing in Anne Boleyn's masque. Did you see it?"

"I did not. I was in attendance upon the queen."

"Oh." His words seemed to take the colour out of the evening and made Thomasin feel a little shame-faced, having danced and feasted, while Catherine was quiet in her apartments. "I hope the queen had good cheer."

"Very little. She had her confessor with her tonight, and her closest ladies about her. I fear she is in need of greater cheer than she is being afforded."

"It is a sad situation, with the court split this way. I can't imagine where it will lead."

"I suppose the Boleyns were making merry?"

One, two, three and then turn to the left, and walk, walk and cross and stop. Thomasin cast her eyes down. "It is not possible, is it, to serve two mistresses?"

"No, I should think it quite a struggle for someone with a conscience." Giles offered her his arm and smiled with twinkling blue-green eyes. "Shall I walk you in?"

She took his arm, and they headed back inside together, up the staircase to the hall, where her father, with Barnaby and Ellen, was waiting to conduct her back to Monk's Place.

SIXTEEN

Cecilia and Thomasin were sorting through the haberdasher's chest, which sat on the floor in the parlour at Monk's Place. Pieces of braid, ribbon, buttons and laces were all mixed together in a swirling cloud of colours. They only had the morning to select the items they wished to use before servants called to collect the chest and return it to the merchant.

"There is so much here, and of such beautiful work," said Thomasin.

"It's the best the merchant could find; Father says he imports from Venice and Florence, so we should look very much in the latest style. I heard Anne Boleyn talk about all the Italian dresses at the French court, and their beautiful gardens."

"Perhaps our French bonnets are already out of date, then?" Thomasin asked.

"Not at all. But the latest things are all from Venice. That's where the gold tissue for our masque costumes came from."

"I wish we might be invited to dance again."

"I am sure that we will."

"You sound certain."

"The king told me, and we are well-liked at court. Lady Anne would have us in her household if she could."

"He told me the same."

"But she needs a proper household first, before she can have more ladies. And she cannot do that until the dowager Catherine has left court."

"The dowager Catherine? Who hosted your betrothal dinner? Do you no longer call her queen? How have you changed so completely in your thinking?" Thomasin was shocked.

Cecilia frowned. "It was explained to me, by Mr Hatton and George Boleyn. Anne's court is the new court, and Catherine will soon be leaving for Windsor. I am very grateful for all the kindness she has shown me, for the sake of our parents' former friendship, but the times are changing and we must change with them."

"They are friends still! Do not let Mother hear you speak in this way."

"Friendship aside, we must look to our futures."

"But yours is already secure. These thoughts are lacking in compassion, Cecilia."

Cecilia made no reply, preferring silence, and Thomasin was reminded of how many times her sister had been unable to feel the pain of others.

They returned to the chest of ribbons, foraging around for treasure, but the harshness of her sister's change of heart hung heavy in Thomasin's mind.

Cecilia pulled out a long piece of golden lace. "This might work upon a cap? Wound around the centre?"

"You're thinking of Henry Kytson? It's very flamboyant."

"True," Cecilia said, "he is not that kind of man."

Thomasin's fingers wrapped hopefully about a wide piece of black ribbon. "How about this?"

"It's so sombre. If he wore that to get married in, I think I should cry at the altar. Wouldn't it be some kind of sign? As to how the marriage would be?"

"Of course it wouldn't; don't be silly. There must be something; keep looking."

"I really don't know what to expect," Cecilia said, digging her hands in up to the wrists and swirling the strands about. "It feels like I am looking for a ribbon not just for adornment, but to tie things to keep them together. Does that make sense?"

"Do you think Henry is giving much thought to his wedding apparel?"

"I am sure he has given it sensible consideration."

"Yes, sensible consideration, you are right there."

"He is more a sensible consideration sort of man than a dancing in a masque man, isn't he?"

Thomasin scarcely knew how to answer this, astute as it was, and ominous. "Keep looking, I am sure we will find something suitable."

"How about this?" Cecilia pulled out a piece of embroidered border, with black and gold work, sewn with tiny pearls. "Isn't it beautiful?"

Thomasin took the end of it in her hands and examined the stitches and design. "It is far too beautiful to waste on Sir Henry. You must use it."

"But where? My gown is already complete. I suppose it might be stitched about the hem, or edge the veil? No, it would be too heavy for that. You should wear it, about your waist."

"Oh, I couldn't."

"Why not?"

"The finest must go to the bride. It is your day, after all. Perhaps you might find a place for it in your trousseau?"

They heard the dogs, coming out of Matthew's study in response to some yet unheard sound. Their claws clicked down the wooden floorboards towards the hall, where they started a low whine in anticipation, rising to small yelps of excitement. Feet were crunching on the gravel outside and up the steps, coupled with muffled voices, before the door was opened.

Barnaby, Ellen and Dorothy had been out walking in the city and took off their cloaks. The Marwood girls fell silent as the clatter of feet and voices came closer. Thomasin sensed, and resented, the coming intrusion. She wished she had closed the parlour door.

"Oh, what have you there?" Ellen stood on the threshold. "Are these things for the wedding? May I look?" She stood over the chest, gazing at the pieces inside. "Oh, but this is all so beautiful. Have you chosen anything yet?"

"No luck yet," replied Thomasin briskly. "We're still looking."

Ellen's plump hand had already slipped inside, pulling out a long piece of pink silk. "Oh, but look at this! You must wear this!" She held it up and turned it around. "Look, Dorothy, look at these beautiful things."

Dorothy was hovering in the doorway, looking pale. When her name was spoken, she ventured a step inside.

Ellen laced the pink silk over her head. "Wouldn't this look fetching on a bonnet? My old square grey one needs something to lift it. This would be perfect. It would freshen it up beautifully for the wedding. You don't want it, do you, Cecilia? Barnaby? Barnaby?" She took the ribbon out into the hallway, following her husband down to the back room. "I must have this, to trim my bonnet for the wedding."

Dorothy promptly trotted up the stairs, leaving Barnaby and his wife discussing the merits of ribbons. Quietly, Thomasin got up and shut the parlour door.

"So, has the bride found anything she likes?" Thomasin asked.

Cecilia did not answer. When Thomasin looked up, she saw her sister staring into the chest, her usual composure broken.

"What is it? Was it Ellen?"

Cecilia let out a heavy sigh. "It's Henry. I can't marry him. I can't be his wife."

Thomasin was shocked. "But why?"

"I just can't. The thought of it. Of him."

Thomasin pictured Sir Henry Kytson, with his plain, simple face and the quiet eyes. There was something colourless about him that the chest of ribbons had brought into sharp relief. "I am sure he is a good man and will treat you with kindness."

"But to live with him, every day. What sort of a life will it be?"

"A good, secure one. A dignified, protected one. How long have you felt this way?"

"The past few days. He is so old. It would be like having another father. Can you ever see him dancing, or laughing? I have never seen him laugh."

"But you have seen him very little so far. You will get to know each other well enough. This is nervousness; it will pass. It is quite natural, I am sure."

"But what if I find I cannot love him, or even cannot like him?"

"I know what Father would say to that. You will give him the love and honour that his position deserves."

"But I have seen court life, seen what might be. How can I marry and be shut away again in the country, when I am wanted at Anne's court?"

"There will be many opportunities for you to come to town. The Kytsons have a house. I am sure if you speak with Sir Henry, he will be most kind about your wishes. And you will have children to keep you busy."

"Do you ever wonder what marriage will be like? How it might be different, with different husbands?"

Thomasin fell silent. It was not a question she had ever pondered, but then she was not on the verge of marriage. She thought again of Cecilia and William Hatton, in Anne Boleyn's chamber, and dancing in the masque.

The chest of ribbons sat between them.

"I cannot marry him."

"Is there any other reason why you say so?"

"Like what?"

Thomasin paused, wondering whether or not to broach the question, but her sister was being uncharacteristically open. "The thought of another husband? I only ask because you mentioned it yourself."

"I have barely been at court. How might I think of another husband?" Cecilia snapped back.

"You are sure?"

"Of course I am sure!"

"So what will you do? The contracts are signed, the arrangements are so far advanced, and supported by the king and queen. Do you think Father will be content to call it off now?"

Cecilia stared at the floor. "No, I do not."

"You will feel differently tomorrow."

"No, I will not."

The parlour door swung open and Ellen, decked in strips of pink satin, floated into the room. "He has relented. I can have the ribbon! I have the best husband in all of London!"

Thomasin was seated at her mother's bedside, reading from *The Lives of the Saints*, when the servant knocked.

"Please, my Lady, there is a caller for Mistress Thomasin."

"A caller?" asked Elizabeth, propping herself up on the pillows. "What kind of caller? A tradesman or a guest?"

"A gentleman, my Lady."

"And what is his name?"

"He did not give his name."

"Then, pray, go back down and ask it." Elizabeth tutted in exasperation as the man scuttled away. "I must speak with my brother about his household; you expect more from London servants. Now come, put down the book and let me look at you."

"It is probably just another merchant with velvets or laces."

"But it may not be. Where is the French bonnet? Put it on, just in case."

"Mother, stop fussing. This bonnet will do as well."

The servant came climbing back up the stairs. "It is Sir Giles Waterson, my Lady."

"Sir Giles!" Elizabeth looked surprised, then turned interested eyes upon her daughter.

Thomasin was just as surprised. "I saw him very briefly after the masque, and we exchanged a few words. I didn't expect this. I shall go down to him."

Giles was waiting in the parlour, where the chest of ribbons still stood on the table from that morning. Thomasin caught him off-guard, peering out of the window at the garden, in a fawn and rust-coloured doublet, with a dark velvet cloak. His blue-green eyes smiled at her as he turned round, with the mischief of the diner whose plates she had shared.

"Good day, Mistress Thomasin. I thought I might take the liberty of calling to see how you fare today."

"We are all very well, thank you, save for Mother, who is a little infirm."

"Excellent, save for your mother, to whom I wish a speedy recovery. I have just seen you have very fine gardens here;

would you show them to me? It's so rare to find such good gardens in the city these days."

They walked together out into the end courtyard, through the gate and onto the gravel path where the herbs grew. It was an overcast day and not too cold, with the grey light making all seem a little gloomy. Leaves were starting to clog the verges, turning from the reds, oranges and yellows of the trees to sludgy brown underfoot.

"Mind your step here," Giles warned. "Get your servants to sweep this away."

"If any can be spared from the wedding preparations," replied Thomasin, a little too quickly. "Sorry, that sounded ungrateful, but I will be glad when all this is over, I think."

"Quite understandable. I try to avoid weddings wherever possible."

"Oh?" She looked at him with interest.

"Yes, well, you know. Son of a large landowning family, heirs required; although I'm not the eldest, at least, so there is less pressure, but my father keeps seeking out suitable brides for me. Would you believe he even mentioned yourself?"

"Really?" Thomasin pretended to be surprised. "How terrible. Think of us having to share a table."

He laughed. "Yes, indeed. You'd be stuck with Sir Mustard Pork, although the everyday me is far more agreeable. Or so I think."

"Where do your family come from?"

"Surrey. We have lands near Guildford, not too far away. I came to court as a young man, as a page to the king."

"All this time at court and no woman has managed to catch you yet?"

"Sorry…" He paused, stilled by memories. "I should have said: I was married before, but I am now widowed."

"Oh." Thomasin's heart fluttered. "I am so very sorry."

"It was three years ago. She died in childbed, her and the baby. These things are common, are they not?"

"I believe so," she replied, words failing her.

"Come, show me this lovely long walk down to the river, and let's talk of happier things. Where did you grow up?"

Thomasin led him to the covered passageway, where they had a view across the whole garden, with its different trees and shrubs, its pathways and beds. The line of statues down the side watched them pass, while she chattered away about Suffolk life, the countryside and her own gardens at home, especially the rose gardens and nut walk.

"It sounds a lovely place. You clearly miss it very much."

"I do," she replied softly. "I had not really thought about it much until I started speaking of it, and now I find myself quite longing to see it all again."

"You will, soon enough. But court has its allure, doesn't it?"

"It does."

"I saw that in your eyes last night. You were positively radiant after your evening."

"Oh!" Thomasin was surprised at the compliment. "Thank you. It was the dancing, I am sure."

"You looked very much as if court life suited you."

"Yes." She stared out across the lawn. "I suppose I did feel that way last night."

"And today?"

Thomasin thought. "Today, I think how nice it would be to be two people, one of whom could remain at court dancing forever, and one who might slip away to the country and live among the trees of the nut walk."

Giles smiled. "I think many of us would like to be able to do that, to escape some things."

"I didn't mean to escape, I meant to experience both."

"Yes, I know you did."

She wondered at his meaning, but then they reached the midway point, where the sundial was set in the wall, and he paused to look at the carvings.

"Is this new? How long ago was this made?"

"Oh, I don't know. It's my first stay here, well, since I was little. I think I remember the walk being here then, but I don't remember particular things so much, like the sun dial."

"It's beautiful — Flemish, if I'm correct."

"Oh? You know much about art? Or Flemish art?"

"I've travelled a little in the Low Countries and France. Diplomatic missions, mostly, which sounds more interesting than it is, carrying letters and getting signatures on trade treaties."

"But it is an opportunity to see the world, regardless."

"Oh yes, I have been most fortunate in that respect. Is that something you would like to do; see the world?"

"I had never really thought of it before now, but I suppose I would. This last week has made me aware of the scope of the world outside my Suffolk home."

"Indeed," he smiled. "There is a vast world out there. Antwerp, Mechelen, Ghent and the Empire are most beautiful to discover. And of course, there are courts there, too."

They walked on, towards the little quay that jutted out above the Thames. The smell of the river was soon upon them, with its odd mixture of fresh and rotten tones.

"I suppose," Thomasin continued, thinking of Cecilia, "it depends why you are at court, or how you are there, whether by right, or by marriage, whether by choice or not."

"I suppose it does," he echoed. "What makes you say that?"

"I was just thinking how it must be an unhappy situation to be trapped somewhere that is not of your choosing, in a situation that may be painful."

"Like the queen?"

Thomasin hadn't been referring to Catherine, but she saw the description fitted her well. "Yes, her position must be a painful one."

"The court is, for her, like a gilded cage. One that used to welcome her, entertain and sustain her, glory her name at every turn. Now it has become her prison, poor lady."

"Will she leave?"

"Yes, she departs for Windsor soon, but will return for the Christmas season. She must be seen to be the queen, and the people love her; if she stays away too long, the Boleyns will gain more ascendancy."

"My sister Cecilia is quite taken with them, I fear."

"I had heard," Giles replied tentatively, "that you are too."

Thomasin was surprised. "Me?"

"Am I wrong?"

"I just wonder why you would say so."

"Oh dear." He walked on. "We are only newly friends, and yet I fear we might be about to fall out. I do hope not, it was kindly meant."

"You have not yet said what made you say so."

"No," he said, "I have not. It was merely that I have heard it remarked that you have been seen in the company of Viscount Boleyn's ward. Forgive me if I overstep the mark; that was what led me to think you favour their cause."

Thomasin disliked the thought of being observed and spoken about. "I detest causes and factions. I do not wish to choose between anyone; I go where I am invited and I am grateful."

"And that generous attitude will get you far, my Lady, but where you go, and who you go with, will be taken as an endorsement."

Thomasin fell silent.

"I do not mean to offend," he added, as they approached the river, "only to advise you, as a friend who has been much at court, not to nail your colours to any mast too soon."

They stood, looking out over the water, as the little craft sailed back and forth. A pair of swans were gliding on the current, followed by a string of grey cygnets.

As they walked back, with something of a cloud between them, Thomasin thought of the moments she had spent with Rafe, in the gardens and ground of the palace, in sight of anyone who might have been there to see them. She thought of the kiss in the antechamber, where the door stood open, and he had led her out by the hand; the outdoor banquet after the joust, when he had led her into the palace on his arm. Whose eyes had been upon them? Whose tongues had been wagging? She had behaved incautiously, if such rumours had reached Giles's ears.

They spoke a little of the weather, of the gardens and the wedding, until the point when they had almost returned to the house.

"I will take my leave of you, my Lady," Giles said with a small bow. "I do hope you have not taken offence at my words; they were kindly meant. You are new to court and you do not yet know what a cruel place it can be. I hope you will still think of me as your friend, as I intend to remain the same, as often as I can be."

"Of course."

She extended her hand and he kissed it, then departed smartly for the stable.

Thomasin turned away from the house, away from the covered walk, and into the gardens themselves, where small paths led her in winding and roundabout routes. And she followed them slowly, as her thoughts were racing, and among the flowers and trees, she hoped to find some peace.

It was easy, she mused, all too easy, to be drawn in by a handsome face. When she first saw Rafe, in the walled garden at court, when she was walking with her father, she had been quite overwhelmed by his beauty. The blue-black hair, the dark tapering eyes, the broad shoulders: she had never seen anyone who looked quite like him. It had clouded her judgement, perhaps making her see him as more than he was. And he still had that effect upon her, she admitted. If he were to appear now, in all his beauty, she would struggle to resist him.

But just how much did she know about Rafe Danvers? Beyond the fact that she longed for him to hold her again, and kiss her again, with his hands in her hair, as he had in Anne's chambers, what did she actually know about him? He was a ward of Viscount Boleyn, but otherwise, he was as a blank slate to her. His childhood, his family, his experiences at court, his thoughts, his wishes, remained a mystery to her. What path was he destined for? A man of his age must have formed attachments, dreamed of certain things, and yet he had shared none of them with her. There was no doubt that he desired her, and she remembered the sight of him in the moonlight outside the front of Monk's Place, begging to be let in. And what then, had she acquiesced? Would he have shared her bed? Married her, or left her, having taken her honour?

Thomasin passed between the rose bushes, where the last pink and yellow blooms were dying. And then there was Giles, who, if she understood correctly, had made the trip out to Monk's Place in order to warn her about Rafe. The Rafe whom she had seen speaking secretly with the viscount, who seemed to have a heavy hand in his business. Then she thought of Cecilia, who was about to be wed to Sir Henry Kytson, yet had declared her aversion to him just that morning, and also of Queen Catherine, caught in the gilded cage she used to love. It was time to step back a little, to breathe and observe, time for reflection and caution.

"Thomasin! Mistress Thomasin!"

It was Ellen, coming tentatively down the path. The moment of solitude had passed.

"I am sent by your mother to tell you two things. Jane Dudley, wife of John Dudley, has had her child. It came early. It is a boy. And the other thing is that you are summoned to go riding with the queen in the morning."

"Wait, what?"

"The two messengers came at the same time. It was quite a lot of excitement, and I am very jealous that the queen favours you."

"And Cecilia?"

"No, the invitation is for you alone."

Thomasin felt this mark of favour profoundly. "Very well, thank you."

"Are you coming in? It is almost time for supper."

"By and by, I will come."

SEVENTEEN

"When I was a girl in Spain," said Queen Catherine, slowing her horse down to a trot, "we would ride for days, from one palace to another, and then on again, all over the country. It was nothing like this. England is so green and so wet; there it was mountains, mountains everywhere, dry and hot, with the earth baked and the trees heavy with olives and oranges and pomegranates."

She was dressed in the most magnificent gown of green velvet, slashed to show the tawny tissue below, laced and tied with gold. Her long hair, once red-gold, now streaked with grey, was twisted up under her headdress, studded with jewels, and she looked at the countryside ahead with pale blue eyes.

"And the spires of great churches," added the man at her side, "rising out of the walled towns, pointing towards God."

"You never forget the place you were born, Juan," Catherine sighed, "and as you arrived in Aragon, and I was born in Castile, we represent the best of Spain between us."

"The very best, as Your Highness knows, as your dear parents knew, God rest their souls, when they united those two kingdoms."

"And Cardinal Mendoza?" She turned back to look at one of the riders behind them. "He is also a Castilian, I believe, as is my Lady Willoughby, so we have the greater numbers."

Thomasin was riding behind the queen, on a horse trapped with red velvet. It was a mare, steady and sedate, which was why, Catherine explained, she had been chosen for Thomasin, although she was a little larger than Thomasin was used to. Trotting through the park and into the forest, Thomasin held tightly to the reins with their little silver bells. Beside her rode Maria Willoughby, who was smiling as she listened to them talk.

"They will be picking the green olives now," Maria called forward, her mind burrowing deep in the past. "Laying sheets under the trees and shaking the loose ones off."

"Oh, that sound," reminisced Catherine, "that gentle thud, thud, as they fall on the ground."

"The sound of harvest. Manna from Heaven."

"And do you remember," Catherine replied, "lying awake on winter nights at Alcala de Henares, and listening to the howling of wolves?"

"I do, I do, we could not sleep. We thought they would creep up into the castle and eat us in our beds."

"Perhaps they still will," replied Catherine wistfully.

They had reached the crest of a hill, rising slow and gently for the last half mile. The valley lay ahead, stretched out in its greenery, the path winding its way through clusters of trees. Pausing for a moment, to enjoy the view, Catherine turned her horse around and looked back at her company, perhaps twenty companions she had chosen, and the same number of servants and guard following behind.

"Is it not glorious?" she asked. "I think you can almost breathe England, breathe its greenness, like taking a long, cool drink. And this is my land! My adoptive country. For eighteen years I have been queen of all this realm!"

"Long live the queen!" cried a gentleman from the back.

"Long live the queen," Thomasin echoed along with the others.

The party rode on, two by two, until they reached a clearing in the forest, where tents had been set up and braziers were burning. Servants, sent on ahead, came to help them dismount and led away the horses. Thomasin watched the queen's ladies, in their elegant dresses, as they saw to her attire and made sure she was comfortable. Some were Spanish, some English, some young and some older in years, led by Maria, chattering among themselves. Remembering the queen's words on the day they met, Thomasin wondered what it might be like to do such a job, going wherever the queen went and sharing her joys and sorrows.

"And now, we shall feast and celebrate this beautiful day," commanded Catherine. "Come, I will have Vives and Fisher on one side, and More and Mendoza on the other."

Thomasin was shown to a spot a little further down the table, between Lady Willoughby and a young woman in her early twenties, with intense eyes and a long, sharp nose that had the look of investigation about it.

"This is Margaret Roper, Thomas More's daughter," explained Maria, as they took their seats. "And beside her, her husband William. She is fearsomely clever and has read hundreds of books, more than I read in my lifetime!"

Margaret's lips curled pleasantly. "There is still time, Maria. You may borrow some of mine."

"Ah, I prefer to dance and sew and pray and think of the old times. Too much reading will strain my poor eyes."

"You are Thomas More's daughter?" asked Thomasin. "I think my uncle may have plundered your library for my sake a few days ago. Sir Matthew Russell?"

"Russell? Oh yes, he did come and take some books — a strange mix, though. I hope you found something useful among them."

Thomasin did not like to admit she hadn't returned to the pile that still sat upon the window ledge in her chamber. "He had one upon the stars, which I confess I have found difficult to follow."

"Have you read Erasmus?"

Thomasin shook her head at the unfamiliar name.

"Erasmus of Rotterdam, our good friend, who has stayed with us in Chelsea, and in London. He has written so many books, on so many things, but you might start with *In Praise of Folly*, as I judge that to be his best."

Thomasin laughed. "I know folly well enough. Does any man praise it?"

Her neat answer pleased Margaret, who smiled again, as their glasses were being filled with wine. "Only Folly herself, in the book, before she starts to point her finger at the Church!"

"At the Church?"

"For all its excesses and superstitions. Because she is Folly, she can see it in others. It is really a book that will open your eyes. You have not heard of it?"

"No," Thomasin replied, "it has not yet arrived in darkest Suffolk, but is it one of these banned books? Even I have heard of dangerous books that threaten our souls."

She remembered sitting in the little Suffolk church while the vicar preached against a German monk called Martin Luther. She hadn't followed all the finer points of theology, but she understood the general theme, that Luther was attacking the old ways of worship, like the shrines of Saints and pilgrimage, and that copies of his works were to be burned before they spread like a disease.

"No, heavens no, there is nothing heretical in it — reformist, certainly, but no heresy. It is clever and amusing; the king himself was greatly amused by it, so there can hardly be any harm in it. Erasmus writes Folly as a goddess and her ladies as all the vices, like pleasure, inebriation, self-love and flattery."

"Now, why do you pick out those of all the many possible vices?" asked her husband, attacking a suckling pig in herbs that had been placed before them. "Surely you mean to draw no parallel with the court today?"

And Thomasin at once made the leap to a comparison with Anne Boleyn's circle. Was that what Mr Roper had intended?

"Nothing of the sort," said Margaret, with playful archness. "But it has always struck me as unjust that Erasmus made Folly a woman. Don't you agree, Thomasin? Which is the more foolish sex, men or women?"

Thomasin smiled. "I am sure there are equal numbers of fools on both sides."

"And all here at court," Margaret laughed. "Does not Folly say that life would be dull without her?"

"So she must make endless noise and mischief," answered Roper, "and as we may conclude, no man is wise at all times, or without his blind side."

Thomasin thought of King Henry, blinded by the dazzling dance of Anne Boleyn, prepared to put aside the virtuous Queen Catherine, creating scandal and division at court. And then, with a flush of shame, she thought of herself, of the blindness brought about by her lust for Rafe. One glimpse from those dark eyes and her reason and good sense flew out of the window. Not all attraction was wrong, surely, but it must be kept in check, seen for what it was, in balance with the world. And some attractions, perhaps, might even be dangerous.

"And pleasure," added Roper, with a smile, "surely there is always room for pleasure? It is what makes life so enjoyable, and God himself created us with the desire for it. Such a pleasurable occasion as this contains no folly, don't you think, Mistress Marwood?"

"None that I have seen," replied Thomasin.

"It is best to stay away from folly of all kinds," said Maria Willoughby, on her other side. "It only leads to danger, like treaties and marriages and wars. We know all about those."

"But that's the very problem," added Roper, speaking across Margaret and Thomasin. "How do we know folly when we see it? It might be dressed up as a goddess or decked in gold chains like a king. Folly itself is good at making fools of us all."

The servants brought jars of wine. Thomasin held up her glass to be filled.

"Is this not perfection?" asked Catherine, raising her voice to address the table. "Surely there must be a scene like this in your Utopia, More? A queen and her court, feasting in the forest, talking of philosophy and theology?"

Thomasin recognised the man she had previously seen at York Place: middle-aged, close-shaven, with the same intense eyes as his daughter.

"You are right, as always. It was remiss of me," replied More, in all seriousness. "I confess I forgot to include such a scene. I must return to Bucklersbury at once and write an additional chapter, just as this is, an idyll of perfection, with every leaf painted in full, and each beetle crawling upon it, and get it out to the printers by the morning."

He pretended to rise in his seat as he said this, making a show of leaving, so that the company laughed at him.

"Stay a while, another day will not matter," said the Spaniard Vives, on Catherine's other side, "when you have already been so foolish."

"Foolish indeed," agreed More, resuming his seat, "when there is such venison to be had at this table, for I should be quite unable to write from lacking it. I always write better on a full belly, such is the way God has created man."

"And woman," added his daughter, "but where is the venison? We have only pork down here."

"For shame!" cried Catherine. "Venison for the poor scholars at the end, that they may better recover their wits."

"So tell us," said a lean-faced, ascetic-looking man seated beside Vives, "ten years on, would you write it differently, your Utopia, if you could? Can time change what we consider perfection?"

More looked up at his questioner. "Fisher," he pronounced, "I know that Bishops must ride and eat, but must you also trouble us with such difficult questions? I cannot begin to rewrite a book I wrote ten years ago whilst I am digesting this meat. Please, my friend, do it for me. Pick up the pen and create your Newtopia. Then I will take my turn again in ten years' time."

Fisher laughed. Thomasin would not have guessed that he was a bishop, for he was dressed plainly, without any trappings of the Church, in a simple dark riding suit. Looking closer, though, she could see that he wore a great ring on the fourth finger of his right hand, a square block of gold, set with a pale stone.

"I would not presume," he replied to More, eating most delicately.

"Whyever not? Your sermons are lively enough. I still recall the one you wrote after the Field of Cloth of Gold, all about riches disappearing into dust. You have the gift, John, why not use it?"

Fisher smiled wryly. "I hope I use all the gifts God was good enough to bless me with."

"Are you new to court, then?" Margaret Roper asked Thomasin. "I've not seen you before, although I am not a frequent visitor there."

"Yes, we've only been here just over a week, for my sister's wedding."

"Oh, who is she, and who does she wed?"

"Her name is Cecilia, and upon Thursday she will become the wife of Sir Henry Kytson."

"Henry Kytson?"

"You know him?"

She looked to her husband. "Well, perhaps Will knows him better than I, but he is a wonderfully learned man, and a great favourite of the queen. Has he spoken to you of his mathematical tract?"

Thomasin was surprised to find Kytson spoken of in such glowing terms. "No, no, he hasn't mentioned it."

"Intelligence and wit combined," Margaret smiled, "and he is well known for his singing and playing upon the lute — I hope you will have heard it — and there is no man in England, even the king, who is such a true shot with the bow. Your sister is indeed a fortunate woman."

"From what you say, I am inclined to believe you, although I do not think my sister has had sufficient time yet to view all Sir Henry's good qualities."

"I hope she will see them as he deserves. He is too modest to push them forward, as he is always thinking of others first. Such a husband is to be prized."

Thomasin ate thoughtfully, as the servants brought fruit tarts and wafers. People were often not what they seemed, at court. Some were upfront and wore their characters like their clothes, colourful and showy, for all to see, while others hid their lights, burying their worth under politeness. It wasn't possible to know people's true value after such a short period of time, either for good or bad.

"Look, here he comes," smiled Catherine, turning to face the direction of the road and rising to her feet.

The party ceased their chatter and watched the tall, lone figure approach on horseback, wondering who it might be. A tall man in his late twenties dismounted with a smile.

"Reginald," called Catherine, as he knelt before her. "We are happy to see you again. I hear you are made Dean?"

Reginald Pole was the son of Margaret, Countess of Salisbury, in whose care the Princess Mary currently resided at Ludlow Castle.

"Dean of Exeter, by the king's grace," he smiled.

"And how is your dear mother? Does she keep an excellent eye upon the princess?"

"I saw them only last week and they are both in the best of health."

"God be praised. Thank you for your news. Come, sit with us, it is so good to see your face."

As soon as he was seated, Queen Catherine raised her glass and called for silence in her heavy accent. "My friends. Now we are all here, I would say a few words."

The daylight showed her age, in the lines about her eyes and mouth and the sallowness of her skin, but it was an age of dignity and experience.

"It is unusual for me to have you all here in one place: bishops, deans, scholars, friends, under this leafy canopy together, far from the court. I confess, it is all deliberate. I wished to have only my friends with me today, whom I can trust, to come together where there can be no watchful eyes and twitching ears to hear us."

The guests smiled back at her, with their sense of having been chosen. Thomasin blushed to be included among them on such a slender acquaintance.

"Dear friends, as you are aware, through no choice of my own, I am about to embark upon the fight of my life. I was destined to be England's queen since I was three years old. I left my beloved homeland and my mother's side when I was little more than a girl, to come to a strange country. I was married and widowed, then eighteen years ago, I was married again and crowned in Westminster Abbey, as my parents and the late king decreed.

"Yet, in all my years as Arthur's widow, through penury, illness and broken health, I never suffered as I am suffering now. My husband of eighteen years, the king, once so tender and loving, who rode in the lists as my knight, Sir Loyal Heart..." Her voice wavered for a moment, but she recovered herself quickly. "My husband seeks a way to put me aside, so that he might remarry. He wants this Boleyn girl who was in my service, a mere servant, to replace a queen. A family who have risen up through trade. And in order that he may bed her, he asks me to retire to a nunnery, me, the daughter of Ferdinand of Aragon and Isabella of Castile. And my daughter, our dear Lady Mary, Princess of Wales, what of her inheritance? Is she to be set aside as a bastard for the sake of children that whore might bear?

"Tomorrow there opens a court at York Place, run by that butcher's son Thomas Wolsey, who will presume to investigate my private affairs, my intimate moments and secret griefs, which I have laboured long and hard to conceal, being known only to God. They are now to be pulled apart by a man like that! It has been God's pleasure to grant me many children by the king, but in his wisdom, it has also been his will to take them from us, and his will must be accepted."

Murmurs of sympathy ran around the table.

"So I will fight this matter, this questioning of God's choices, for the sake of my own soul and that of my husband, and the future of my daughter. I have dispatched messengers to my nephew, the Emperor, and the Pope, who I am sure will not permit these calumnies to be taken seriously. My dear friends, difficult times lie ahead. It is your love and loyalty upon which I must rely, as you have proven to me time and time again, and for the sake of which I may need to call upon you for testimony. I thank you, before I depart for Windsor, from the depths of my heart. Brace yourselves for the week ahead. Pray for me, and I will pray for you. Your good health, my dear friends."

Thomasin found her words unexpectedly moving. The pride and stoicism of a woman against whom time had turned. A woman who had once been the glittering jewel of the court, with all lying before her, and the hopes, certainties and dreams of youth. The years had surprised Catherine, creeping up behind the young queen who had danced at Henry's side, who shared his bed, bore his children and seen all but one die. One morning, suddenly, her beloved husband was trying to consign her to the past. And Henry was a man who got his way.

Cardinal Mendoza climbed unsteadily to his feet, seeming older than a man of his years. "Dearest Lady, be assured of our constant prayers on your behalf. I will write again to the Emperor and appraise him of your situation. So long as I am able to hold a pen and have lips to speak, you shall have an advocate in me."

"And in me," echoed Bishop Fisher, "as I will defend your marriage as legitimate in God's eyes, as well as the rights of the Princess Mary."

"And I," added Thomas More, "for all that is right and true in Christendom. A toast to Our Lady, the queen, God preserve and protect her in this time of trial."

Thomasin drank with the others, and listened to their talk, wondering at her place at the table. Cecilia had not been invited, but that had been judged quite rightly, for her sympathies had been swiftly seduced by the glamour of the Boleyns. It might have seemed, to anyone who had watched Anne's masque, that Thomasin, too, was won over, but the thrill of that evening sat in her heart alongside a well of sympathy for the queen. It was almost as if whoever had invited her to the picnic today had seen inside her heart.

The feast was over, and the horses were being brought round, when Thomasin found Catherine at her side.

"I hope you have passed a pleasant day, Mistress Marwood."

"Most pleasant indeed. I thank you, my Lady."

"I wonder if you are surprised at your presence here?"

Thomasin smiled at her recent thoughts. "A little, I confess."

The queen nodded, her splendidly decked headdress shaking like a galleon. "You are a good, kind girl. Court has not yet spoiled you, as it does with many. As the daughter of one of my old friends, I feel as if I know you better than our brief acquaintance would allow."

"You are most gracious, my Lady."

"It is important, Thomasin, at all times of life, to find the right friends. Today, you have seen some of mine: good men and women of learning and faith. I would be pleased to count you among them."

"I am honoured…"

"You would do well to cultivate friendships with such good men and be mindful of those who try to influence you for their own sakes. It is too easy to think of earthly things and take our minds off the spiritual. Pray often and go to confession. Remember God sees all."

Thomasin had not been to church since arriving in London, and resolved to speak to her mother about it once she returned to Monk's Place.

"You are aware that I depart for Windsor shortly. I am aware of your sister's forthcoming wedding and your mother's illness. Under other circumstances, I would already have asked whether you might be willing to join my household, as a lady in waiting, and accompany me, but I know that family matters could make this difficult for you."

The queen took Thomasin's hand. She felt the heaviness and cold smoothness of her many rings. "If I were to ask you, now, to come with me to Windsor, I would expect the answer to be no, so no, do not reply now," she said as Thomasin opened her mouth in gratitude. "I know the time is not right for you, but I want you to know that the offer is open, and you are most welcome. If at any time you would like to join me, you need only send word. You would always be welcome."

"Thank you. I am so honoured, I scarcely know what to say."

"Then say nothing, until you are ready. Up, into the saddle. Give your mother my fondest love."

Thomasin obeyed, climbing up onto the large mare with the tinkling silver bells, and watching the queen walk away, to where her own mount was waiting.

As they made their slow procession back to court, with Thomasin riding between Margaret and Will Roper, she reflected on the dignity and strength of Queen Catherine, and the cruelty of her position. So many years given in service, so many labours resulting in miscarriage and stillbirth, so many prayers offered to God. And she had loved her husband, truly loved him, and still did, Thomasin was in no doubt about that, and yet she was being cast aside after age had crept upon her.

As they came out of the trees and back into the park, the palace lay ahead, beginning to light up in response to the daylight fading. Windows blazed bright, gates and paths were lit by beacons. The roof of the chapel caught the final dying rays of the sun.

They made the last distance in dignified silence, with heavy thoughts of the queen's situation. The palace looked pretty with its mix of roofs and walls, and the collection of life and activities taking place within. In the hall, servants would be sweeping and laying out the tables for dinner and the horses were being groomed in the stables. In the wardrobe departments, servants of the body were cleaning and preparing the king's clothes, wiping the dust off his shoes, laying out his hose in lavender. The kitchens were hot with life and activity, as pans seethed on the stove, pots boiled, herbs were scattered and pastry was being rolled.

"To my chamber," Catherine said softly to her people, tired after her exertions.

Thomasin watched as she was led away to her private entrance, then dismounted with the help of a groom. A stable lad was sluicing the cobbles and another was brushing off the excess water into the central drain.

Margaret Roper was waiting where the flares burned outside the stables. "Mistress Marwood, will you permit us to conduct you back home, as our carriage passes through the city?"

"Oh, that is most kind, thank you."

Thomasin gladly took her place in More's carriage, interested to know the family better. The two women sat on one side, while More and Roper sat opposite.

"I heard a little," began Thomasin, looking up bravely at the sage-faced scholar, "I hope you don't mind me asking, of your book discussed earlier. I forget the name…"

"*Utopia*," he supplied with a gentle smile. "An imagined place of perfection, an island in the far away seas, where governance and society are run along different lines."

"What made you write it?"

"It was something my good friend Erasmus said, when he last visited us, about a painting he had seen, a vast triptych he saw being painted in Brabant, called The Garden of Earthly Delights."

"Oh, it sounds wonderful."

"Doesn't it? When I heard that name first, it set my imagination going. The Garden of Earthly Delights. What might one find there?"

"Endless feasting, jousting and pleasure," laughed Will Roper.

"And an endless library, don't forget," added Margaret.

"What would it mean to you, Mistress Marwood? The Garden of Earthly Delights? What would you find there?"

Thomasin thought of her first night at court, when Rafe had drawn her away from the fire, and given her the pink rose. "I think it would be exactly that, a garden, where everything is untouched, unspoiled and perfect, where people live together in harmony."

"Like the Garden of Eden," said More, "before the Fall?"

"Yes, I suppose so."

"But, do not be fooled; just like Eden, there is darkness in it, and warning, of the pleasures of the flesh. Erasmus described it to me as a vast, ideal landscape being spoiled by mankind's lusts. It made me think of such a place in isolation, perhaps an island, where the people matched the beauty of their surroundings, and everything could be just as it should be. And I wondered what that might look like."

"And where such a place might be found," added Thomasin, full of wonder, thinking that perhaps her gardens at Eastwell might count.

"There's the trick of it," said More. "It's actually rather a sad story, and the clue is in the name. This is where your Greek is needed. Margaret?"

"Utopia," supplied his daughter, "comes from the Ancient Greek, meaning no place."

"No place? So it does not exist?"

"Nor, as I conclude," explained More, "can it exist, due to human nature."

"Oh, I see," said Thomasin thoughtfully, her mind racing with the speed of their conversation. "Yes, that is sad. But it is worth trying, surely, to come as close as possible, perhaps closer than we are now?"

"Not everyone is of your opinion," More added. "Kings will always seek war and riches and glory."

"And new wives," added Will Roper.

"Yes, I felt the queen's grief deeply today," said Margaret. "I don't know what can be done."

More nodded. "Very little. Tomorrow I am summoned to attend the Cardinal's court at York Place, along with Fisher and other theologians and thinkers. The king hopes we will smooth his way for an annulment, but we cannot grant the king what God does not wish for him."

"But surely King Henry will assume that whatever his will, God will fall in line?"

"Now, Margaret, watch your tongue. God created the gulf between thought and speech for good reason."

The carriage pulled in through the gates at Monk's Place, and it was time for Thomasin to bid her new friends goodnight.

"Do not be alarmed, Mistress Marwood," added More, as his parting speech, "by what you have seen of court. Keep true to yourself, true to your beliefs, and God will be true to you. Goodnight."

EIGHTEEN

Thomasin was sitting by the parlour fire. On her lap, a copy of More's *Utopia*, bound in red leather, had fallen idle as she stared into the flames. The others had retired, and sleep was creeping closer, but she had wanted to wait up for her father, to see how the court at York Place transpired and whether the queen was spoke of fairly.

The room was silent but for the crackling of the flames, and she slipped in and out of a half-doze. There was nothing in particular in her mind, just tired musings about the day and her enjoyment of the fire's glow and warmth. Her limbs were growing pleasantly heated.

The commotion in the hall roused her from her reverie. Stepping out to see what was happening, she saw her father, muddied and limping, leaning heavily upon the arm of Rafe Danvers. Rafe, with his dark eyes full of urgency and the hair falling forward across his face. It seemed like a dream to see him, there. Her surprise at his presence was swiftly overridden by her father's need.

"Quickly, into the parlour, sit him down here."

She guided Rafe towards the chair she had just vacated, pushing aside her book and shawl, calling to the servants to fetch hot water and brandy.

"It's nothing, just a sprain, probably, nothing to worry about," said Richard stoically, as Rafe helped him down.

"What happened?"

Her father tried to stretch out his leg and winced.

"It is entirely my fault," said Rafe, "mine and my fellows. We were on an errand, carrying a letter back to court, and we did not think there would be anyone in the streets. We did not see him."

"You knocked him down?" Thomasin was aghast.

"No, no," her father insisted, "they did not touch me. I stumbled as I stepped out of their way."

"We should not have been riding so fast."

"I should not have been in the street. I should have returned to the river, as I had planned."

"You left your boat, Father?"

"Yes, it is my fault. I got to London Bridge and I fancied walking the rest of the way. I know it sounds foolish now, at this late hour."

"Not foolish at all," said Rafe. "We were the ones who were riding too fast. My fellows galloped off at such speed they were unaware of you, and that I had stopped. It was only because I was the last, that I saw you fall."

"Folly on both sides, perhaps," said Richard, bringing to Thomasin's mind the book that Margaret Roper had told her about. "But I am truly grateful, Mr Danvers, for your assistance. I might have managed without it, but it would have taken me much longer, and my spirits would have been far more bruised than they are after your kind attention."

"Might I have a look at your ankle?"

"By all means."

Rafe knelt and carefully removed the brown leather boot to show the lower leg in its black hose. It looked red and a little swollen. With gentle hands, he felt round the ankle and rotated the foot a little. "Yes, it will be swollen up nicely by morning. I do not think it broken, rather a little sprained, as you suggest. I will send a doctor to you first thing in the morning, but it is likely he will prescribe a herbal poultice and plenty of rest."

"Thank you. You know something of medicine?"

"Only a little, from watching my uncle work, when I was a boy."

"Oh. You did not wish to enter his line of work?"

Rafe smiled, his dark eyes softening. "He said I did not have the patience for it. Now, you should try and get up to bed as soon as you can."

"I will, by and by. It has been a most trying day."

Thomasin remembered the trial, the reason for her father's absence. "How was the queen's cause received?"

Her father frowned. "Very ill, indeed. Only Fisher and More dared speak for her, and the king was most displeased." He looked to where Rafe was listening, conscious of his allegiance to the Boleyns. "But we should not speak of this now. It is late."

A servant returned with Matthew, a gown thrown over his night clothes. Between them, they hoisted Richard up to a standing position, sharing his weight. He put a little pressure upon the foot and managed to walk out to the staircase.

"There, I shall be mended in no time. Thank you for your assistance, Mr Danvers."

"If I may, I would like to call in the morning, to see how you fare."

"Very well, if you wish, but for now I will bid you a good night."

Between his two helpers, Richard slowly began to mount the stairs, pausing every few steps. Eventually, they turned the corner on the landing and climbed the second portion, up to the first floor. Rafe and Thomasin were left alone in the hall, listening to the receding footsteps. And again, in spite of herself, she felt the beauty of those dark eyes, with their tapering corners and long lashes.

He turned towards her, hopefully, in anticipation that she might invite him into the parlour.

Quickly, she indicated the front door, saying, "It's late."

"Yes," he admitted, with an air of disappointment. "But would you turn me out so soon? Might I not warm myself by your fire a little, before I go back out into the night?"

She hesitated, sensing this could be unwise.

"Mistress Marwood, I fear I may have offended you somehow. The other night in the gardens at court you left so abruptly, it left me concerned that I may have said or done something that displeased you, and the thought of that troubles me greatly. I would undo whatever harm I may have done, if you would guide my hand."

Her mind was racing. None of her doubts were firm enough to voice, or even to withstand her own private scrutiny. As her father's saviour, it would be rude not to permit him that small kindness.

"You may warm yourself, but not for long, because of the hour." She watched him walk in, with his powerful broad shoulders and back. "Would you like wine?"

"I have drunk enough wine tonight, thank you."

She led him back into the parlour, where he stood before the fire. His dark eyes held her in the flickering light, boring into her with intensity. Her book lay open upon the floor, along with her shawl; she scooped them up and hugged them to her.

"You did not answer my question before, which leads me to believe I have offended you somehow. I offer my sincerest apologies if that is so; it was entirely unintentional and causes me much pain to think on it."

"You have not given me offence," she said quickly.

"Then what?"

Thomasin sighed and pulled the shawl about her shoulders. "It is hard to say. This is all so new to me. I am finding my way through dangerous waters."

"There is a directness about you," he replied, "an honesty, which I like. It is rare at court."

It was the first time she recalled him speaking of her character. "In which case," she added, emboldened, "I cannot help but wonder at the way things are at court. It seems such a glittering but such a cruel world."

"It is exactly that, but it is the only world."

"No," she said in surprise, "it is not. It is like one bright fruit hanging upon a tree, but there are other places, other branches. Until two weeks ago I had never been here, at least not when I was old enough to recall. I lived quite happily in Suffolk, with my gardens and the house, and knew no different. And there are a thousand such houses and gardens, and more, where people live quietly and happily."

"And they are just stars, basking in the light of the moon, wondering where the light is shining from. The court is the world where the rules and lives and tastes of the country are set."

"But yet they are not touched directly by it, nor do they play these tortuous games of allegiance."

"Tortuous games of allegiance? What has upset you?"

"Truthfully, I feel I cannot find my way here. I do not feel certain of it, as if I am walking in shifting sands. It is very difficult to know people here, to judge their characters and see the truth of them."

"Well, I cannot disagree with that. Remember many of those whom you see have grown up at court. They have been shaped by its rules and customs, made for the flattery and games and know no other. In truth, it is one giant game, like chess, knowing where to move next, and how far."

This seemed like an apt metaphor, and Thomasin was encouraged to believe that Rafe understood. "And you? How long have you been at court?"

"I became a ward of the viscount upon the death of my uncle, when I was twelve years old. So I had a brief, quiet life before it all, and I can see the contrast of which you speak."

"What happened to your parents?"

"My mother died soon after childbed and my father of the sweating sickness, when I was just a small lad, so I was sent to my uncle, in St Albans, who worked as a doctor."

"How did you find court, when you first came?"

"Well, I was too young to question it. I was grateful to be taken into such a good household and I did as I was bid, minded my manners, did my lessons, completed my chores."

"And now?"

"Now? I suppose it is my life. When you are at court so often, you get used to its ways, the excitement it brings, all the people. It gives you a feeling of importance, as if your life matters more than just the survival of it, as if God has some plan for you. I have seen the visits of the Emperor, exiled kings, cardinals, bishops, envoys, foreign ambassadors."

"While in Suffolk, I have seen the visits of the butcher, the tailor, the blackbird and the stray sheep."

He laughed. "Can you say, now, that you could go back to Suffolk unchanged? That even if you were happy there, you could rid yourself of the memory of dancing before the king, or feasting in the hall?"

Thomasin thought for a moment.

"Can you say that you would never long to feel that thrill of excitement again, while you are young and strong, full of good health? Fortune's wheel turns so fast."

This was a sentiment against which she could not argue.

Rafe was looking down at her. "Once you have bitten into the court, you never forget its taste."

She met his eyes directly. "Like the forbidden fruit? One bite and all is spoiled?"

"No," he laughed, "no, no, that is not the way to look at it. It is there to be enjoyed. Do not fear it, let it carry you on its wave and see how far it will take you."

"Is that your intention?"

"I suppose so. The Boleyns are on the rise. The king showers them with titles, lands, gifts. Who would not wish to be the recipient of such good fortune? There is nothing immoral in it; it is simply how things have always been."

"And when his favour turns from you? I can't help but feel for Queen Catherine."

"Of course. Everyone feels for the queen, but what is to be done? She can live out her days in comfort and Anne will provide England with an heir. The Boleyns' fortunes will be made, and mine with them."

"And what do you propose to do with that fortune?" Thomasin asked, aware that she was seeking some reassurance about his feelings for her, some suggestion that he intended to settle and marry.

"Why, enjoy it!" He laughed, but seeing her serious expression, added, "Are you sure I have not offended you in some way?"

He was moving closer, but she took a step back. "I am due to leave for the country at the end of this week. I do not know where my path will lie."

"And this makes you doubt me?"

"It makes me fear forming a connection."

He nodded, leaning back from her. "I understand. I will be honest with you: I can't promise you marriage."

It hadn't been the answer Thomasin was hoping for, but his absolute refusal was harsh, heavy. His words were bitter in her ears. "I don't believe we ever spoke of marriage. Or anything even close. And," she added, trying to redress the balance, "my mother already has someone in mind for me."

It was merely a defence. Although Thomasin's mother had spoken once or twice of Sir Giles Waterson, there seemed to be little movement in that direction, and Thomasin had not thought of him as a husband, despite his merriness and kindness.

And all the time, in spite of everything, a little voice inside her was screaming for Rafe to lean in and kiss her.

"Well," said Rafe, his black eyes burning, "if that is the case, you should not be dallying with one such as me."

"Dallying? Is this dallying?"

"Maybe," he said, stepping closer again.

"How do I know?"

"Dallying is … it's a feeling you get."

This time she did not pull back, as the proximity of him made her senses dizzy. Gradually the realisation crept through her that she longed to surrender to him. It was like a warmth spreading through her limbs. In spite of everything, of all that was wrong, she longed to be in his arms.

Both moved at the same time. Their lips met, hot and hard, as he drew her to him. With more passion and more energy than the night in Anne's chambers, he kissed her deeply, drawing out such emotion in her, that she felt overwhelmed. His arms were about her shoulders, dropping down to her waist, and she gingerly lifted her hands, to touch his arm, his chest, his cheek.

His mouth opened, covering hers, as he took control of the kiss. She felt the surprise of tongue, gently against her lips, playfully, then probing inside her mouth. The sensations sent thrills through her, as her head tipped back upon his shoulder and her body relaxed into his arms. And though doubts still swirled at the back of her mind, she pushed them away, wanting to lose herself in the moment. His kiss moved her. It wakened her body and parts of her mind she had been unaware of. The closeness of his body was thrilling. The hands travelling over her shoulders, down her arms and across her breasts. She gasped as he lingered there, stroking the skin above her bodice, as he claimed her again with his mouth. She curved towards him, unable to stop herself, feeling as though she might lose her balance.

He moved her carefully, up against the wall, one hand on her hip, the other tracing downwards along her thigh, trying to bunch up her skirts. Reeling with his kisses, she sensed his intention, and longed to feel his touch. His mouth was more ardent as his fingertips found her skin, just above the knee. The hand was cold and urgent. She wriggled and pulled her hips back, but his fingers moved further up her leg, coming close to touching her intimately. Still, his mouth was on hers, and she gasped for breath between his kisses. She had some idea what happened between a man and woman, having heard tales of local women seduced and shamed, forced to repent in the church, but the feeling was too good. Again, she was torn. Duty called her, but desire mudded her senses. She felt his fingers nudge against the space between her thighs, usually so hidden away and secret under her petticoats.

"Oh God, I want you," he murmured into her mouth.

Thomasin was just trying to regain some breath in order to reply, when she felt the insistence of his fingers, pushing up against her defences.

Her hand went down at once, instinctively, to block him, hold him at bay. She held back his hand, but his fingertips gently stroked against her, and the need that arose in her was almost overwhelming.

"Is there somewhere we can go? Your chamber? I must…"

Suddenly they became aware of footsteps on the staircase. It was painful to break apart, but Rafe walked to the fire just in time, as Thomasin rearranged her skirts.

Matthew pushed open the door and looked inside. "Ah, here you are. Your father is settled in bed. He sent me down to check that all was well."

Thomasin could only nod, stunned and speechless with passion.

"Well, the hour is late. We are truly grateful for your assistance, Mr Danvers, but I believe it is time to lock up the house for the night."

"Of course," Rafe replied, shooting a look at Thomasin. "Please convey my best wishes to Sir Richard; I may call in the morning to check his progress."

He headed for the door, pausing halfway to look back, as if he wished to speak, but was unable to. In desperation, he met her eyes with a pleading apology. At the door, he said again, "Goodnight, goodnight," and disappeared into the darkness.

"Now you, Thomasin," said her uncle, "should not detain a young man, alone, at such an hour. Up to bed with you, go. I will lock up."

She needed no further warning, understanding the dangers entirely, but hurried up the stairs to the seclusion of her waiting bed.

NINETEEN

The stone flags were hard and cold under her knees, even through the folds of her skirts. Thomasin screwed her eyes tight shut and waited. Incense swirled around her, heady and spicy, as the priest swung the censer, back and forth down the aisle towards the altar. She clasped her hands and joined in as the congregation began to recite the prayer.

"Our father, who art in heaven, hallowed be thy name."

Thomasin clung to the words, each one solid as a stone, to shut out her memories of Rafe the night before, to shut out her guilt, and the immodesty of their lust.

"Thy kingdom come, thy will be done, on earth as it is in heaven…"

Thomasin had been grateful when her mother had risen early that morning, descended the stairs and announced her intention to go to church. Her mother was feeling much better in body and required the same treatment for her soul. She proposed attending the little chapel of Our Lady, which was tucked away on a corner of Thames Street, just a short walk from the gates of Monk's Place, in the direction of the Tower. Thomasin had readily agreed to accompany her, feeling that her soul could also do with absolution, and also in the hope of avoiding Rafe's visit that morning.

Pulling on her fur-lined cloak, Elizabeth had looked at herself in the glass and tutted. "Such bags under my eyes, despite all that rest. I must use my rose water before the wedding, and you too, Thomasin. We shall all use it."

"What matters most, Mother, is that you are well again for Thursday, especially now that father is injured too."

"The doctor will see to him this morning. He will be well enough."

"And Cecilia?" Thomasin had asked, realising she had only seen her sister in passing the last few days. "Is she well? Is she ready?"

"Of course she is ready, what do you mean?"

"Is she coming to church with us this morning?"

"The king's carriage called for her earlier; she has been gone this past hour. He has kindly allowed her to choose a small gift from the royal treasury, for the ceremony."

Thomasin was genuinely surprised. "That is an honour I would not have predicted. Is the king really that taken with her?"

"He favours her," Elizabeth had said, almost dismissively. "Why should he not?"

An unpleasant thought occurred to Thomasin, but she had felt it too important not to voice. "You do not think, Mother, that he has any… I don't know how to say it, any expectations of her?"

"Expectations? What do you mean, expectations?"

"You know what I mean, Mother. He does not mean, you know, to have her in his bed?"

To her surprise, Elizabeth had scoffed. "That is what your mind runs on? There is no chance of that."

"Well, you seem certain. But he does seem to favour her." Thomasin had wondered if she should mention Cecilia's outburst the other day over the chest of ribbons. Whether it would be wise to let her mother know about the doubts she expressed, or if it would cause more concern than was needed. It may be that Cecilia had already overcome her fears. She had dismissed the thought. Better to talk to her sister first.

Thomasin opened her eyes. The morning light was streaming down through the windows behind the altar, bright with their pieces of coloured glass. Our Lady was a little, snug church, small enough for only a cluster of people in the congregation. A carved image of the Virgin Mary, in her blue robes and the holy child, white upon her lap, was set upon the altar while the shafts of light from behind brought the pink, green and blue down in pools onto the stone flags beside the spot where she knelt. Again, the censer was wafted by unseen hands, and clouds of incense billowed about them.

The priest was moving along the line, bowed and heavy in his robes. To Thomasin's left knelt her mother, her eyes intent upon the gilded cross and flickering candles, while on the other side waited Ellen Russell, next to her husband Barnaby and her sister Dorothy. The three had appeared at the moment of their departure and had determined to accompany them. Thomasin had walked down Thames Street with Ellen, watching the strange, sedate form of Dorothy walking with Barnaby, having finally emerged from her chamber, after her illness.

"God bless you and keep you, my child," the priest murmured, laying his hand upon the headdress of Elizabeth. Thomasin's mother received a sip of wine from a silver chalice, followed by a small piece of white bread from the platter carried by the altar boy. Crossing herself, she rose slowly, with a twinge and an ache, and returned to her seat.

Closing her eyes, Thomasin felt the blessing land gently upon her head, the slight weight discernible through the plain lines of her black bonnet. Then the chalice bumped against her lips and she opened her mouth to receive wine and bread.

"God bless you and keep you, my child."

As the priest moved on to Ellen, Thomasin felt a rush of shame. God saw everything, he knew everything, he heard everything, even the most secret of acts and the thoughts buried deep in her heart. He knew what had transpired the night before, between herself and Rafe: unclean acts, driven by lust. She had allowed him to use her body for pleasure, and had taken pleasure in it herself, even though she had known it was wrong. The arrival of her uncle Matthew had been timely. She shuddered to think of what might have occurred had they remained alone, but her guilt was tinged with the thrill of excitement. It was that very strength of her desire that scared her the most. There was a well of passion inside her she had never suspected, waiting to spill over. It felt dangerous.

Ellen was nudging her to rise. The next line was waiting to kneel, to receive Communion. Thomasin followed her back to the pew and took her seat. There would be a final hymn, and then the service would be over. Surely Rafe had already paid his visit to Monk's Place by now, and would have had to accept her absence, and go away again? It was for the best. She could not be tempted into sin again if he was not there. Then, after the wedding, she would return to Suffolk, or perhaps go to Windsor with the queen. That possibility had been on her mind the last few days.

Elizabeth was standing on the coloured tiles at the end of the aisle. The bells began to peal out overhead, marking the end of the service. They paused before the little chantry chapel that was devoted to Matthew's aunt, Bridget Russell, paying their respects. A stone plaque set with a bronze figure topped the square stone tomb and winged angels guarded each corner. After a moment of reflection, Elizabeth lit a candle, and Thomasin took a wax taper between finger and thumb. Holding it above her mother's candle, she watched the wick kindle, before setting it upon the stones. The tiny lights flickered in the gloom, bringing to mind the shortness of life, the eternal flame and the memories of loss.

"It is hard to believe ten years have passed since her illness," Elizabeth murmured. "It brings to mind my own frailty, and how easily we pass."

"You are nowhere near your time, Mother."

"We cannot know. We must go when God calls us. We are his humble servants."

Thomasin laid her hand upon Elizabeth's arm and they turned towards the door, where the others waited.

Dorothy was speaking, unusually for her; Thomasin had barely heard her utter a single sentence since her arrival.

"The most charming church and a very moving sermon. If I lived in London, I should come here every day. I know a lot about such things and I make a point of only attending places of the highest quality."

Her words made Thomasin frown. "God is to be found in the most humble place as well as the grandest. He sees everything, no matter where we are."

Dorothy's sallow face turned an unexpected shade of red and clasped hold of her sister's arm. Ellen patted her hand as if to comfort her. They headed for the daylight outside.

A desire to unburden herself came over Thomasin. "Mother, please go on ahead. I wish to make my confession."

Elizabeth's pale brows frowned. "Confession? Now? You have it the wrong way round. You are supposed to confess before you take Communion. And what sins have you been committing whilst I have been laid up in bed, that require such urgent action? Apart from being rude to Dorothy?"

"Nothing, Mother, there is no urgency. I was not rude to Dorothy; I spoke the truth and she did not like it, for some reason."

"Yes, some people do not like to hear the truth."

Thomasin thought this was a strange answer, but the arrival of the priest diverted her attention.

"I will confess, if you don't mind. It seems like a good idea as we are here, and I have not made any confession for weeks now. Look, the priest is free. I will walk back to Monk's Place straight after you."

"Hmm. Mind that you are careful, after your father's experience."

"It is broad daylight, nothing will happen to me."

"Very well. Come straight back. But do not let me discover that you have been up to mischief!"

No, thought Thomasin, watching the others walk away, *you must not discover*.

The little confessional box was cool and dark, made from carved wood. A plain plank for a seat was set alongside the intricate grille, through which she would speak to the priest. Its enclosed privacy was a relief. She sat and waited until she heard the creak of the wood on the other side and saw the blurred shadow of someone enter.

"How may I help you, my child?"

"I need to unburden myself," she replied softly, "of certain sins."

"Sins of the mind or sins of the flesh?"

"Both, I fear. There is a man."

"You are unmarried?"

"Yes, but there is a man whom I have permitted to take certain liberties with my person."

"You are with child?"

"No, no," replied Thomasin, aghast, "nothing like that. But when I am with him, privately, I feel overcome by my desire for him."

"Lust," said the priest. "You are young?"

"Yes."

"It is quite natural in young, unmarried people. Can you marry?"

"No, it is not something we … no, he said as much."

"Why can he not marry?"

"I don't know. He is in service in a great household. I am sure he lacks the means."

"Does he have prospects? Could you marry in the future?"

"I don't know."

"What intimacies have you allowed him?"

Thomasin flushed with shame to put it into words. "I allowed him to kiss me, more than once."

"Anything else?"

"He touched me, in a secret place."

"Outside or underneath your clothing?"

"Underneath. But only briefly, then we were interrupted."

"And if you had not been interrupted," the priest asked, "what then?"

"I cannot say."

"You are intact, you have not been carnally known by a man?"

"No," she whispered, blushing, "I have not."

"I absolve you, my child, on condition that you do not permit this man to come to you again in private. Is he of your household?"

"No."

"And you have protection? Parents or guardians?"

"Yes, I do."

"Then you are fortunate. I counsel you to maintain your distance. If you encounter him again, ensure you are in company. Make excuses to leave if you must. You must remove yourself from the path of temptation. Sinful thoughts are one thing, easily forgiven, but sinful actions have greater consequences. I have seen many young women in your position, who have ended in great trouble and woe after giving in to their desire. If you cannot contract marriage with him, speak to your parents about marriage to a good, honest man. But you must not permit him further liberties with your person."

Thomasin hung her head. "It is the strength of feeling in me. I do not know how to curb it."

"You must pray. When you feel that way, ask God for strength and he will help you. These are tests sent to prove your character, my child, common to all mankind. You are strong enough to resist. God would not send you that which he does not believe you can withstand."

She was silent, torn between the desire to do what was right and submit to the strong emotion within her.

"Remember God sees all, my child."

"Why does he plant such desires in us, if he does not wish us to follow them?"

"To give you a chance to prove yourself. What kind of a life would it be without trial? If everything was easy and there was no struggle? This is how we earn our path to heaven. Use your strength for good. You know this, my child."

"Yes, thank you, Father."

"You are absolved. Go out into the world and be a virtuous child of God. Cherish the body and soul with which he has blessed you. Sin no more with this man, in thought, word or deed."

"Thank you, Father, I will not."

"Return and speak with me if the temptation becomes great again."

"Thank you, I will."

"Let my words plant themselves in your soul like a seed. Water the seed and let it grow, to fill you with virtue and strength. As you go into the world, picture yourself full of the holy spirit."

TWENTY

Monk's Place was quiet upon her return. Thomasin was relieved to see there was no sign of Rafe. She was greeted instead by the dogs, Caesar and Brutus, loose from their usual place in Matthew's study, and roaming freely. Their claws clicked upon the wooden floorboards and their hot muzzles pressed into the palms of her hands. She gave them some attention, rubbing their ears and backs until their tails wagged hard.

Through the back window, she could see Matthew and Barnaby practising their archery, loosing arrows at the colourful butts set up halfway down the lawn. Ellen and Dorothy were walking arm in arm along the paths between the herbs. She watched them for a while, with little inclination to join in, until Elizabeth appeared in her sight, carrying a basket of apples. She headed towards the house and entered by the back door, seeing her daughter standing there.

"There you are, at last. I have just picked these for the kitchen."

"Here, let me take them." Thomasin relieved her mother of the heavy burden. "You should have asked one of the others to bear it for you."

"No, I am well enough, only a little tired. The doctor's diet seems to be working. And we have had another doctor this morning, to look at your father's ankle. I can't keep track of them all. It is just a sprain. He will rest today and tomorrow, to be ready for Thursday."

"Is Cecilia here?"

"Not back yet. That Mr Danvers called while we were at church — and the gifts that have been sent to your father, from Mr Francis Bryan and his friend, Mr Nicholas Carew! I think he should be knocked down more often. You will see them when you take the apples down."

"I will do that now."

"I have taken the liberty of inviting some guests, as we have so much food."

"Guests? Which guests?"

"The gentlemen who sent the gifts. I thought it would be a pleasant opportunity to show that we harbour no hard feelings about the accident."

"You invited Bryan and Carew? And..." Thomasin stammered. "Mr Danvers?"

"Yes, all of them, although Mr Bryan has sent a messenger to say he is attending upon the king tonight. And I invited Cecilia's Henry and that lovely Mr Hatton, and Mr Waterson. We shall be a jolly party."

The list of names horrified Thomasin. All of them, together, around one table? "Does Cecilia know?"

"Lord, child, how can she know, when she has been at court all day? Now, take those apples down for me and find your best dress."

Thomasin made her way down the stone steps into the busy kitchen below, where servants were bustling about the hearth and tables, preparing dishes for that evening's dinner. There was an ominous feeling in the pit of her stomach, bigger than just Rafe's imminent presence, if that was not bad enough. Just as she had resolved to avoid him, he would be here, dining, under the same roof. At least the house would be full, and there would be no opportunities for him to seek her out. But her nerves sensed something more, an unease, which she could not quite define.

She deposited the basket on the table beside a brace of pheasants and a huge boar.

"Compliments of Mr Bryan," explained the cook, who was beginning to pluck the birds. "Mr Carew sent three cheeses and a hand of rabbits, and Mr Danvers himself brought up six carp, which he had out of the royal ponds, with the approval of the king."

Thomasin felt a twinge of emotion at the sound of his name. "We will feast well tonight, then?"

"You will feast better than the king himself!"

The dinner hour was almost upon them when the royal carriage brought Cecilia back to Monk's Place. Thomasin and her mother were seated in the parlour, putting the finishing touches to their embroidery as the light was fading, and saw it pull up before the steps. The king's arms glittered upon the door as Cecilia climbed out.

Thomasin rose to greet her as she came through the door, intending to warn her, but Cecilia was in a hurry. She ran upstairs, calling back.

"I need to change my attire. I will be down at dinner."

"Cecilia? It's Sir Henry."

She paused at the turn of the stairs. "What do you mean?"

Thomasin went up a few steps in order to speak more quietly. "Mother has invited him for dinner, along with Hatton and a few others."

"She has what? She did not consult with me."

"You were at court all day. Surely you have seen Henry? Did he not tell you?"

215

Cecilia drew back into herself. "Perhaps the message had not reached him. No, oh no, I cannot. I must say that I am indisposed."

"But why? You are to marry in two days!"

"I can't, I can't!"

Cecilia hurried up the rest of the stairs into her chamber. The door closed firmly. Thomasin followed her.

"Cecilia? Cecilia? We must speak."

"Go away!"

"What is the matter?"

Cecilia came to the door, tears streaking her face. "I can't marry him, I can't. It is hopeless. I have no choice but to go through with this and live in misery."

"But why? Mother and Father would not want that. What is your objection?"

"I simply can't."

"But he is a good man. I have heard people speak glowingly of him."

"It doesn't matter. He could be a saint as far as I care."

"Then what? You don't want to marry?"

"I can't tell you."

"Well, you must speak up soon, or else you will have to go ahead and marry."

"I would rather run away."

"Where to? Why? How would you live?"

"William would look after me."

"William?" Thomasin's mind swam. "Which William? Not Hatton?"

"Yes, of course Hatton. I love him and I cannot marry Henry."

Thomasin looked aghast at her sister's tear-streaked face. All her feelings and experiences with Rafe, all her struggles, and the priest's words that morning, came rushing down upon her. How had she been so blind? While she was fighting to resist one man, her engaged sister had fallen for another. At once, Cecilia's confession gave her a clarity that she had lacked herself.

"Cecilia. We have been in London almost two weeks. At the start of this month, you did not even know that William Hatton existed. The marriage with Sir Henry has been arranged between our two families for three years. These feelings are infatuation, nothing more. They will soon pass and your calm will be restored. Henry is a good man. If you look closer at him, you will come to admire him, even love him. It is your duty."

"It is not infatuation. I love him."

"In such a brief space? Does he love you? What does Hatton say about it?"

"He will not discuss it."

"There you are," Thomasin replied, as Rafe's admission the other night, that he could not offer her marriage, came back with a sting. "He understands that you must wed. He may feel something for you, but he has made no commitment to you. He knows he cannot. Henry is his friend, too."

"He has only not spoken because of Henry. Otherwise he would, I know it."

"Has there been anything between you? Any gestures or intimacies?"

Cecilia blushed. "Do not ask me, do not ask me that!"

At that moment, a door along the landing opened, and Richard appeared, leaning on the shoulder of Barnaby, with Matthew on the other side, preparing to assist him down the stairs for dinner.

"Get ready for dinner," whispered Thomasin. "Wash your face and come down."

"I can't. Not if they are both there. Tell them I am indisposed."

"I will not. You have to face this; your wedding is in two days."

"Thomasin? Cecilia?" Elizabeth was calling up the stairs. "I hear horses!"

"Coming, Mother," Thomasin replied, before turning back to her sister a final time. "Come down to dinner!"

William Hatton and Henry Kytson were already seated at the table, with Ellen and Dorothy. Thomasin smoothed down her skirts and took a deep breath, before she entered the room. Her mother was fussing around the outside, arranging who should sit where, preparing her husband's chair with cushions.

"Good evening," said Thomasin to the company, dropping a brief curtsey.

Henry sat solemnly, as he usually did, and she wondered whether he had any suspicions about his future bride's reluctance. At his side, where Elizabeth had unfortunately seen fit to seat him, William Hatton was glowing in his blondeness, with ruddy cheeks and bright eyes, like the cat who had got the cream. He knew he had Cecilia's affections, Thomasin was certain, and he was basking in the possession of them, seated beside her intended husband. The realisation made her stomach turn.

"Thomasin," said her mother, "I have put you here, beside Ellen, with Sir Giles Waterson on the other side when he arrives."

Thomasin took her seat dutifully. Ellen gave her a wide smile, but Thomasin felt too unsettled to return it with much sincerity. Nor did she feel able to meet the eyes of Hatton or Kytson opposite. Before her on the table sat a bowl of shelled walnuts. She kept her eyes on their gnarled shapes, listening as her father made his steady progress down the steps, one by one, until he appeared in the doorway.

"Here I am, fit as a fiddle!" he announced, as Matthew and Barnaby helped him to the chair at the end of the table closest to the door. Usually his place was by the hearth, but Elizabeth had swapped their positions, to make his access to the table smoother.

The company rose out of respect, but he waved them into their seats.

"Oh, pray, be seated. I am not the king!"

"My Lord, we were so concerned to hear of your accident," began Kytson, "but your appearance puts paid to many of our fears, especially given how close we are to the wedding. I understand you have already been visited by a doctor, but if there is anything we can do to alleviate your discomfort, you must speak it. Here." He placed a small leather pouch on the table. "My mother sends you some of her herbal mixtures and a special tincture to rub upon the swelling."

"That is most kind," replied Richard. "Do pass on my grateful thanks. I shall use it this night, and thank her myself on the morning of the wedding."

"Which is only two days away," beamed Elizabeth. "Are you almost ready, Sir Henry? Our preparations advance apace, dresses and all. Are your sister and mother happy with their choices?"

"I believe so," he smiled. "I rather let them alone to sort themselves out."

"But you have been busy too?"

"I have been making arrangements for our future home. Mother and Lucy will be departing for the country, so we shall take over the house in Blackfriars, and I wish to have it in readiness to receive Cecilia, and for you all, before your departure."

"Oh, I am glad to hear you say so," said Elizabeth. "We should so like to see the place before we return to the country."

The door sounded and a servant showed in Sir Giles, bearing a gift of comfits and candied fruits. He looked about the room, wearing a chestnut-brown coat and a wide smile. Thomasin found it a relief to see his good-humoured face, and this surprised her. Hard upon his heels came Rafe, dark and brooding, as he repeated his words of regret and his gratitude for the invitation. Her heart beat hard at the sight of him. At his side was Sir Nicholas Carew, a slight, sandy-haired man, who made profuse apologies for the part he had played in Richard's accident, riding on without realising he had fallen.

"Be content," her father replied, "all of you. Your generous gifts and your presence tonight have more than made up for a little discomfort. Come, now, be seated and we can enjoy this splendid feast."

Thomasin dared not look at Rafe. As Giles took his seat by her side, and made merry small talk, she was aware of him out of the corner of her eye, being seated close to her father on the other side of the table. Yet his presence hung heavy in her limbs, and she sensed his eyes upon her, searching for a response. What had passed between them last night remained unresolved, and he must have been surprised, and disappointed, not to have found her at home when he called that morning.

The seat beside Henry Kytson remained empty.

"Where is Cecilia?" asked Elizabeth. "Thomasin, you were speaking to her just now; is she almost ready?"

Thomasin composed herself quickly. "I believe her to be a little indisposed."

"Indisposed?"

"I hope it is nothing serious," added Kytson.

"I don't think so, just fatigue."

Elizabeth frowned towards the stairs. "All the more reason that she should eat."

But Richard dismissed her concerns. "She will be down, by and by, do not fret. I can't wait; I have been on an invalid's diet all day and I am starving!"

The servants brought in the first course, with dishes piled high with roast boar and beef pastries, pheasants, chicken golden with saffron and larks in wine. The smell of meat, spices and herbs circulated through the room.

Richard rubbed his hands. "Delicious, well done, very well done. Matthew, I compliment you upon your cook."

Thomasin saw Rafe lean forward for his wine glass and take a long draught. He was dressed in his usual dark clothing, furs and velvet, combined tonight with a clean white collar and cuffs, but he seemed quiet as Ellen and Dorothy chattered at him, and she was certain he was thinking of the previous night. Perhaps also, he had noted her lack of welcome. A pang of guilt stirred her conscience. She should, at least, meet his eyes, or bid him good evening, even if she had no intention of engaging with him further. After their intimacy, it would be most appallingly discourteous not to speak with him and show him some cheer, but not too much.

He met her eyes with curiosity. His own were black, full and liquid in the candlelight, burning her. Thomasin nodded in greeting, thankful for the table between them, and tore her eyes away before he could respond. Instead, by way of distraction, she turned to where Giles was playfully dividing up the portion they were to share. Yet her stomach was in knots and her hands, even though she hid them in her lap, were trembling due to Rafe's presence.

They were halfway through the first course, and the talk was all of hunting, led by Nicholas Carew, when Cecilia slipped through the door. In a simple, plain dress, her face washed and her hair hidden under an old bonnet, she took her place beside Kytson.

"My lovely bride-to-be," he greeted her. "I was concerned to hear that you were indisposed."

"I am not indisposed," she said, shooting an angry look at Thomasin. "I was tired, but I rested and now I am well."

Thomasin tried to concentrate upon the dish before her, but her usual good appetite failed her and the meat was eclipsed by her nerves. William Hatton seemed untroubled by Cecilia's entry, her state of mind, or the awkwardness of the situation, and was tucking into a great dish of meat with enthusiasm.

"Well, this really is a most jolly company," pronounced Nicholas Carew, raising his glass. "I propose a toast to the speedy recovery of Sir Richard and the good health of his family."

The words were repeated around the table and the glasses clinked together.

"You are most welcome," Richard replied, "and even if our acquaintance has begun under difficult circumstances, I hope it will continue with warmth and mutual regard. You are all most welcome at Eastwell Hall if you ever have cause to visit Suffolk."

"You are most generous in your hospitality," replied Carew.

"I can afford to be, my good Sirs, when I am sent such generous gifts."

"Sir Francis Bryan would have been among us tonight, but it is his turn to serve the king, and he charged me to pass on his warm regards and best wishes for your recovery. He hopes he will see you at court soon, and that you will drink a glass of wine with him before you depart."

"He should attend us at court on Thursday, to see our Cecilia married to Sir Henry, and partake of our wedding feast. You too, Mr Carew."

"Of course you should," added Elizabeth. "You would be most welcome."

"Yes," added Henry, "come and join our celebration. The preparations are almost complete. All that is needed now, is for the day to come and the vows to be spoken."

"Where do you marry?" asked Carew.

"The king has been kind enough to offer us his own chapel," replied Henry, beaming with pride, "and he told me only yesterday that he intends to attend in person."

"Oh, Cecilia, you did not tell me this," said Elizabeth, with something like indignation in her voice. "I would like to have known that the king himself was to attend."

"It doesn't really change anything," replied Cecilia sullenly, drawing surprised eyes from around the table.

"What do you mean?" questioned her mother. "Of course it does. Having the king at your wedding confers a special blessing. No doubt he will make you a handsome gift. Has he spoken of it to you? Perhaps when you saw him today?"

"I saw him but little; he was busy. I am to choose a piece from the royal jewel collection on Thursday, after the ceremony. That is quite enough."

"That is an unusual honour," replied Carew. "Does your family have a royal connection? It is rare for a knight's daughter, forgive me, to be so honoured."

"The king has taken a special liking to Cecilia," said Elizabeth, a little formally, then she turned to Ellen and Dorothy, as the closest distraction. "And you, ladies, you have your gowns and bonnets trimmed and ready for Thursday?"

Dorothy continued to eat as if such things were beneath her, but Ellen began to bubble over at once with excitement about ribbons and gold laces and pearls.

"And is your dress ready?" smiled Giles, offering Thomasin a dish of baked larks.

"Ready and waiting."

"I am glad to hear it. I had feared that I had upset you last time I called, with my talk."

"No," she smiled in reassurance, "you did not upset me."

"I see that the gentleman of whom we spoke is present at the table."

Thomasin blushed hotly. "I had no idea. It was Mother who invited him. He was the one who helped Father home after his accident."

"After being the cause of it, as I hear."

Thomasin was surprised to find that her first instinct was to defend Rafe's innocence, but she overrode it.

"So," continued Giles, changing the subject, and offering her a new dish, "do you relish the thought of a wedding? Food, dancing, eternal vows?"

"Food and dancing I always enjoy," she replied, as she spooned a piece of chicken onto her plate.

"But you are not ready for the vows, perhaps?"

She smiled. "It is Cecilia's day. So long as she is content, that is all that matters."

Prompted by this thought, they looked in unison across the table at Cecilia and Henry, who were seated almost opposite them, side by side, yet eating in silence.

"Is she happy in this match?"

Thomasin longed to confide in him, but was unsure whether to speak to someone outside the family. "It is her duty. She knows that."

"Your answer does not inspire confidence. Has she expressed doubts to you?"

"I cannot say. Don't all brides feel that way, on the verge of a new life? Some element of doubt is normal, is it not, especially when her acquaintance with her future husband is so slender?"

He said nothing, but continued eating. After a bit, he added, lightly, "I heard she has been much at court."

"Indeed she has. The king himself sent his carriage for her."

"But yet she saw him little today, as he was busy?"

"Yes, as she said."

"I wonder who she did see."

He picked at the larks, basting them in mustard.

Thomasin processed his words with unease. "Is there something you know?"

"Perhaps you are best placed to speak with her, sister to sister, just to see she is as committed to the match as we would hope."

Cecilia's tears from earlier came back into Thomasin's mind. She looked over at her sister, who was focused on her plate, although she seemed to be eating little. Then, as she watched, Cecilia lifted her pale eyes and cast a glance down the table in the direction of William Hatton. Not at him, but more at the place in front of him. Ellen was doing her best to interest him in her lively talk, but his attention was elsewhere. Thomasin could not say that he was looking at her sister, but his face was turned that way, in readiness, in case she should try to meet his eyes.

Thomasin spoke softly to Giles. "She has already spoken with me about the matter, and I confess I am at a loss to know what to do about it. Between ourselves, I believe her affection may have been bestowed elsewhere."

"We should not speak of it here," he replied softly. "After dinner, we will go into the garden."

"Yes, that is best."

"It may not be too late to overcome this."

"I hope not."

"Be assured, I will do all I can to help."

Thomasin took a deep breath and looked around the table. Rafe's burning eyes met hers, containing a mixture of annoyance and surprise. She was confused and dropped her spoon upon the cloth. Was it her conversation with Giles that had provoked such a reaction?

"Here." Giles picked up her spoon but took it into his napkin. "Let me wipe it for you first." He handed her the cleaned utensil with a smile.

And looking at Rafe again, Thomasin saw his face burning with rage at the attention she was receiving. He was jealous of her conversation with Giles, even though he was her dining partner.

"All was very merry at court the other day," spoke Ellen loudly, trying to draw in the whole table. "We did enjoy our visit very much, seeing the king and the dancing. We don't get very much of that kind of excitement in the country."

"If I recall," laughed Carew, "there isn't much of anything in the country, save for sheep and fields."

"There is quite good company to be had in Derbyshire, in fact," replied Barnaby, rankled by this reply, "obviously not to court standards, but we do not go without. We count ourselves to be very fortunate."

"And the most pretty countryside to drive in," Ellen added, seeking to please her husband. "But I am still looking forward to Thursday so much. It reminds me of our own wedding."

"How long have you been married?" asked Giles politely.

"Five years and all of them happy. He made the right choice, did you not, Barnaby?"

Barnaby's reply was muffled as he received a dish of pies.

As the servants circulated, filling the wine glasses, Thomasin chanced another look at Rafe. There was no denying his beauty: the white brow, the blue-black head of hair, the chiselled jaw, the black eye. Somehow, he had a visceral hold over her, of the kind she had never encountered before and found hard to resist. Her body responded to him in ways that alarmed her, but she remembered the priest's words. So long as she kept her distance, all would be well.

A chair scraped back. Dorothy had been quiet throughout the meal, eclipsed by her sister as usual, but now she rose shakily to her feet. "Pray excuse me, I feel unwell. I will go and lie down." She leaned upon the back of the chair, her face pale, even waxy, her eyes dull. The plate before her showed she had eaten little.

At her side, her brother-in-law Barnaby rose to help steady her. "I will take you up."

"No, you continue your meal," said Ellen, placing down her knife. "I will take her." She placed her arm through her sister's. With Dorothy swaying slightly, the pair made their way out of the dining room.

"I do hope it is nothing serious," said Elizabeth, looking after them in concern. "Dorothy seems to have experienced poor health since her arrival here."

"She is of a weak disposition, after a childhood illness," replied Barnaby. "Too much rich food disagrees with her."

"Please, my Lord." A servant appeared in the doorway. "Mr Cromwell has called. He is waiting in the hall."

Richard frowned. "Here? Now? Well, I cannot go to him without difficulty, so I suppose you had better show him in."

The minister was invited into the dining room, still in his cloak and hood from the night outside. He pushed it back to reveal his face when he saw the spread upon the table and the guests.

"Forgive me for intruding, gentlemen, ladies, blessings upon you all. Sir Richard, I had hoped to find you alone."

"I am not, as you see. Will you not join us, Mr Cromwell? There is plenty to go around. We can make another place at table."

"Thank you, but I will not. I have already dined tonight."

"Very well, then how might I help you?"

"Well…" He cast a look round at the company, as if reluctant to speak before them. "I heard about your accident. I hope you are well and recovering."

"Quite well and recovering. I thank you for your concern. Forgive me, it is also the reason I remain in my chair."

"I am glad to hear that. I would hope this will not prevent your attendance at York Place on Thursday, for the second session of the Cardinal's court?"

At these words, the table fell silent. There were those at the table who supported the king's great matter, and those who believed it to be the most grievous insult to the queen. As yet, those differences had not arisen at what had been a harmonious dinner, but all were aware that Thursday was Cecilia and Henry's wedding day.

"I was able to attend the court yesterday," replied Richard, "as you requested, and it was upon my return that I was injured. My daughter is getting married on Thursday and my attendance is required there."

"Perhaps that will not take the entire day? May I remind you this is a matter close to the king's heart."

Richard frowned, feeling the weight of expectation, and the difficulty of the conversation taking place in company.

"I am sure you are aware of your duty," added Cromwell, "and the king's desires."

"Mr Cromwell," spoke up Elizabeth, unexpectedly and boldly, "I do believe you were not yet at court when my husband and I first held office, but let me assure you we are both fully aware of our duty and the king's desires. On Thursday, the king intends to be a most special guest at our daughter's wedding. He himself wished to bear witness to her nuptials and intends to make her a special gift. No doubt he would be most surprised not to see Richard partaking of the celebrations. I am sure he would overlook my husband's attendance in your court on this one occasion. I am happy to speak to the king about this, if you require confirmation, or if the task is arduous, Mr Cromwell."

Thomasin looked at her mother in awe.

"Very well, Madam," the minister replied stiffly, eyeing her with a particular look, "I wish to concur with the king's wishes in all things. I will bid you goodnight."

There was a pause around the table, as they heard his footsteps in the hallway, followed by the opening and closing of the door.

"That was most splendidly said, Lady Marwood," offered Giles, to the general agreement of the table.

"Most splendid," added Barnaby.

The feasting resumed, but the mood had changed. There was a general air of complicity, but Thomasin could not help noticing that both her parents were quiet, even when the fruits and spices were brought up; the part of the meal they usually enjoyed the most.

She favoured the sweetness of candied oranges, the sharpness of lemon peel, selecting pieces from the dishes Giles offered her. The warm wine made her feel drowsy and comforted. The wood in the fire crackled, candles guttered and were replaced. In the park outside, an owl screeched. A servant brought a lute and began to play.

"You are having a pleasant evening?" Giles asked her.

"More so than I had feared," she replied, although between Cecilia's expression and Rafe's burning eyes, she feared it may be the calm before the storm.

TWENTY-ONE

Above Monk's Place, the clouds had blown away. The clear skies revealed a thin, cold sliver of moon and a host of bright stars. In the garden, the last flowers of autumn wore a grey cloak over their brownness, with petals poised to drop and scents fading. The maze of paths that snaked through the beds and lawns were partially lit by torches, with others dissolving into shadows. At the far end, the little sparks of lanterns glowed from late night boats bobbing on the river.

"Shall we?" asked Sir Giles Waterson, offering Thomasin his arm.

The party inside was breaking up, with guests taking spices and sweets, and seeking a breath of air, as the table was cleared. Before they slipped outside, Thomasin had seen Rafe detained by Barnaby, who was asking him many questions about attaining a position at court. Cecilia had made her excuses and headed up to her chamber.

Arm in arm, Thomasin and Giles headed off towards the rose path, which led down the side of the lawn, dark and obscured by the large trees overhead.

"It was a pleasant dinner," began Giles, "for me, at least."

"For me too," agreed Thomasin, speaking the truth despite the awkwardness of certain moments.

"Your mother spoke with a certain authority to Mr Cromwell. I suppose she has the ear of the king."

Thomasin thought of their first visit to court, when Henry summoned Elizabeth to sit beside him, and spoke to her at length. "I suppose she does, from the early days. She was a lady-in-waiting to Queen Catherine, back at the start of his

231

reign. He is quite taken with Cecilia too. She was born at court."

They walked on a little further, passing through an archway which afforded them greater privacy.

"I would speak with you about your sister," he replied. "Come, let us walk a little, to where we can't be overheard."

Thomasin followed his lead towards the trees, still holding his arm, wondering what he had in mind.

"From my observations tonight," said Giles, when they were a distance from the house, "I do think that Cecilia has some aversion to this match. I must also tell you that she has been observed at court, frequently in the company of another. Did you know?" He shot her an uneasy look.

Thomasin's stomach churned. She knew what was coming, but feared to discover the full extent of it. "Another man?"

"William Hatton. I am afraid she has not been discreet. There is gossip in certain circles. I am genuinely surprised that none of it has reached the ears of Sir Henry or his friends yet."

Thomasin stopped, thinking of the times she had seen Cecilia and Hatton at court, whispering, talking, dancing. "This is worse than I thought. Cecilia; the subject of gossip!"

"Gossip always seeks out new material; it will be something else next week, but she must prevent any harm being done to her reputation. She must not consort with Hatton again and accept this marriage with a good grace."

"I fear she will not comply. Earlier this evening, she admitted to me that she loves him. Hatton. She refused to come down to dinner at first because she could not face Sir Henry. I told her it was mere infatuation, but she will not listen. I was surprised to see her so composed at the table."

"Hatton will not wed her. He has prospects of a grand match with a title. He will not wish to throw those away or displease the king."

"She said as much. He will not speak to her on the matter."

"And yet he dallies with her and keeps private company with her."

"Are you sure, private company?" Thomasin thought of the private, snatched moments she had shared with Rafe, and how quickly and easily temptation could arise.

"I believe so, today, while the king was busy about council business. Hatton has his own room at court, where they would have been uninterrupted."

"Yes, she was out all day."

"She was seen arriving at court, and leaving later, but where she was between those times, is unknown."

"A few days back, as I recall, she went out, saying that she was visiting Lucy Kytson."

"Lucy Kytson has been away for almost a week, visiting a friend in Surrey. She returned this morning."

Thomasin felt a wave of despair wash over her. Private company could only mean one thing. "What is to be done? How can we save this? Can we, now, in good conscience, send Cecilia to Sir Henry as his bride on Thursday?"

"Of course. We have no evidence to confirm her seduction. We must proceed as if all is well." He walked on a little, then turned, thinking aloud. "The best course of action is for me to appeal to Hatton. I will ask him to remove himself from court until the ceremony is complete."

"Yes, yes, that is a good plan. Do you think he will go?"

"If he thinks that his position at court is compromised, he will. That's all that matters to a man like that. I could threaten to take the scandal to the king if he refuses. Henry is keen for this marriage to go ahead, so he will not look kindly upon any interference from Hatton. I do not doubt that will be sufficient to send him away, tail between his legs."

They had walked round in a circle and now came back to face the house. Lights shone in the windows, revealing movement as the party dispersed. A few people had stepped outside for the air, talking and looking up at the stars, or out across the Thames to the scattered lights on the far bank.

In the moonlight, William Hatton was unmistakeable with his shock of blonde hair, hurrying away from the party, down towards the covered walk.

"If I am not mistaken," said Giles, "he is going to meet someone."

Quickly, they walked across the centre of the garden, towards the wooden structure, Thomasin's emotions in turmoil. Giles was correct. As soon as he entered the shadows of the walk, a second figure appeared, and rushed into his embrace. Their lips met.

It was unmistakeably Cecilia, her fair hair tumbling over her shoulders, dressed in a long, loose gown. Meeting at that point in the shadows, they had believed themselves to be unobserved from the house, but had not reckoned upon others being further down the garden, who might be able to observe their hiding place.

Thomasin was shocked. "I thought she had retired to bed!"

"That is what she intended you to think. They must have planned this, before tonight."

As soon as the pair broke apart, Giles went forward. "Hatton? Is that you?"

The two figures froze.

"Hatton, we have seen you, come out."

After a moment, Hatton appeared, alone. Stepping away from the walkway, he came down into the garden before Thomasin and Giles, allowing Cecilia to shrink back into the shadows.

"Sir Giles," he said, lightly, smoothing down his hair, "you are taking the air too?"

"I am set to leave. My carriage awaits at the front, and I can carry you back to court with me."

"You are most kind, but I had intended to remain a little longer."

"The night draws on. Neither of us wish to cause our hosts offence by exceeding our welcome. It is best to withdraw now."

"But I had wished…"

"I say again, Sir," said Giles more forcibly, "you must retire now before offence is given; I am sure you understand my meaning. There is something particular I wish to speak with you about, which touches the king. So come to my carriage, if you will."

Hatton threw a glance into the shadows, then appeared to comply.

"I will see you anon," Giles said softly to Thomasin. "Hopefully tonight will end this, and we will meet at the wedding." His green-blue eyes glowed with warmth as the moonlight caught his face.

"Thank you," she whispered, captivated by his expression for a moment. "I cannot thank you enough."

He pressed her hand. For a moment it felt as if he desired her, as if he felt some emotion for her, but she shook the sensation off.

"Come, Hatton, let us depart."

Thomasin watched the two men striding across the garden together, towards the house, to bid farewell to their hosts. They disappeared within, and stillness descended upon the garden. Thomasin wondered whether she should approach her sister, or pretend that her presence was unknown to her.

She turned towards the walkway, but then Cecilia's white figure appeared, hurrying around the outside, through the shadows towards the kitchen door. Thomasin was too late to catch her, but no doubt she would be full of fury against her sister for the part she had played in it.

Thomasin let her go. There would be time enough for recriminations in the morning, or else, by then, Cecilia might have come to her senses.

She had almost reached the house, seeing the figures inside lit up brightly through the windows. Guests were bidding farewell, pulling on cloaks and departing; servants were clearing the room, transporting dishes, lighting fires and candles in the upstairs bedchambers. Thomasin paused and watched the activity. In a few moments, she saw a moving light in the window of her sister's chamber, as if someone was walking with a candle. Thomasin saw it flit about like a ghost and guessed at Cecilia's distress. The situation had profoundly shocked her, with all its implications for the family. She was thinking it over, when another figure appeared from the bushes at the side of the lawn. A tall, broad-shouldered man in dark clothing. Thomasin gasped to recognise Rafe at close quarters, thinking him long gone.

His face was dark and scowling, his heavy brows ugly with anger. "I saw your lover leave. I thought to challenge him, but I would not spill blood on your uncle's land."

"What? There is no lover."

"Sir Giles. He walked right past me, having come straight from your arms."

"No, no, you have it wrong, he…"

Rafe's face was dark and contorted with anger. "I came here this morning, hoping to find a warm welcome, but you were not here."

"I was at church!"

"And I was glad to receive your mother's invitation, thinking it another opportunity to see you, but the coldness you have shown me tonight, flaunting your connection with another man, after the liberties you allowed me yester night, have quite sickened me."

"No, no, this is a misunderstanding. Cecilia…"

"I think not. You have barely met my eyes, and were walking with him in the darkness, seeking privacy. What might have happened, had Hatton not appeared? Would you have let him kiss you, touch you, as I did?"

"No, not at all…"

Thomasin's instinct was to go towards him, wanting to reassure him with a touch, but he stepped back, away from her.

"No, don't touch me. I don't want you now, behaving like a common whore."

Tears and indignation arose in her throat. "You don't understand. We were acting to prevent a scandal concerning my sister. You should not use such words to me!"

"Then you should not deserve them."

He broke away from her. Desperation and desire arose in her chest.

"Rafe! No, no, please! Let me explain!"

He did not look back.

The violence of his response had shaken her. Choking back her tears, Thomasin hurried round to the kitchen door, which Cecilia had used only recently, and raced up to her chamber.

TWENTY-TWO

It was in the early hours of the morning that the rain began to fall. Heavy, streaming rain which beat against the windowpane and woke Thomasin after she had finally fallen into a fitful sleep. It was dark, very dark. She had drawn the heavy curtains around her bed before she slept, longing to disappear into the cave they created. As the house fell quiet, she had sobbed at Rafe's brutality, telling herself it was for the best, trying to purge him from her mind. But, as soon as she woke, there he was again, with his compelling eyes and the sharp, cruel words falling from those beautiful lips. The pain set in again.

She pulled aside the curtain a little. The embers in the fire were almost cold and the water was pouring down the diamond-paned glass. As she lay, looking out, the rain gave way to thunder, deep and rumbling. Then, through the gap she saw flashes of lightening, three or four, white as day, showing the tree-tops outside. There were footsteps on the landing and creaks on the stairs, no doubt because the storm had woken someone else, or the servants had been called. Finally, after the clouds passed, and the thunder dimmed to a grumble, Thomasin was able to sleep again.

Dawn broke over London. Grey clouds pressed in from the west, bringing more rain. It fell upon the roofs of the houses in Thames Street and saturated their gardens, upon the people passing down the narrow city lanes, upon those seeking shelter in the alleys down to the river. It splashed upon the river itself and the boats bobbing on the waves, upon the houses spanning the bridge and the brick façade of York Place, where

Wolsey called the servants to build up more fires against the damp. It fell upon the church of Our Lady, upon the palace of Westminster and the grey face of the abbey, upon the royal park and the tiltyard. Standing in his oriel window, King Henry lamented the loss of a day's hunting and, nestled on cushions by the fire, Anne Boleyn turned her back upon the rain and fed treats to her dogs.

Further across London, in Bucklersbury, Thomas More and his family sat poised in their parlour, as the new German painter, Mr Hans Holbein, sketched their outline for a portrait. More sat centrally, with Margaret at his feet, amid the rest of the household. Captured together in stillness, they looked serene on the page, as the artist's hand moved swiftly to endow them with immortality. In Chelsea, Thomas Cromwell pored over his accounts, looking for a way to release funds to send another ambassador to the Pope. He looked out at the rain, with eyes pinched in his thick-set cheeks, wondering if he dared risk the ride to court. At Windsor, Queen Catherine sat at her desk, dipping her pen in a pot of ink, writing a letter to her daughter in Ludlow.

Thomasin was combing out her hair when the discovery was made. It was Elizabeth whom she heard first, speaking loudly down the corridor, her tone urgent, insistent, rising to shrillness. Thomasin paused, tried to hear her words, but her mother was coming closer, with hurried footsteps. The door burst open.

"Is she here? Is she in here with you?"

"Who, Mother? I am quite alone."

"Cecilia, of course!"

Elizabeth rushed towards the bed and pulled back the curtains. "Is she hiding?"

"What do you mean?"

"Cecilia is missing. She has gone. Some of her clothing, too."

Thomasin felt cold. "Gone? She can't be gone."

"I assure you she is. We are searching the house from top to bottom, but she is nowhere to be found."

Elizabeth swept out of the room, moving along to the next, knocking at Ellen and Barnaby's, then at Dorothy's.

Thomasin pulled on a gown and hurried down to the chamber where her sister slept. True enough, the bed did not look slept in and the chest was empty, save for a few odd pieces of clothing. The better pair of shoes were missing. Looking around for anything that might suggest what had happened, she found nothing that could be of use. No sign of flight or struggle, no note left behind, nothing broken or disturbed. The window was still secured. She thought of the footsteps she had heard last night, in the middle of the storm.

"Nothing?" Elizabeth was standing in the doorway.

Thomasin shook her head. "Her good shoes are gone."

Matthew came down the stairs from the attics. "The servants know nothing, save for Jane, who found the kitchen door unlocked when she went down this morning. She swears she locked it before retiring last night; it is always part of her routine and she particularly remembers doing it, because she checked it once the rain started."

"That is how she left. Foolish girl! Wait until I get my hands on her."

Matthew put a hand on her shoulder. "Calm down, sister. Remember your health. Save your strength."

Richard hobbled into sight, leaning on Barnaby. "Still nothing?"

"We think she left by the kitchen door, sometime in the night."

"But why? Where has she gone? Amid this rain, too! She will catch her death of cold and wet."

Thomasin's unease had been mounting. She knew they had reached the point where she could remain silent no more. "I fear she may have fled to avoid the marriage."

They all turned to her, each enquiring face filled with a dozen questions. Elizabeth took a step closer and looked intently into her daughter's eyes. "What do you know? Do not hold back."

Thomasin took a deep breath. "I believe Cecilia did not wish to be married. She said she could not do it. I thought it was just nerves and it would pass, but last night she wept about it, before dinner."

"And you did not think to speak of this, to your father and I?"

"Of course, but I thought it was nerves, and there was no time last night. When she came down, eventually, she seemed calmer and resigned. And I spoke with Giles, and he said..."

"Sir Giles Waterson? Does everyone know our business?"

"Mother, I regret to say there were already rumours. Sir Giles raised this with me at dinner and was most solicitous on our behalf. He spoke to me of it, Mother, think of that!"

"Rumours? Rumours circulating about us, at court?"

"I do not know how much; it may have merely been one observation, but Giles said he would act, speak to the gentleman involved, and bring the matter to an end."

"The gentleman involved? What is this I am hearing? Can it be worse? What compromising situation has Cecilia got herself into? Oh God, she is ruined!"

"Now, you must wait to hear," spoke Richard. "Thomasin, tell us everything you know. Who is the man you speak of?"

For a moment, Thomasin hardly dared answer, aware of the floodgates she was about to open, but she drew a deep breath.

Cecilia was missing, no doubt run away to join Hatton, and the marriage, and the family, would be ruined. Her own prospects would be tainted by such a scandal, along with those of her younger sisters.

"I did not speak earlier because I trusted Cecilia to come to her senses. I was also afraid to upset you, Mother, in your state of health."

"Come, come, tell us, do not hold back. Every moment will count."

"Cecilia was upset yesterday, saying she could not marry. She said she was in love with someone else. I told her this was mere infatuation, which would pass, but she would not accept it. She believes herself in love with William Hatton, but I do not think he has made any kind of promise to her; she said he would not speak of marriage."

"Hatton! Marriage?" exploded Richard. "Who dined in this house only last night, who has been our guest before? How dare he take such a liberty?"

"And, as he is a close companion of Sir Henry," added Elizabeth, "it is a despicable act."

"Giles promised to speak with him last night. He said it would displease the king to hear of Hatton's behaviour, and he would warn him off."

"Giles again," raged Elizabeth, "who seems to have known everything before we did. Her own parents!"

Thomasin struggled to remain calm, although she felt the tears rising. "He would have spoken with Hatton last night. He has been our friend in this, Mother, and most discreet."

"But he must have failed, as she has gone! Gone!" And Elizabeth broke into sobs.

"We must act," said Richard, "although I am sadly limited at the moment by this injury. Send round the carriage, at once.

Matthew, Barnaby, we must seek her at court, where she may be in the chambers of this wretched Hatton. If we act swiftly, we may prevent a scandal."

"Lean on me," said Matthew, offering his arm. "We go to court at once."

"Is there anything we can do?" asked Ellen, who had been listening further along the landing. "Go out searching, or write letters?"

"You are best to wait here, in case of news, but I thank you," said Richard, making his way painfully towards the staircase.

"We could look in her room again," suggested Dorothy, beside her, "in case there is anything that has been missed."

"It is intolerable," uttered Elizabeth, marshalling her senses, "that a daughter of mine, my eldest child, should have brought us to this. I cannot bear it. I am retiring to my bed before I fall into an apoplexy."

"We depart at once," said Richard, before she could leave. "Hopefully we will return with her. Offer up your prayers, those of you remaining."

The day crept past slowly. The women kept to the house, mostly in their own chambers, although by the dinner hour, as darkness arrived, even Elizabeth had reappeared. All four sat quietly before the parlour fire, where they could best hear any carriage approach.

"Tomorrow should be her wedding day," Elizabeth mused, full of regret and anger. "All is set, after years of negotiation. I suppose we must inform the Kytsons that there will be no bride in the morning. The shame of it. We will have to return to the country in disgrace."

"Not yet," Thomasin counselled. "They may still bring her back."

"But we cannot offer them a spoiled bride. Morally, how can we do that?"

"They would not know, Mother. All this could be forgotten."

"And the court rumours?"

"We do not know yet. It is difficult, I know, but you must be patient."

"I have been patient all day. I am running out. I do not have the strength for this."

"What was that?" asked Ellen. "I thought I heard the gates open."

They rose and hurried to the window, where a carriage was visible drawing up before the front door.

"Oh, dear Lord, let them have found her," urged Elizabeth, making her way into the hall.

As the men entered, it was clear at once that they had failed in their task. Barnaby and Matthew supported Richard on each side, who was moving slowly, as if fatigued. They helped him into the parlour, to a chair by the fire.

"Bring wine," Matthew called, "at once."

Richard looked up at the women's expectant faces and shook his head. "I'm afraid we didn't find her, nor Hatton, whom no one has seen today. We were very discreet at court, and I do not believe the king knows of the situation, but we failed in our task. Tomorrow we will have to face this, admit she has gone, and call a stop to the wedding."

Elizabeth, who had been containing her emotions for hours, could no longer do so. "Wretched, ungrateful, sinful child, no child of mine! After all we have given her, to treat us in this disgraceful manner. And the king, waiting to attend her wedding tomorrow, waiting in his own chapel, to offer her gifts. I will have to go to him myself tomorrow and explain. We must depart for the country at once. I cannot bear to stay in London any longer. Our names will be whispered everywhere and people will laugh. She has brought shame upon us."

"People will not laugh," said Richard. "No one relishes this."

"Of course they do! What nonsense you speak. There are always enemies at court, gladdened by another's misfortune. Sir Henry will snatch up another bride, who will enjoy his title, his lands and estates. Foolish, selfish girl."

"We have done all we can for now. I do not know where else to seek them. I suppose we must speak with Hatton next. If they are together, there must be a match between them, to save her name. Or else she will just be his mistress."

"Where are their estates?"

"The Hattons?" Richard shook his head. "I do not know. We must ask for the king's assistance, although I am loath to."

"You are loath to ask the king for help?" asked Elizabeth. "When it comes to the future of our daughter?"

"Yes," he said pointedly, "I am. It is a task more suited to your tastes."

Thomasin noted the sting in the words, but knew not what occasioned it. Her mother did not react, but turned away, as if they made her heavy.

"Unless," said Matthew, "unless. This may be madness on my part, I know not, but it occurs to me as a solution. Sir Henry Kytson is expecting a bride tomorrow morning, and you still have a daughter."

The meaning of his words slowly sank in for Thomasin, as those in the room turned to look at her.

To become Sir Henry Kytson's bride, instead of Cecilia, was a horror she had not imagined. The expressions on the faces of her family showed that they were considering this as a serious option.

"No," she said, "no, no, I can't be married in the morning. It isn't fair that I should pay the price of Cecilia's misconduct."

"She is right," said Richard. "The mantle should not fall to her."

"But it is worth considering, is it not?" asked Elizabeth, narrowing her eyes as she surveyed her second daughter. "She is young, but not too young. I wonder what the Kytsons would say to it, that is, if they still want an alliance with our family after this scandal."

"Please," said Thomasin, "do not ask me to do this. Father, I beg you. Nothing has prepared me for this."

Richard put his hand upon her arm as a gesture of reassurance, but Thomasin did not feel reassured. Her mother still eyed her critically, as if resolving a plan.

"Let's go in to dine," suggested Matthew. "Nothing was ever resolved well upon an empty stomach."

TWENTY-THREE

Dinner was almost concluded when they heard the front door. Thomasin had eaten little, her stomach in knots, but she had appreciated her father's attempts to keep the subject of conversation off her and the forthcoming marriage. He spoke instead of the storm, the falling rain and the rising river.

It was a simple meal, reusing the remnants of last night's feast, and Thomasin could not but reflect upon the difference a single day might bring. They ate steadily, but uncomfortably, and she could not wait until the moment arrived when she could retire to her chamber. She was seated at the end of the table, closest to the door, so when the front door clicked, the sound reached her ears clearly. Thomasin could not have said what prompted her, but something made her rise and go into the hall.

Cecilia was standing there, alone. She was drenched from head to foot, with her cloak heavy with rain, her head bare and hair plastered to her face.

"Oh, Cecilia!" Thomasin went to her sister, and threw her arms about her, despite her state. "I am so glad to see you home safely."

"She is back!" called Ellen, who had followed Thomasin into the hall. "Cecilia is back."

Elizabeth and Matthew laid down their knives and spoons, appearing in haste, with Richard limping afterwards.

"You dare to show your face, knowing what disgrace you have brought upon your family…" Elizabeth began.

"Now, this is not the time for that." Richard urged his way towards his daughter. "You are drenched, and probably tired and hungry. Let's get you warm and dry and fed, and then we will have some answers."

With a trembling chin, Cecilia surveyed them all with her pale eyes. "I need to rest. I will be marrying Sir Henry in the morning. I will go to my chamber."

A stunned silence followed this announcement.

"I am sorry for the concern I have caused. I will be ready in the morning." She turned, limp and dripping, to the stairs.

"I will come up and help you," offered Thomasin.

"And I, too," said Ellen, whose unexpected kindness was welcome.

"Very well," said Richard. "I shall look in upon you when I retire."

But Elizabeth was not satisfied. "Well, I never! Was there ever such scandalous behaviour?" She stood with her hands on her hips. "You have not heard the last of this!"

"Our child is back," said Richard, as Cecilia began the slow climb, moving her limbs as if she ached. "She is back, and that is what matters."

"And she is prepared to marry tomorrow," added Matthew, "so there may be no need for anyone else to know what happened today."

"But we do not know what happened today! I must go up with her and find out."

"No," said Richard, "you saw her. She is exhausted. She looks broken. Let the girls attend her until she is well again, and then we will have our answers. Be patient a little longer."

Thomasin took a deep breath and then entered her sister's chamber. It was just as she had left it that morning; empty and cold, the bed still made, with the chests open to reveal their missing clothes.

Questions were racing round inside her mind. Again, she thought of those words of William Hatton's, about the individual taking their own destiny into their hands, about acting not reacting, and making your life what you wanted it to be. She could not help but feel that his attitude had caused this situation, and that his new beliefs about life had created a sort of recklessness that had infected her sister. The old Cecilia, before they came to London, had such faith in convention and duty, that she would never have behaved in this way.

Cecilia was standing, staring into the cold grate, arms wrapped about herself, the picture of misery. Her breath came out short and broken. Thomasin had not seen her in that passionate state before, not even when they had argued as children, not even when Cecilia's beloved puppy had run away when she was twelve. She turned to Ellen, who was behind her.

"Go and fetch a servant to light the fire."

Ellen hurried away, her footsteps filling the awkward silence, until she returned with a maid carrying a coal bucket, and a large glass of wine.

"Here, you need this."

Cecilia accepted it gratefully and raised it to her parched lips. The serving girl knelt in the grate, and Ellen helped her to build up the fire and light it. Their bustling briefly provided another focus in the room, drawing the sisters' eyes as they laid the pieces of fresh coal upon the kindling. Taking a long, thin spill, Ellen lit the candles along the mantle, one after the other. They guttered slightly at first, then slowly, their warmth brought the room back to life. The smell began to spread and the coal crackled as it caught. Finally, as the blaze kindled, and the maid closed the door, the three women were alone.

Thomasin turned to her sister. "The room will soon warm up, but we must get you out of these wet things quickly. Lift your arms."

Cecilia did as she was bid, but it was a languid and defeated gesture.

Carefully, on both sides, Thomasin and Ellen peeled the soaking wet dress up over her head. It came slowly, the material sodden, ruching about her arms. She stood shivering in her white shift. Her skin was cold as ice, her arms covered in gooseflesh.

"That must come off too, or else you will catch your death. You're shivering. Go closer to the fire."

Thomasin looked in the depleted clothes chest and pulled out a plain, dark dress and a clean shift. "I suppose this will do. Where are your clothes?"

"I lost them. I don't know." The tears streaked down her face.

"Come, never mind now. Let's get you warmed up."

"I can do it."

Cecilia pulled off her wet shift and let the dry one cover her, with a single sweeping gesture from the women's hands.

Thomasin saw the dark drops gathering on her sister's back. "Look, your hair is dripping. Let me wring it out and put it up."

"It's all right." Cecilia twisted her dishevelled hair about her fingers and tucked it into a temporary bun at her nape.

"Now the dress."

She shook her head. "I will sleep soon, if I may. I won't need a dress."

"As you wish. Here, be seated for a moment and warm up."

Thomasin drew a chair up beside the hearth and her sister sank into it. They stood before her, questions burning on their lips, yet wanting most of all, in that moment, to be patient, to be kind. Thomasin could almost feel Ellen's curiosity, nudging against her, and prayed that she would not speak.

Cecilia sighed. Her hands lay heavy in her lap. Her head bowed low, shoulders drooping, as if they carried the weight of the world. The minutes hung like lead between them, with only the sound of their laboured breathing above the flames.

Eventually, it came, as Thomasin knew it would. The confession.

"I waited," Cecilia said, choking back sobs. "I waited for him, all day, but he did not come." She did not even try to wipe the tears away, just let them fall. "I waited. I watched for him, and the hours passed and I kept thinking he would come, but he didn't. I thought he had been delayed, and would come rushing in, but he didn't, and then I feared him injured, or even killed, but no word came. He just left me there."

Thomasin knelt before her sister and took her hands in hers, as if somehow, this could hold the pieces of her together.

"I would have given him everything, gone away with him, wherever he wanted, but he never came."

"Perhaps it was a misunderstanding."

"He wanted me, I know he did. He told me to come; he promised we could go away together."

"Did he offer you marriage?"

The question unleashed the last of Cecilia's restrained emotions. She shook her head. "He did not."

Thomasin could not help but wonder if Hatton's absence was not down to chance or cruelty. It may have been the result of Giles speaking with him, or not, and she longed to hear a word from him on the subject. Yet no other messenger had come to the house that day. "Was this at court?"

"Yes. I waited all day in his chamber."

Ellen cleared her throat. "You were actually going to run away with him?"

"Yes," Cecilia flared up, "I was. I love him! No, I thought I did. I thought he loved me. I can't stand this terrible feeling, this pain."

"I cannot condone what you tried to do, you know that, but whatever the rights and wrongs of it," said Thomasin swiftly, "he has treated you with cruelty, with disregard for your person, for the honour of this family and that of his friend. He is not worthy of your love."

"I know it," Cecilia said bitterly, "I know it. When we came to court, it was all so new, so exciting, overwhelming; there were so many people, it was all so thrilling."

"I understand that all too well," replied Thomasin. "I felt that too. It draws you in; it's very easy to imagine you feel something, that the court is the only place to be."

"You too?" said Cecilia, lifting her wet eyes to her sister's for the first time. "That's it, and the king and Anne gave me such favour. She encouraged me to meet him."

"Anne? Encouraged you to meet Hatton?" Thomasin was shocked. "Are you sure?"

"Yes, she spoke to me of him, praising him, and I confided in her about my feelings."

"Did the king know this?"

Cecilia shook her head. "No, she told me he must not. She said love was the only worthwhile pursuit."

"And not your marriage?"

Cecilia sighed. "I wonder where he might be."

"You must not! You must put him from your mind as a deceiver, a base creature, a cruel trickster of women, and betrayer of his friends. Look at the dance he has led you."

"Do they know?" Cecilia asked suddenly. "The Kytsons? Does Henry know?"

"There have been rumours at court, but so far as we are aware, he does not. He still remains in ignorance."

Cecilia breathed a deep sigh of relief and drank from the wine glass.

"You would still marry him? In the morning?"

"It is my duty. I will not let everyone down again."

"You are sure?"

"I will go to the chapel tomorrow, with the king's blessing, and become Sir Henry Kytson's wife, and I will do my best," Cecilia added, her voice breaking, "my best to be a good wife to him."

Thomasin was torn. "But you do not want to, I fear, not in the way that you were content to, formerly, before we came here."

"It is a matter of honour. I still have the chance to make it right. I will honour the families' agreement."

Thomasin took her sister in her arms, holding her as she felt her sobs. "That is a good and noble sentiment."

"It is all I can do, now. Otherwise I am lost."

"No, you are not. This will be forgotten. In a short while, it will no longer be spoken of, no longer remembered."

"Do you think it possible?"

"Fulfil your vows and no one would dare to criticise you. People will move on; there will be something else to speak of in a week's time."

"I will throw myself into this marriage and make it a success. I will never be such a fool again."

Thomasin frowned. "But it must not cost the sacrifice of yourself, not if it comes at too high a cost. We could speak with Father in the morning. I am sure he would not wish you to be unhappy."

"I will not be. I will be happy in the fulfilment of my duties as a wife and mother."

"If you are sure?"

"I am resolved." Cecilia wiped away her tears. "And do you think Mother will ever forgive me?"

"I am certain of it. And Sir Henry is a good man, a very good man. But now, if you are intent upon honouring your promise, you must get some sleep."

"Yes," Cecilia agreed, "everything will begin again tomorrow."

Thomasin rose and held out her hand to Ellen. "Come then, let us leave the bride to her rest. We will return in the morning, to help you dress. Good night, sweet dreams, sweet sister. Until the morrow." She blew out the candles. The room filled with smoke and darkness.

TWENTY-FOUR

The morning brought visitors. The rain had cleared, the sun came up over Monk's Place, and carriages drew up before the door, with servants hurrying in and out. Thomasin woke feeling hopeful and hurried into her sister's room, her stockinged feet soft on the floorboards.

There was a doubt, just the slightest of doubts in her mind, like a mote in the corner of her eye. Perhaps Cecilia would have flown, leaving the bed empty, the room cold. Perhaps the pain of her broken heart had proved too much, in the dark hours of the night, and even now she was seeking the arms of her lover.

But Cecilia was sitting up in bed, pale-faced, with their mother standing at the end.

"Look," said Elizabeth, pointing towards her daughter's hands, which lay in her lap, "see this."

Cecilia's fingers were laced around a small gold figure of a hart, with clear crystals for eyes.

"It is a gift from the queen, a wedding gift. She writes that she regrets she is unable to attend, being at Windsor, but will always think of you kindly and gives your marriage her blessing."

"It is beautiful," said Thomasin, seeing Cecilia's lip beginning to tremble. "A treasure you deserve. Now come, you must rise, dress."

Their mother walked towards the door, holding herself very erect. "The dressmakers are waiting downstairs. Prepare yourself. I shall send them up to you now."

As she opened the door, about to step out onto the landing, they heard the sound of feet rushing up the stairs. Dorothy Springe ran past Elizabeth in her nightgown, heading to her room at the far end of the landing. The door closed firmly and they heard her struggling with the key in the lock.

Matthew followed hard upon her heels, with Dr Elyot behind him.

"She is refusing to see the doctor, in spite of all her illness. I don't know what's to be done with the girl."

Elizabeth shrugged. "She will be returning to Derbyshire in a day or so, and her parents can take care of her then. She is not your responsibility."

"She is saying now that she will not go back to them, but wishes to live with Barnaby and Ellen."

"She is a strange one indeed. Perhaps her mind is troubled?"

Matthew strode down the landing and knocked upon the far door. "Mistress Dorothy. The doctor is here, waiting, and you are a guest under my roof. You must open the door, it is my wish."

"I ... I wish to sleep," she called back falteringly. "I am well."

"The doctor is here, outside with me. It is foolishness not to let him attend you. There is time enough for sleep."

"I am well."

"I do not think so. Unlock the door, I command it! We have a wedding today!"

There was a reluctant scraping as she turned the key. Matthew led Dr Elyot inside. At the same time, the dressmakers came sailing up the stairs, billowing with their armfuls of satin and silk.

Elizabeth beckoned them in. They entered the chamber with a rustle, filling the space. "Forget about the nonsense with

Dorothy. We have just a short time now before the wedding, and nothing more must prevent it, so let the dressmakers attend you and let's have no fuss."

Cecilia rose and stood in the centre of the room, preparing herself to be dressed. Her mother took a brush and ran it through her long, fair hair. The stokes were drawn and hard, snagging upon tangles; she winced as the teeth bit each time.

"Now shake out the dress."

The two dressmakers, women of middle age in sombre clothing, had been chosen specially for the task. Between them, they held up the special gown they had been busily sewing for two weeks, with its gold-coloured silk and lace, its full white skirts embroidered with flowers and the border of red and yellow.

"It's breath-taking," said Elizabeth, her voice awed almost to a whisper. "Isn't it? Doesn't this dress make it all seem worth it, Cecilia?"

Her daughter inclined her head, and lifted up her arms so that the underdress might be lowered. It slipped smoothly down, hugging her closely at the front, gaping wide at the back where it needed to be laced.

There came a knock upon the door.

Elizabeth jumped. "God in Heaven, what now?"

"Please, my Lady," spoke the servant through the wood, "Sir Giles Waterson has called, to speak with Mistress Thomasin."

"Has he indeed?"

"Mother," insisted Thomasin, "he has been our good and loyal friend, I promise you. Fear not."

Giles was waiting in the parlour below, where Ellen was fussing over a string of pearls and Barnaby was reading stoically beside the window. He turned in relief as Thomasin arrived, out of breath from running down the stairs.

"Shall we take a turn in the garden?" he asked, not wishing to speak on a sensitive matter before the others.

When they were under the covered walkway, with only the statues and sundials for welcome, he turned to her, his blue-green eyes full of hope.

"She is back? I understand she came home last night?"

"Late last night. She was very upset but now seems resigned to marry."

"That is most excellent news. I am glad he heeded my warning. She went to court?"

"Yes, she disappeared. We discovered her absence yesterday morning and Father went to seek her, with no luck. She was waiting for Hatton at court, determined to run away with him, except he did not come to her, so she waited all day."

Giles shook his head. "Yes, he left. It was worse than I feared."

"You spoke with him?"

"When I took him home in my carriage, I explained that the king was in favour of the marriage, and that he would be most displeased to learn of any impediment to it."

"And what did he say?"

"Very little. He listened, and then he agreed to not return to court until after the ceremony. He went to the house of William Compton last night and has been there since."

"Without complaint?"

"Yes. He made none. I believe it was only a dalliance for him, that his heart was not engaged."

Those words stung Thomasin. "Poor Cecilia. She believed herself in love."

"It was her first experience. She was naïve but she will recover and live reputably."

"Yes, she has sworn to make Sir Henry a good wife."

"Excellent, then my work is done."

They were almost at the end of the walkway, by the river. Giles nodded at a vessel moored there. "I came by barge. I had better hurry back now, to dress. I will see you shortly, at the chapel."

She put up a hand to stop him. "Please, don't hurry away before I have had the chance to thank you, for myself, for my family, but most of all for Cecilia."

He nodded. "It was a small service, nothing worthy of any great thanks. There was one thing," he said, as he departed, "which struck me as odd."

"Oh?"

"Yes," he recalled. "As Hatton was getting out of the carriage, he said that the king always looks after his own. He muttered it under his breath. At the time I took it to be insolence, meaning he thought himself above punishment, but now, I do not see how that could be."

"It is strange," agreed Thomasin, "and I am sure I have heard similar words spoken before. I don't recall when." A sense of unease crept over her. "Can he mean Cecilia?"

Giles frowned. "I don't see how. Probably some arrogance of Hatton's. But I must depart. All will be well. This is only the briefest of farewells."

Thomasin stood at the steps, watching as he climbed into the barge and the rowers pulled him away upriver, but those words kept turning around in her mind.

Back at the house, Thomasin found her father in the hallway, issuing orders to the servants. Richard was resplendent in his new red, gold and brown wedding clothes.

"Ah, daughter, see how well I am able to stand! I will be walking Cecilia down the aisle shortly."

The servants scattered about their tasks, adding another layer to the noise and bustle of the place.

"Father, Sir Giles has just departed. He has played an invaluable part in resolving this mess of Cecilia's. I believe it is his actions which have resulted in this wedding taking place today; we owe him a debt of thanks."

Richard looked grave. "Very well. I shall speak with him later. Are you going up to dress? There is little time now."

She looked down at the plain gown she had thrown on that morning. The hem was splashed with mud. The thought popped into her mind that Giles must have seen her in that state, but she pushed it to one side.

"Father, can I ask you something?" She looked about the hall, waiting for the servants to move out of earshot. "It was a strange comment that Hatton made."

"Oh? What was that?"

"Giles told me, so he may not be reporting it aright, but as he departed, Hatton said that the king always took care of his own. What did he mean?"

Her father's cheeks coloured, something she had rarely seen. At once, from his demeanour, she could see she had touched a nerve.

"What is it? I can see it means something to you."

He took her by the arm, heading into the quiet doorway of the front parlour. "It's nothing. He must be referring to the time when we were at court, when we were close to the king. He means our friendship, nothing more."

But Thomasin wasn't convinced. Her face showed her doubts.

"Now, leave this subject. Go up and get ready."

She hesitated, her mind troubled, wondering whether she dared risk his wrath by asking again.

"Go and dress. This is not your business. Go and dress, that is your task now!" And he hobbled away as swiftly as his ankle would allow.

Thomasin climbed the stairs slowly, reluctantly, sensing something in the shadows, a secret of which she was only able to see the edge. Her father's brusque response only added to her confusion.

The maid dressed her slowly, clumsily. The new dress was tight about the arms. It sat uncomfortably on her shoulders. She wriggled and twisted, to settle it, feeling the material shift. The maid pulled at the laces behind her, tugging her backwards, robbing her of breath. And her father's reaction, and his words, would not go away.

She emerged into the upstairs corridor, a mixture of blue and green silks, with silver laces.

Elizabeth was waiting and cast her eye over her younger daughter. "Those colours become you very well."

"It's a little tight."

"Never mind, stand up straight; it is just for one day. Cecilia is ready. The carriages are waiting outside. We should make our way down."

As she spoke, Cecilia emerged from her chamber, dressed head to toe in white and gold. She had not chosen to wear the French headdress, which had been Anne's gift, but had selected a gable design, with gold beads, lace and pearls. She had never looked more beautiful, with her clear, pale skin and blue eyes.

"Cecilia, you are a picture!" their mother enthused, as if her beauty could make up for her misdemeanours.

Thomasin remembered something. Reaching inside her bodice, she picked out the little scented bag given to her by Dr Elyot. His presence in the house earlier had jogged her memory. "Here." She handed it over to Cecilia. "These are herbs and flowers for good luck and happiness. Wear it inside your dress."

Cecilia gave her a quizzical look, but took the little bag in her cold fingers and tucked it between her breasts, as she was bid.

Elizabeth led the way downstairs, slowly, sedately. Richard had reappeared and was standing at the bottom, watching them descend, full of pride. Cecilia followed, then Thomasin, and then Ellen, proud in her new gown of grey and silver, with her pink-trimmed bonnet.

"Now, we are all set," he said as they descended. "Let us forget what has happened and celebrate this day together."

Through the open door, Thomasin could see the carriages waiting, the horses patient in their harness, the Marwood sun and moon design painted on the side. She felt relief at the sight. Perhaps the gnawing doubt in her stomach could now subside. The wedding which had brought them to court was finally taking place.

As they descended, Elizabeth spotted her brother standing down the hallway, still in his plain coat. She called to him above Cecilia's head.

"Brother? You are not dressed, but the hour is upon us. Is the doctor still here?"

Matthew looked up. "No, he has left."

"And Dorothy? Will she join us? Is she unwell?"

"No," he said slowly, as if processing his thoughts. "She is not unwell. But it appears that she is expecting a child."

There was an astonished silence.

"A child?" asked Elizabeth. "Whose child?"

"Whose child indeed?" asked Ellen, on the stairs behind her.

Matthew raised his hands in caution. "I am as shocked as you. She remains in her room, refusing to speak or come out. We cannot solve this matter now, but it will be solved. Today, we must put it aside and celebrate the wedding."

"That is most generous of you," replied Richard. "Today we will celebrate with Cecilia, and then we will turn our minds to the problem of Dorothy."

"To the carriages," added Matthew, "and to the chapel."

TWENTY-FIVE

The palace loomed before them, autumn sunshine warm on its red bricks and galleries of windows. Against the skyline, its many domes and spires, castellations and twisted chimneys, sat regal and timeless. The place was heaving with life. People hurried under archways, through gateways and along corridors. Courtiers were strutting in gold chains and slashed sleeves, hounds running and falcons flying. The marble courtyards were set with fountains, running with clear water and carved with roses. Up the grand staircase and through the guard room, the presence chamber and the privy chamber, the footsteps of the king rang out. Henry was angry, with that particular explosive fire that only the king could give vent to.

The carriages rattled into the courtyard and drew up before the main gate. Heraldic beasts, painted in gold, stood above the entrance, beside the king's initials, carved alongside those of the queen. Those inside saw only the colour, the gold, the jewels. They knew nothing of the events in the presence chamber that morning, the words spoken in the chapel, the angry exchanges between one man and another. And nor did Richard, climbing out first, smiling, pausing to look about him in pride, and test his weight upon his ankle, before he turned to hand out his wife and daughters. One by one, they emerged from the carriage, decked in their finery. Silk, tissue and satin gleamed bright and untainted in the sunshine, but not for long.

Gathering up her skirts, Thomasin followed her father out of the carriage. She could not but wonder at her sister's mood and her secret feelings. Cecilia's face had regained its composure, with the pale expression of her eyes and the determined set of her mouth, and she had the protection that beautiful clothes and jewels might confer. Yet only a few hours before, she had been waiting here, holding back her tears, desperate for the arrival of her lover. Outwardly, she was composed, but Thomasin knew that inside, she was struggling to keep the broken pieces together. Beneath her white and gold dress, her heart was in fragments. She went forward to this sacrifice with the numbness of one who had lost herself.

Thomasin turned. Cecilia was climbing out behind her, so she offered a smile of encouragement. A touch upon the arm, warm fingers upon silk.

Descending from the second carriage, Matthew, Barnaby and Ellen followed them across the cobbles towards the main gate, their mood subdued by the startling news about Dorothy.

"We shall not mention it again," Elizabeth had said to her family, in the secrecy of the carriage, "but this might prove a terrible scandal for Matthew to weather, if my suspicions are correct."

"Your suspicions?" Richard had asked.

"I will keep them to myself, in case I am wrong. I am sure all will be revealed soon."

As they reached the bottom of the grand staircase, two figures emerged. The duke and duchess of Suffolk, Charles and Mary Brandon, were descending to the courtyard, their fine clothes covered over by cloaks, about to depart.

Elizabeth and Richard bowed low and their daughters followed suit, but the Suffolks walked past them, towards the stables without a word.

"Perhaps they are in a hurry, or indisposed," said Richard, seeing his wife's look of dismay.

"I had hoped they might attend the wedding," Elizabeth replied, "but they do seem in a hurry."

"Don't give it any more thought. Come on."

The corridor was empty, save for its heavy scent of stone and wood. The brick walls and flagstone floor reflected no warmth, and Thomasin shivered as they made their way along the passage towards the entrance to the king's apartments. Heavy wooden doors stood open between the stone archway ahead. On the other side, the steps rose, wide and high, to carry them up to the first floor. The walls either side were hung with tapestries, heavy and dark.

Slowly, Thomasin followed her family up the stairs that led to the royal apartments and the king's chapel. Before her eyes, the hem of Cecilia's gown, with its brilliant red and yellow border, swished and swung before her. Later, she remembered that moment as the last image before. Before they knew. That swish of red and yellow silk, the colour and patterns of hope.

Feet came clattering past them, merry, young feet, in fashionable square-toed shoes. The group of young men hurried past like the wind. Thomasin recognised Thomas Wyatt and Henry Norris. They made no greeting, but Wyatt gave a laugh which had a note of cruelty in it. That laugh brought a realisation with it. Thomasin had the sudden, uneasy sense that all was not well. Surely, on another day, those men would have spoken in greeting, in welcome, not rushed past thus. Not on the morning of a wedding. Wyatt, whom she had met in Anne's chamber, Norris with whom she had danced. Something was amiss.

"Father," she whispered, "Father." But Richard was too far ahead to hear her, with Cecilia between them. His broad back was intent upon the climb, his focus upon balancing his weight, leaning upon the wall for support. Instead, she turned back to Matthew, who was climbing the stairs immediately behind her. "I fear something is wrong," she said, stumbling over her skirts.

"Careful! Just get to the top."

At the top of the stairs, Richard and Elizabeth forged ahead, leading their party into the watching chamber.

"Uncle," Thomasin said again, addressing Matthew, "something is wrong, I feel it."

"You are unwell?"

"No, not me. This situation. The marriage."

"By what signs? I see nothing. Has Cecilia asked you to speak?"

"No, no. I sense it. The lack of warmth in the faces of those who should be our guests."

He frowned. "We shall see. I will be watchful."

Thomasin looked to Ellen, and to Barnaby, but they seemed to be held in some strange spell of their own, not meeting her eyes, as silent communications passed between them. There was nothing to be done but to press on.

The king's presence chamber was busy, thronging with voices, but there was a strange atmosphere of unease. Thomasin felt it at once. Among those gathered, she recognised Francis Bryan, watching them steadily out of his one good eye, and the king's friend William Compton whispering to Nicholas Carew. Men from whom she should have received a greeting; Bryan for his part in her father's accident, and Carew who had dined at their table just the night before last. A little further along, John Dudley was speaking with William Roper, who paused to look up at them with wide eyes. Beside, in the alcove stood Margaret Roper, dressed as if to attend the wedding, but facing Thomasin with an expression of despair, as if she would speak but could not. Yet still the Marwoods led the bride forward, seeing nothing amiss, or choosing not to see it. Ahead, the doors to the chapel invited them, bright and hot inside with the flames of dozens of candles. The light seemed to draw them like moths to be burned.

Matthew was at Thomasin's side. "I see what you mean. It is in their faces. I fear some impending act, or some news."

Spotting them pass, John Dudley had broken away from his group, and hurried after, in their wake. "Sir Richard," he called softly. "Sir Richard."

Again, her father did not hear, but Thomasin and Matthew turned.

Dudley was shaking his head, as if to warn them, beckoning, but he was too late. Into the chapel doorway stepped Viscount Boleyn, blocking the entrance. Blazing in black and gold, with a jewelled collar and heavy gold chain about his shoulders, he was regal, prepossessing. He paused, as if present by chance, looking the approaching party up and down. Yet there was nothing about his performance that was accidental.

Richard stopped at once.

"The errant bride," he pronounced with a smile.

Cecilia recoiled.

"Have you really dressed up and come to court, expecting a wedding?"

"Please," said Richard, attempting civility, "let us pass."

"But to what purpose?" Boleyn raised an eyebrow. "What can you imagine your business is here today?"

Thomasin watched her father trying to steady himself. He turned to his wife. "Are the Kytsons in the chapel?"

"Oh no," laughed Boleyn, "they have long gone, like the bride's lover."

Even Thomasin heard her sister gasp. Taking hold of Cecilia by the arm, Richard turned on the spot, and began to walk back towards the door. Thomasin made way for them to pass, then followed, feeling her legs beginning to shake.

The chamber erupted in sound around them. It had clearly been waiting for this moment.

Matthew was the last of the party remaining. He bid Boleyn stand aside, put his head through the doorway and had a quick look into the chapel. It was empty. Only the candles burned bright on the altar. "It is empty," he confirmed, turning to Barnaby and Ellen. "Let us follow."

"Keep your heads held high; be proud," Richard instructed, leading them on the difficult walk back through the chamber.

Thomasin felt the eyes of those present upon her, like needles. Only the sympathetic faces of John Dudley and Margaret Roper gave any relief.

"Where is the king?" asked Elizabeth. "Let us find the king."

"Yes, run to the king," Boleyn called after them. "You'll remember the way to his bedchamber."

Thomasin turned cold, and the tears rose in her throat, even as she fought them back. The king's bedchamber? "What does he mean?" She turned to her uncle, bitterly, as soon as they passed through the doors. "Was my mother once in the king's bedchamber?"

"Ignore his barbs. He speaks from malice."

"Was my mother the king's lover? Uncle, please."

Matthew's face was taut. "Not now."

But the realisation took hold of Thomasin, with the voices and laughter of the court ringing about them. Her mother had once shared King Henry's bed. Back in the days when they were courtiers, in the early years of his reign, in the king's youth. But when? Her father must surely know. She thought of his refusal to discuss the matter with her earlier. And what did it mean? Her heart felt like lead and the walls came crowding in on both sides. She took a deep breath, rasping and difficult.

"Here? You are here already?" It was Giles, hurrying up the stairs into the chamber. Then he saw their faces. "Oh, by our Lord, you are here, you already know! I sent another message, then I set out to meet you on the road, but I am too late. Come, quick, come with me."

He led them into an antechamber. Somehow, they grouped together, stunned and silent. Thomasin could not take her eyes off her mother's face.

"Somehow Boleyn had received word of Cecilia's presence here yesterday, from someone in Anne's household. I only discovered this when I returned from visiting Monk's Place this morning. I believe they have already informed Sir Henry Kytson, or else he will be told shortly, and advised to withdraw. I am so sorry. There is to be no wedding."

Cecilia stumbled a little against her father. Thomasin reached and took her hand.

"Who has done this?" muttered Richard. "Who has done this to us?"

"I have done it," said Cecilia. "It is all my doing."

Elizabeth's mouth was set firm. "Can you take us to the king?"

Richard turned to his wife. "The king? Our friend the king? Where is his protection now?" The tone of his voice confirmed everything Thomasin suspected.

A devil arose inside her. She looked her mother in the eye. "The king, Mother, whose bed you shared?"

She saw the shock enter the blue eyes. It was followed by a cold composure.

"Do not presume to speak to me of things you do not understand."

"So it is true?"

"Do not speak to me of this again."

Thomasin looked to her father. He met her eyes with resignation and warning.

"The king is indisposed," said Giles, uncomfortably. "He is closeted away with Anne, and they are arguing fearsomely. The best thing you can do is to get back in your carriages and return to Monk's Place."

"Come," said Matthew, gesturing to Ellen and Barnaby, "we will do exactly that."

"No," replied Elizabeth, with determination in her voice. "I will not run away. I will see the king. He was to have attended the wedding. He gave it his blessing."

"But…" began Giles.

"No buts. I have never asked anything of the king before and it is fitting that he receives me, and hears me, now."

And without waiting to hear another objection, Elizabeth Marwood walked with purpose out of the antechamber. Thomasin and Sir Giles followed, both compelled and concerned, while Richard hung back.

They heard the king's raised voice as they approached the door, which stood open. Guards were posted on either side, and crossed their spears as the group approached, to signify that they may not enter. Yet Henry's angry voice reached them loud and clear.

"You must always meddle in matters that do not concern you," he was saying, in tones of anger and frustration. "You forget that you are but Boleyn's daughter, only as high as I have raised you, and no more. Everything you have, you have due to my generosity. These are my gifts to you. And in return, you behave as if you are already queen and these people are yours to command."

"I only act as I see fit," they heard Anne reply, "in honour of yourself, my Lord, and the favour you have shown me."

"Then why meddle in this match? It is to no one's glory, not to the girl, nor the family, nor to yourself."

"But it is no longer to anyone's dishonour."

"You speak of honour. Honour. How do you know what duty and honour look like in this world? It was an honourable match, honourably made. And it had my blessing. Now it is undone, for the sake of a few rumours. Why so, Madam?"

"I acted to prevent a scandal. When I heard the rumours, I could not simply stand aside. So yes, I asked him to speak to Sir Henry, and his reaction was just as I thought. What should I have done? Looked away?"

"Yes, Madam, looked away. That is exactly what you should have done."

"I am not one to look away!"

"You think this your role? To involve yourself in my decisions — my decisions, Madam, which I have been making as England's king for the past eighteen years? You think you know better? You challenge my judgement?"

"Not at all, my Lord. I thought rather that we would be in agreement, and that I would be acting in accordance with your wishes."

"But my wishes have already been stated, irrefutably, to the contrast."

"Yet that was before you knew, before Rafe brought me the news."

At the sound of Rafe's name, Thomasin's stomach turned over. So, he was involved in this mess, too. Not only involved, but instrumental in her sister's disgrace.

But it was Cecilia who surprised them all, stepping forward towards the open chamber doors.

"My Lord?" she asked, curtseying.

Henry and Anne were mid-argument, pacing the floor, and came to a stop within sight of those outside.

"Cecilia!" said the king, and in response to some gesture from within, the guards stood at ease.

"My wedding has been halted today," she said, in a clear, firm voice.

"So I have heard," he replied. "Let me assure you, it was no doing of mine."

"Thank you, my Lord. My family, they are here too." Cecilia gestured behind her.

"Lady Elizabeth, Sir Richard!" Henry added, his face a mixture of emotions while Anne chafed at his side.

"Come, we shouldn't intrude," said Thomasin, thinking it wisest to withdraw, but Cecilia felt the need to speak, and would let nothing deter her. Through the door, she dropped a curtsey to Anne, whose black eyes were flashing in fury.

"My Lady Anne, pray forgive my impertinence. When I came to court, you welcomed me and included me in your circle, for which I was grateful. When you saw that I was impressionable, and swayed by Hatton's attentions, you encouraged me to think of him, you spoke to me of love above all, and I followed your example. Yet now I find you speak against me; you turned your own advice upon me, and informed my intended. Why did you push me to act as you did, with these results?"

Anne half turned away, as if to dismiss her, or gather her thoughts. Then, she whirled back to face them. Her expression was indecipherable, almost mocking. "You come here, asking questions of me? As if I am somehow beholden to you? Are you too much of a fool to see the truth, or too afraid to speak it?"

"Cecilia," urged Thomasin, fearful for her sister.

"What truth is that?" Cecilia half spoke, half whispered.

Anne laughed. "Have you not been humiliated enough today, that you would ask for more? Very well. You hardly needed any encouragement; you jumped at the chance of love, to escape marriage to a dull man. You were desperate for love, for escape. I merely told you what you wanted to hear and you ran to him, like a lovesick puppy. Kytson has had a lucky escape."

Before Cecilia could reply, Elizabeth spoke, directly to Henry. "Please, my Lord, will you not intervene and end this cruelty?"

"What should I do?" the king asked, in frustration. "It is out of my hands now. The damage has been done."

"For the sake of my family," asked Elizabeth again, "I respectfully ask you, Your Majesty, to speak with the Kytsons, to resolve this…"

"No, Mother," replied Cecilia. "There will be no marriage. The Lady Anne is right. This is a mess of my own creation. The best we can do now is to leave."

Elizabeth lifted her chin. "I had hoped," she uttered tautly, "to find that the old values still prevailed at court; those upheld by the court in days past, of kindness, charity and forgiveness, especially towards those who may have erred and repented." She looked directly at Anne. "But I find that things have changed. The court is not what it was."

"No," replied Anne, looking her straight in the eye. "It is not. You will find it much improved."

"And so, my King," continued Elizabeth with dignity, "I request your gracious permission for myself and my family to leave court and return to the country."

King Henry looked evenly at her; a woman he had once loved. "I see your wisdom, Madam. Your request is just, and it is granted."

"Thank you, my gracious Lord. I regret that our reunion was but short-lived. I will continue to pray for your eternal soul."

These words were followed by silence, as those present waited for the wrath of the king to be unleashed upon Elizabeth's head. Yet old affection remained, the moments passed, and the darting blue eyes moved over her and alighted upon Anne.

"Madam," he said finally, "I do not like your part in this. I do not like it at all."

And with that, King Henry turned and strode away, leaving Anne Boleyn watching after him. Thomasin was close enough to see that his face was red with fury.

Picking up her skirts, Elizabeth rose slowly to her feet. Then, without a word to Anne, she headed for the staircase, the Boleyn woman's black eyes boring into her back. Thomasin followed in her wake with the others, her heart beating hard at the insight into her mother's past and the power of her words.

Behind them, in the watching chamber, someone had started plucking a lute. The tune reached them, giving sound to their unvoiced emotions, each note taut.

They had reached the bottom of the stairs when Elizabeth faltered and put out her hand to steady herself against the wall.

Cecilia was closest. "Mother, what is it?"

"Elizabeth?" Richard supported his wife and she sank lower.

With her face pale, Elizabeth fought to regain her breath. "It is just a turn. My old complaint. I need to rest."

"Of course." Richard put his arm under her shoulders and took her weight on to him.

"I will get the carriage brought as close as possible," said Matthew, hurrying away.

"Here, it is lavender, to revive her," offered Ellen, holding forth a small, dry bundle.

Between them, Richard and Barnaby took Elizabeth's weight and, in slow, tentative steps, headed for the courtyard. The others followed, close behind.

Then, down a side corridor, Thomasin caught sight of Rafe and George Boleyn, speaking together. The anger within her rose close to boiling point.

"You!" she said with force, hurrying down to face him, undeterred by his beauty. "Are you here to gloat? Your meddlesome work is done, is it not? See my mother, led away, as her illness overcomes her, my sister disgraced, my family humiliated. I had thought you our friend, and mine."

Rafe turned away from Boleyn and advanced a little towards her, under the light of a burning torch. His dark brows were furrowed, his jaw set firm. "Your friend? I had thought so too…"

"You were welcomed into our house, and you act against us like this. Why did you take it upon yourself to tell Sir Henry?"

"Of your sister's whoring? If it had not been me, it would have been someone else. No one is to blame for her waywardness, only herself."

"But the active part you took in it speaks of malice. It is your revenge upon me."

Rafe shook his head. "You little fool. You have been at court for a mere two weeks. To whose household do I belong? Who pays for my bed and board? To whom do I owe my allegiance?"

This perspective shook Thomasin. She recalled her first ever meeting with Rafe, when he had appeared in the rose garden with Viscount Boleyn, and showed no interest in her whatsoever, compared with the times she had seen them whispering together, and Rafe's companionship with Anne. Of course he had never been hers. The harsh words spoken to her father by the viscount reminded her that there had formerly been animosity between them. She, and her family, had only ever been a diversion to them, players in a wider scheme.

She fought against the sinking, breaking sensation in her chest. "You never cared for me, did you?" It was a realisation rather than a question. "Not for me. It was part of a game for you."

"I had my instructions."

"Yes." She looked at him in disgust. "Yes, I suspected that. I did not recognise its meaning before."

Giles placed his hand upon her shoulder. "Come away now."

But Thomasin could not move. "Instructions?" The word was distasteful to her. "I was less than a person to you."

At the sight of her distress, Rafe's face softened slightly. "No, I... It was not that simple."

But Giles had her by the arm and was leading her away, in the direction of the courtyard, where her mother was being helped into a carriage. "Forget them," he said gently. "None of them are worth your thoughts. Let us see to your mother instead."

"What did he mean, he had his instructions?"

"He was trying to wound you, nothing more."

"No, I saw him with Boleyn. From the start there was some intention on their part."

"I imagine that, if anything, it was to win you over to their cause."

"By any means?"

"I could not say. Everything is a battle to them: you are either a soldier for their cause, or you are against them. It is as simple as that."

"But why break my sister's marriage?"

Giles paused. "Because they could. I only know that there were things in the past between your family and the Boleyns. I cannot say more."

"Cannot or will not?"

"It was before my time at court. Look, your father beckons. He wishes to depart."

Giles led her out of the gateway and across the cobbles. Richard was waiting to hand his daughter into the carriage where Elizabeth and Cecilia were already seated. The second carriage, with Matthew, Barnaby and Ellen, was pulling out of the gates.

"I will call on you, before you leave London," Giles promised, handing Thomasin over to her father. "But remember, there is a whole world beyond the court, where happiness can be found."

But his words were lost. Thomasin sat wedged into the corner, as if deaf and dumb, as the carriage pulled away.

TWENTY-SIX

The sun shone upon the roofs of Monk's Place and made the windowpanes golden. It shone upon the paths snaking through the garden, the dogs frolicking on the lawn and the distant river. It lit the edge of the pile of books in Thomasin's window, the sleeve of the wedding dress hanging on Cecilia's wall and the carriage of the dressmakers, who were sombrely removing all traces of the wedding.

In the back bedroom, Thomasin and Cecilia were sitting on either side of their mother, who lay upon her back, as Richard paced the floor.

"This all took place many years ago. It belongs in the past and should remain there," he was saying, tugging at his beard in frustration. "As our daughters, and as young women, it befits you not to know the details of your parents' marriage. Such things are the secrets between man and wife, not for meddlesome girls."

"It is hardly meddling," replied Elizabeth, weakly.

"No, do not try to speak," replied her husband. "The doctor said you must not exert yourself. You need rest if you are to make the journey back to Suffolk."

"Then you must speak for me," Elizabeth whispered, "but they must know now. They cannot be left with half-truths."

"I am certain," replied Thomasin, "that this is a matter we would never have wished to have known, or pried into ourselves from mere curiosity or any love of secrets. But, surely, if it has had an effect upon Cecilia's marriage, she must know it?"

"I cannot!" stormed Richard, leaving the room.

The sisters looked to their mother, pale between the sheets.

"We must wait until you are strong," added Thomasin.

"No," Elizabeth said softly. "The time is now. I will speak of it now. And then it can be forgotten."

"Only if you can, Mother," urged Cecilia, "without tiring yourself."

"I promise I will stop if I feel too weak." Elizabeth took each of her daughters' hands. "We must go back twenty years, more, in fact. I came to court in the old king's reign, when I was very young. My mother brought me, as she was in service in the household of the old king's mother, and I was of an age to be useful. It was a very different place then, if you can imagine."

She paused to draw her breath, her eyes misting as if she was staring back into the past.

"We were mostly at Richmond, in those final years. The old king was increasingly ill and the prince, King Henry as is now, was impatient for the throne. He was denied much, at a time when he was ready for manhood. Your father was then a page in his household, close in age, his constant companion in the field. We wished to marry, but my mother had other ambitions for me; she wanted me to make a better match and did not consider the Marwoods a worthy connection.

"When I came of age, Richard obtained the blessing of the old king to marry, on account of his good service, but my mother was furious that I had gone above her. She denied me and cut me off with nothing. We went ahead and were wed anyway. A year later, I had Cecilia and we lived in lodgings outside Richmond Palace, close to penury, dining occasionally at court, although I had to sell my plate and dresses. This is what brought me close to Queen Catherine, who had known great hardship when she was a widow. When the old king died, she brought me into her household.

"Soon after her marriage, the queen conceived a child. It was then that the king's interest lighted upon me. He sent his messengers, to usher me into his bed, but I refused, for love of the queen, and for love of my husband. Finally, he made promises to advance us, so that Richard's career would prosper; he was to be appointed an ambassador and would travel, in a position that Thomas Boleyn had coveted."

"If you would share his bed?" asked Thomasin.

"Yes, if I would share his bed. I understood that otherwise, Richard would be overlooked. So yes, I went to the king, half a dozen times. We had so little and he promised so much. The queen never knew of it, and still does not to this day, I believe. But your father was unhappy. He was never ambitious in that sense. When he was offered a diplomatic mission to the Low Countries, he refused it, because I was with child again. Boleyn went instead. He saw himself as your father's rival then. But while he was away, Richard inherited Eastwell Hall, so after my confinement, we left court for the country."

"Your confinement?" asked Thomasin.

"I shared the time of my confinement with Queen Catherine; she bore a son soon after I bore you, Thomasin. After we returned to the country, her little son died."

"You bore Thomasin after your liaison with the king?" Cecilia asked.

"Yes, later that autumn."

"And you did not think…"

"It was never a suggestion," replied Elizabeth. "And she is the image of Richard, everyone can see."

Thomasin's head swam. She thought of the king, that first time she had seen him upon their arrival at court, and how his sharp eyes had borne down upon her. "No, it cannot be. The timing must be wrong."

"I always felt that you were Richard's daughter. I never doubted it."

"Who else knows of this?"

"Barely anyone at the time, and that was seventeen years ago. Many of those who were at court at the time have moved on, or lie in their graves."

"But not Boleyn."

Elizabeth sighed. "The situation with Anne is very delicate. Precarious. The viscount fears that the king will tire of her and replace her, or else the Pope will rule against him, or the Emperor invade. He feared the return of your father, as his old rival, in case the balance tipped back in favour of the queen. Or perhaps Anne feared he would take to Cecilia. I believe he set out to cause trouble in our family."

"He has succeeded," affirmed Cecilia, "but only because I was foolish enough to walk into his trap."

And Thomasin blushed as she thought of the many times she might have gone down the same path, floundered in the same danger and been ruined as a result. Only her caution and the good advice of the priest of Our Lady, had prevented such infamy being heaped upon her head.

"But we will leave court," said Elizabeth, "and have no more part in this disgraceful, shameful business. Cecilia is too beautiful not to attract another suitor in the country and you will both make good matches, you need not fear." She squeezed both her daughters' hands in hers. "This has been a trial for us all, but we shall overcome it, and the matter will be forgotten. It is my fault. I should have remembered how it was and known better than to return."

It was at that point that Richard re-entered the room. He spoke in clipped, disbelieving tones. "Matthew has been closeted with Lady Dorothy Springe. He has forced her to a confession. It would seem that the father of her child is her own brother-in-law, Barnaby Russell."

"Ellen's husband? Her own sister's husband?" gasped Elizabeth.

"The very same. She is around three months gone with child. It seems that Dorothy's extended visit to their home proved fruitful."

"And Ellen?"

"Is at this moment packing her bags."

Thomasin rose. "I will go to her. I have a suggestion that may ease her suffering."

Thomasin drew her cloak about her and looked up into the sky. Above the rooftops of London, it stretched a clear, pale grey, with a few light clouds, but towards the west, the colour lifted and became brighter. Somewhere in that direction lay Windsor and the queen's court. Thomasin had been grateful for Catherine's swift response to their dilemma, grateful for the Spaniard's interest in her and her kindness, grateful for the new opportunity she offered, for the new chapter in her life.

The dogs came out and roamed about her feet, scenting life among the stones of the driveway. It felt far longer than two weeks since they had arrived at Monk's Place, drawing up in the carriages from Suffolk. So much had happened. So much that they could not have predicted, in ways that had left them all affected. And there were things she had learned, about the past, her parents and their world, that changed the way she viewed them. Thomasin's heart felt packed in tight with mixed emotions. What she needed now was a change of place and some distance.

Cecilia appeared in the doorway, calling to her sister outside. "Mother's down."

Thomasin turned back to the hall, where Elizabeth was being helped down the final stairs by Richard. Her face was pale and drawn, with a bed jacket thrown about her shoulders. Dr Elyot had prescribed complete rest, but having examined her, he had hopes for her subsequent recovery. She, Richard and Cecilia would stay on quietly at Monk's Place for another week, before making a slow return journey to Suffolk.

"Mother, I would have come up to you."

"She wanted to come down," explained Richard. "To see you off."

"But you must go right up to bed again afterwards, or else I cannot leave!" Thomasin embraced her mother, and then her father. "I will write to you as soon as I am settled, and you must write to me all the time about Mother's improvement and life in Suffolk."

He nodded. "You know we will; you will be drowning under a flood of letters. But daughter, are you certain this is what you want? It's not too late to return to the country with us."

"Of course it's what she wants," said Elizabeth. "Given a choice between a place in the queen's household and being shut away in the countryside, what girl would not choose the former? So long as you do not repeat our mistakes; but you have a sensible head on your shoulders, and Queen Catherine will keep a good eye on you and guide you well."

"Thank you, Mother. I hope I shall be of use to her."

"You will," Elizabeth nodded. "I know that you will."

Thomasin turned to her sister, who stood waiting at the side.

Cecilia gave her a rare smile. "I promise I will look after them."

"And look after yourself," said Thomasin, pulling her close. "We'll meet again soon." She threw a look back up at the house. "Has Matthew decided yet what to do with Barnaby?"

Elizabeth nodded. "Barnaby is upstairs packing, right now. He is returning to Derbyshire in the morning, and Dorothy is being sent back to her parents, taking her little surprise with her."

Footsteps on the stairs drew their attention to Ellen, who was descending, dressed in a riding habit. "I am ready," she said, her round face a mixture of emotions. The news of her husband and Dorothy's liaison had caused her much grief, especially as she had not conceived a child of her own. Perhaps it was the betrayal by her sister that hurt the most and had made her decision easier. "I can't wait to get to Windsor and away from here. Please do not take that the wrong way, but I need a new place to be, a new life."

"We quite understand," said Elizabeth kindly. "This is quite the right thing for you, my dear. You will flourish under Queen Catherine's care."

"You have said your farewells to Barnaby?" asked Richard.

"I have. He does not approve of my going, but I do not approve of his conduct. I am glad to be leaving, glad that he is returning north."

Queen Catherine had been more than generous when she heard the details of Ellen's situation and had extended her invitation to Thomasin to include her cousin. Now both were to be taken into the Windsor household.

"Here come the horses," said Cecilia, indicting the courtyard outside, where hoofs could be heard on cobbles.

They appeared from the stables; two chestnut mares trapped in Russell livery, and a large black stallion with a Spanish saddle. The largest beast was being led by the reins by Giles Waterson, who was dressed in a grey habit, ready to ride.

"All is in readiness," he assured them. "I have checked the chests of clothes; they are all secure and likely to reach Windsor by nightfall. Are you ladies ready to depart?"

He assisted Ellen and Thomasin into their saddles. From that position, Thomasin looked back up at Monk's Place, so newly familiar, and yet so tired now, wondering if she might see it again.

"I promise to deliver them both safely," Giles assured the party waiting on the threshold, joined by Matthew, who had come out to bid them farewell. "The weather looks to be set fair with no sign of rain, so it should be a clear ride."

They passed through the gates and out into the street, heading West. The city was not too busy at that early hour, but the church bells pealed out and the street traders were already crying out their wares. They passed the little church of Our Lady and the tight-fronted houses and inns, the conduit flowing with water and the sheep being herded in a drove. Heading along Cheapside, they rode under the spire of St Paul's Cathedral, crossing themselves, and on past the Franciscan Friary until the Newgate came into view, and the green fields beyond. The sight of them filled Thomasin with a surge of excitement. Here, finally, was a new start, a new adventure lying beyond the hills.

As they approached, a rider passed them by, circling about on a dark horse. It was a man in black, with a flowing cloak, bringing his horse into rein, as he turned about to face them, waiting at the side of the road.

Thomasin recognised Rafe at once. His distinctive hair and eyes marked him out, as did the strong, sinuous movements of his body in the saddle.

Giles saw him too. Yet he did not stop, but pressed them forward.

Rafe watched as they rode ahead, on towards the gate. Thomasin shot him one brief look, meeting his black eyes, before tearing her own away. Keeping pace with Giles and Ellen, she covered the last distance and passed under the shadow of the gate. Whatever Rafe Danvers had hoped to say, or do, went unspoken.

"And onwards," said Giles, kicking his spurs.

The three horses surged forwards, carrying them to Windsor and the court of Queen Catherine of Aragon.

A NOTE TO THE READER

Dear Reader,

Thank you for choosing this book. I hope you enjoyed it.

Welcome to the world of the Marwoods. Their story, set at the court of Henry VIII in 1527, has been a long time in the making. Some of you may have come to this work after reading my non-fiction, but it was always my ambition, from the age of eight, to write novels. A number of Tudor families have formed themselves in my head over the intervening years, slipping through my games as a child, haunting my later dreams, clamouring to be written. Various characters blazed briefly into life in stories, drawings and even several full-length novels before the Marwoods came into being. Whilst I was researching the key figures of the period, tracing their journeys through the primary sources, I always saw the potential of weaving fictional characters into the Tudor world, to represent the eyes and ears of a modern readers, being both part that world and set apart from it.

I am a great fan of fiction and its prerogatives. It allows authors and readers to transcend normal boundaries of time, space and reality, providing the ultimate escapism. It can perform a kind of magic, and its only responsibility is to itself, to be good art. However, what we mean by "good art" may vary significantly. Historical fiction as a genre in its own right has its own specific freedoms and limitations. It also offers the greatest thrill of escapism, the closest we can come to having been there, a witness to the past. I suppose one of the reasons I write Tudor fiction, is to allay my own frustration of not having been there.

Growing up reading the historical novels of Jean Plaidy, I quickly absorbed how much the genre could also be educative, and deeply rooted in fact. The Marwoods are a fictional family, but they are also representative of many potential real Marwoods living in the sixteenth century. Although they are atypical in their closeness to the throne, I created them by assimilating the lives of many other historical figures I had read about whose experiences are known to us. Other characters close to them are also fictional, especially those men relevant to the romantic plot line: Rafe Danvers, Giles Waterson, William Hatton and Henry Kytson, to allow me greater scope to flesh out their roles without altering what is known about existing people.

However, the lives of many real Tudor men and women remain distant and full of holes. Whilst I have researched the lives of individuals like Henry VIII, Catherine of Aragon and Anne Boleyn in much detail, a gulf remains between biographical work and the creative fleshing out that allows them to come to life as people in fiction. Thus, there will be times when I have taken the liberty of putting words into their mouths, describing their words and actions that I believe are compatible with what is known, or can be inferred, about their characters over the passage of five centuries. Individual readers' views on Henry, Catherine, Anne and others can often be strong and surprisingly varied. It may be that my presentation of known figures at this moment in their lives does not always fit with that of my readers, but I have always had sound reasons for doing so. The same is true for locations and events of the era, as well as details such as clothing, food, furnishing, protocol etc; I have embellished the known facts in keeping with their essence.

Beginning in 1527, I plan for the Marwood series will run over several decades to come. Thus, I will be tracing developments in character and events as they unfold. The Thomasin Marwood and Anne Boleyn of 1527 will not be the same as their depiction in 1530 or 1535; they will grow and change through ups and downs. I hope readers will enjoy following their journey.

Reviews do matter to writers and I would appreciate a review on Amazon or Goodreads. Often, we're writing in isolation, working in something of a vacuum, living most intensely in our heads, sending out manuscripts into the ether. It's lovely to receive feedback and contact from readers, to know our work is being enjoyed and see the ways we can improve when planning our next part of the story. You can contact me **on Twitter** (@PrufrocksPeach. I am a T.S.Eliot fan) via **my author page on Facebook** (Amy Licence Author), or **via my website**.

I am currently completing the second book in the series, *Troubled Queen*, following Thomasin through her service in Catherine's household, and hope you will be inspired to follow her adventures. Thank you for reading *Dangerous Lady*, and I hope we meet again soon.

Kind regards,

Amy Licence, Canterbury, June 2022

www.amylicence.weebly.com

Sapere Books is an exciting new publisher of brilliant fiction and popular history.

To find out more about our latest releases and our monthly bargain books visit our website:
saperebooks.com

Printed in Great Britain
by Amazon

25666787R00165